LOW-GEE HIJACK

Sesh was tied completely and gagged, and the line was towing her toward the emergency exit, faster than Jak could airswim to her. Their eyes met for just a moment; he could see her terror pleading for rescue, in that bare instant, before the rotation shifted again, and he lost his orientation as the netting flew around him, grabbed him in a fierce hug, and spun him in a dizzy whirl.

Her final scream, smothered by the gag, felt to Jak like a kick in the stomach. Sesh was dragged out of his field of view. The net yanked brutally. Jak saw boots touching down all around him. Then there was a flurry of fists, feet, and clubs, fading rapidly into terrible pain and utter darkness.

PRAISE FOR JOHN BARNES

"Astonishing speculations combined with brilliant extrapolations."

—*Kirkus Reviews* on *Mother of Storms*

"Sheer storytelling power."

—*Booklist* on *Mother of Storms*

Also by John Barnes

Orbital Resonance

A Million Open Doors

Mother of Storms

Kaleidescope Century

Encounter with Tiber (with Buzz Aldrin)*

Earth Made of Glass

Finity

Candle

The Return (with Buzz Aldrin)

The Merchants of Souls

The Sky So Big and Black

*The Duke of Uranium**

* AVAILABLE FROM WARNER ASPECT

THE DUKE
OF URANIUM

JOHN BARNES

ASPECT®

WARNER BOOKS

An AOL Time Warner Company

WARNER BOOKS EDITION

Copyright © 2002 by John Barnes

Cover design by Shasti O'Leary/Don Puckey
Cover illustration by Matt Stawicki

Aspect® name and logo are trademarks of Warner Books, Inc.

Warner Books, Inc.
1271 Avenue of the Americas
New York, NY 10020

Visit our Web site at www.twbookmark.com.

An AOL Time Warner Company

Printed in the United States of America

First Paperback Printing: September 2002

10 9 8 7 6 5 4 3 2 1

For
Steve Leon
Neil Caesar
Ted Eisenstein
because they stayed in touch, and
in memory of Elmer Rungate.

THE DUKE
OF URANIUM

"Of course, I've been asked about him a great deal. You might say he's the only thing I've ever been asked about. I suppose it's understandable. No one has the courage and the forthrightness to blame the parents anymore, so now we blame the teacher, so you come and bother me again.

"All right, I confess. Yes, I was the person who was supposed to teach Jak Jinnaka about the Wager; that was the class I taught, and he was in it. Oh, by Nakasen's furry pink bottom, yes, yes, yes, I remember Jinnaka.

"That's always the question they ask; do they think it's clever? No, he does not appear to have learned very much; his behavior across the past century indicates that he never understood a word that Paj Nakasen wrote, nor a single one of the ideas that has so advanced and ennobled our species. He always acted as if the Wager were some kind of obscure joke being pulled on him by society, rather than the fundamental approach to the universe adopted by all of humanity. Or maybe he just thought it was a good idea for other people, but not for him; wolves probably think sheep should believe in meekness, you know, and con men probably regard being very trusting as a virtue. But in any case, I can't teach the unteachable, no teacher can, and with Jak Jinnaka it was doubly unteachable—trying to explain a subject that is so basic that most people don't require an explanation at all, to a person who had no interest in knowing it. It would have been more rewarding trying to teach polypsychronic dipsolodies to a cageful of monkeys.

"Frankly, I'm sick of people blaming teachers, and I wish that our union had the guts to take it up with the Journalists' Brotherhood. Why don't you blame the cafeteria workers or something?"

—From "Fwidya at Age 300, Was Jinnaka's Teacher, Disavows All Responsibility," <u>Reasonably True News</u>, vol. 1042, Story 398, page 22, open distribution at standard terms, stillpic of Fwidya at additional charge, see catalog for over 1 million Jinnaka stillpix

CHAPTER 1

The Dullest Lecture
in the History of the Universe

Teacher Fwidya said you couldn't *not* dak the idea, because it was so central to the way everyone thought about the world, so naturally Jak Jinnaka tried not to even understand the idea. Jak was that way—tell him he couldn't and he'd try. Uncle Sib always said it was a good thing nobody'd ever told him you can't breathe vacuum.

Jak always responded that even if he did precess a little when people said "You can't . . ." he was at least smart enough to do his challenging mostly in situations where that did not matter. And it could hardly have mattered less than it did in this situation. Philosophy and Religion Fundamentals Review was a class that you had to take, but you could be graded only on attendance. Theoretically it could help your application to the Academy but not hurt you. Jak specked it was a sinecure for teachers who really enjoyed hassling younger people with statements of the obvious.

Right now Fwidya was trying hard to get them to see

that the Wager was important. Dujuv, sitting next to Jak, objected, "Teacher, isn't this kind of like saying that space travel, or fire, or the wheel, were important? I mean, we know that the whole solar system daks the Wager, it's about the only thing that holds the whole human race together, and we all know that the Hive is the center of the true version of the Wager, masen?"

"*Everyone* believes that they live in the true center of the Wager," Fwidya said, primly. He paced back and forth. This far up in the Hive, 650km above the black hole, the gravity was at 0.4. Fwidya probably didn't intend to bounce as much as he did, but he was a kobold, and the genies had never specked the singing-on ratio between control muscles and main muscle masses for that breed, so his overpowered, squatty leg muscles were always bouncing him too high in this classroom.

"Everyone, everyone, everyone," he repeated. Teacher Fwidya didn't have that habit of repetition because he was a kobold; he had it because he was pedantic, even if he wasn't a bad old gwont on the personal level. "Everyone thinks that they live at the center of the only true version of the Wager. If they thought elsewise, they'd move. Remember the Wager's very own Nineteenth Principle, the one that Nakasen always stressed as essential to success in life: 'Whenever possible, agree with those in power.' Now, nonetheless, the Wager, despite its many, many interpretations, has allowed unprecedented peace through the simple application of the Two Hundred Thirty-four Principles. By now you surely must at least have learned that—"

They had, so they ignored Fwidya's ten-minute summary of the last thousand years of solar system history, and all the interpolated commentary about the Wager and about what Paj Nakasen had meant by it originally and what it had become. Jak drew a caricature of Fwidya, and showed it to Dujuv, who mimed dying of some horrible disease. The students nearby shifted their balance to make it clear that they had nothing to do with them.

It was their last twenty minutes of gen school. Because the grade was all attendance they had to sit through Fwidya's excruciatingly dull review of everything.

Fwidya talked about the Rubahy, and although everyone in the room had probably not had an hour since the age of two without being reminded that the war with the Rubahy had shaped human civilization, or that the aliens resembled a cross between a terrier and a feathered lizard but were in fact utterly different internally, or that their settlement on Pluto was always a matter of dispute and that many wars had erupted within the solar system over it . . . Fwidya had to tell them all of that yet again. And of course he finished off by piously reminding them that though the Rubahy were very bad, it was bad form and ill-mannered to call them by epithets like "terrier" or to express the hope that they might all be genocided sometime soon, either in a war with humans or because the Galactic Court would sooner or later—probably within a few centuries—be ruling on the continuation of both species.

Fwidya went on to describe the fragmentation of planet-surface societies, the complexity of the aristocratic system, and the differences between the Hive and the Aerie, but said absolutely nothing that would surprise anyone.

Dujuv raised his hand. "Teacher Fwidya, you just told us the position of the Hive and the Aerie. You do that every time you mention them."

"That's right."

"You always tell us that the Aerie is at the L4 point, two months ahead of Earth in its orbit, and the hive is at the L5 point, two months behind. Right?"

"That's correct. Is there some point to this question?"

"Well, shouldn't all that be classified information? What if the Rubahy use it to target us?"

Fwidya gaped at him. Dujuv was a panth, and among the hundreds of genied breeds of human, panths had never exactly had a reputation for brilliance, but this was . . . the kobold drew himself up with his full dignity. "By any chance," he asked, "do you have a bet down with your friend Jak Jinnaka as to which one of you can get me to explain the most trivial possible point?"

" 'Principle 122,' " Dujuv quoted, " 'Consider what use those in authority may make of the truth, and speak accordingly.' "

"Well," Fwidya said, mollified a little, "at least you know one of the Principles, and that's more than I would have bet. But on the off chance that the question was serious, the Rubahy have known exactly where both giant stations are for many centuries, and could hardly help it. The construction process that built a black hole here, at the center of the Hive, would be detectable at ranges of five thousand light-years, easily—"

Time crawled by. Jak couldn't make himself care about anything Fwidya said. Twelve more minutes of gen school. Then, at long last, they'd get their feets, and after a vacation, if they were lucky, the Public Service Academy, and a successful, adventurous life, and if they weren't so lucky, then at least a job and a chance to be a little independent. Dujuv was now miming a snake eating his head, or maybe a man who couldn't get back out of a drainpipe—Dujuv wasn't very good at mime, but Jak still found it much more interesting than Fwidya.

More minutes crept by. Fwidya branched off from the history of the solar system to give a history of science since Einstein and the whole human cultural tradition since Bach. Who could Fwidya imagine wouldn't already know this?

Fwidya began his concluding comments, "And so the key to understanding your own culture, and all the great changes of the past few centuries, is—" The period bell rang and the whole class bolted through the door.

"Could that have been the dullest lecture in the history of the universe?" Dujuv asked his friend as they stood at the Pertrans station. They had already requested a Pertrans car and at any moment one should emerge from the metal doors in front of them, glide onto the boarding track, and let them in. Meanwhile they stood with their backs to the station, enjoying the sight of a girls' slamball team jogging by in the wide corridor.

"Naw." Jak was emphatic. "He's what, a bit under two hundred years old? And he's probably given exactly that lecture three times a year for the last hundred seventy years, masen? What are the odds that that was even Fwidya's dullest lecture?"

"One in five hundred ten. People buy lottery tickets with worse odds."

"Good job, old tove. You're using those math skills they told us were so important, masen?"

Dujuv held up his right hand, then looked down at his left palm, where he wore his purse, the supercomputer in a fingerless glove that was as basic to modern life as a wallet or trousers had been. "Is there a record for the dullest lecture in the history of the universe?"

"I only have access to records for the solar system," the purse said. "Do you want me to check those?"

"Please."

"Well," the purse said, "over sixty ways of measuring dullness have been invented, and for each way, a different lecture wins."

"Were any of the dullest lectures by any of those measures ever given by Teacher Fwidya?"

"No," the purse said. "No speeches of his are even ranked."

"That'll be all, you can go off-line," Dujuv said, and the purse said "G'night" and did. Dujuv squeezed his left palm, a little trick that many people did—having programmed the purse to like being hugged, they could reinforce it silently all the time, encouraging it to become a better and better purse. He dropped his left hand to his side. "Well, not only is Fwidya dull, he's also an amateur at it."

Jak shook his head. "So a failure all around. Speaking of that—let's think about ourselves. Do you want to check our scores now, or wait until we're at Entrepot?"

"Let's get to Entrepot, find a good place to sit down and eat, order food, and then check. Are you scared, Jak?"

"Toktru, yeah. Terrified."

"Me too."

"Good thing we never get too scared to eat."

The Pertrans car glided silently into position behind them, a face-to-face two-seater. The canopy popped open and the two toves climbed in, their knees almost touching. Dujuv said, "We want to go to Entrepot, what's the price for less than five?"

"Less than five minutes?" the car asked. This one had a warm, motherly voice.

"Toktru."

"Which end of Entrepot?"

"Wherever there's the most food places."

"Southeast terminal, then. It will be two utils."

"Authorized," Jak said, before Dujuv could, so that the trip would be billed to him. Uncle Sib always seemed to just throw utils in Jak's direction, so Jak might as well spend them on his less-well-off friends.

"Please speak long enough to verify that the speaker-customer was Jak Jinnaka."

> *"Mary had a little duck,*
> *She kept it in her bed,*
> *And everyone that Mary—"*

"Verified." The canopy closed. The car rose, the door to the Pertans passage opened in front of them, and they accelerated onto the line; they would be at Entrepot in less than five minutes or the trip would be free.

"Amazing how it always stops you at that point," Dujuv said. "I mean, right at that syllable. Singing-on."

"Machines are very judgmental, is all. So it listens to as much as it can and then it stops me before I offend its sensibilities," Jak explained. "It's the same way that we sneaked into the school that time, by showing the camera those pictures—it was so offended it closed its eyes. As soon as we're legally adults—which is what, now?"

"About two hours. They have to verify that we went to Fwidya's last class."

"In two hours, then, we won't be children and the machines won't be offended by our bad behavior, and won't send complaints to our folks. I'm going to miss that. You should have seen Uncle Sib's face the time that Myx and I got caught—uh, I mean Sesh and I got caught—"

"Never mind, we're almost there," Dujuv said. "I think I heard this story already."

Jak thought, *That was toktru stupid.* Dujuv had had a crush halfway to forever on Myxenna Bonxiao, and would have gladly spent all his time gazing into her eyes and adoring her. Myxenna, for her part, was happy to have Dujuv's attention; the trouble was that she was also happy to have the attention of most of the heets she knew, and generally got it. Dujuv was loyal and generous except when he was insane, and Jak had just pushed the insane button.

Dujuv was a panth, and the genies had given the panths singing-on fast reflexes, intense attention, quick thinking, and great burst strength. He was Jak's toktru tove, and had always been, but now he was hurting. If he lost his temper at Jak . . . well, an unmodified human against a panth was like a kitten against a bear.

After a minute or so of brooding, Dujuv's naturally energetic disposition won out. "Hey, so what are we going to do tonight besides celebrate?"

"You need more to do?"

"Well, we'll have a meal and go somewhere for some fun, but it seems like we ought to do more. You don't get your feets and escape from gen school every day. We could dance, or brawl, or maybe just go climb something."

"Let's not climb another light shaft, though, eh?"

That particular stunt had gotten them six days' house arrest last year. The light shafts mixed and carried the bright glow of the sunlight and the actinic blaze of the plasma around the black hole at the heart of the Hive, distributing it to skylights, sconces, and lamps throughout the gigantic space station. They ran out radially from the central black hole space to openings on the surface. In the shafts themselves, many thousands of little catchers—fiber optic-filled pipes with a mirror at the end, like one end of a periscope—jutted into the bright light, and it had occurred to Dujuv that if they got in through a service entrance, the catchers might furnish the hand and footholds for a good long climb. Since the sperical shell forming the Hive from the mirrored face of the black hole enclosure at the center to the outer surface covered with silvery pipes and domes, was about 1250 km thick, they were never going to be able to climb the whole way, but "We can sure see some interesting spaces and do some interesting technical stuff," Dujuv had said. "We can do it up toward the surface, in low gravity, so it's more skill and less strength. Come on, Jak, it will be fun."

Unfortunately, small bends and forces in an optical tube cause big distortions in the light coming out of it; furthermore, the boys had forgotten that their shadows would be cast for very long distances along the tubes. All over one big cone-shaped sector of the Hive, lights bounced and flickered, odd beams swept out from the sides of sconces and chandeliers, and many lights simply went out. The all-powerful Maintefice was flooded with complaints within a second or two; by the time, ten minutes later, when the pokheets caught the two boys, they had probably become the least popular adolescents since people had begun moving into the Hive a thousand years ago.

Jak and Dujuv sat quietly, enjoying each other's company, as light and dark flashed by the Pertrans car windows. Some unknown architectural genius in the Hive's construction agency, many centuries before, had thought to require viewports in the sides of the Pertrans tunnels, so that in nearly every classroom, shop, corridor, park, gym, or office—any space but a private home—you were forever seeing the flash of passing Pertrans cars. But since the cars moved at bullet speeds, the passengers only rarely saw anything other than a flash of light, and people in the spaces tuned out the brief flicker of a passing Pertrans.

Entrepot was about two hundred kilometers northeast of their gen school, and more than three hundred kilometers deeper within the Hive, so the Pertrans would have to take most of its permitted five minutes. After ninety seconds of near weightlessness, weight increased briefly to almost a full g. As the car slowed to make its turn, for an instant Jak and Dujuv looked through a viewport into a big public gymnasium, then into the amusement park under it, and finally into a warehouse below that. Then the g of weight became diagonal, feeling as if the car were climbing a slope, and then each viewport glimpse came faster and briefer, till it was all flashing lights again.

Just after it felt like they were on a steep downslope, the lights flashed more slowly and became glances through windows again, and the Pertrans glided to a halt at Entrepot. Jak opened the door and stepped into the annoying heavy; Entrepot was at .76 grav.

Dujuv planted his feet on the walkway beside Jak. As the canopy folded back he had grabbed its upper lip, swung out and up, done a handstand grasping the top edge of the door, switched hands, and dismounted in a somersault.

"Do you *have* to do that?"

"No, but I *can*. Decision time. Where are we going? Where's a good place to find out if we got into the PSA?"

Jak shrugged. "We need a place where we can both celebrate, or where we can both commiserate, or where one of us can pretend to be happy for the other one."

"Well, when I celebrate, I like to do it at a place with lots of food. When I'm depressed, I just want to eat. And anytime I have to conceal my feelings, I get nervous, which always makes me really hungry." Dujuv raised his left hand to his face, palm inward. His purse—the fingerless glove into which his computer was built—activated, casting a faint glow on Dujuv's face. "Where would we go for a lot of food cheap?"

"The same place you go four times a week, the Old China Cafe," the purse said. "Jak will have sweet and sour beefrat, and you'll have a triple portion of oyster fried rice and an order of fishloaf with Chinese vegetables. Authorize to pre-order? Or are you going to pretend you're having something else until you get there?"

"Pre-order," Dujuv said, laughing.

"Done." The glow vanished from Dujuv's face and he dropped his hand to his side.

"Toktru, you ought to do something about your purse's attitude, Duj," Jak said.

Dujuv shrugged. "I like some spirit in my purse, even if it's a little snotty. It's a good way to check and see if I'm an idiot."

"You could just ask your friends."

"They're all idiots." Dujuv grinned. "And besides, if your purse can have an attitude, it can be your friend, and it won't turn you in if you do something like climb a light shaft."

That poked Jak in a sore spot; his purse had gleefully informed on him as soon as the pokheets had called it, whereas Dujuv's had done its best to hide him.

"I just don't like the idea of them being able to back-talk to people," Jak said. "Before you know it they'll start to think that they *are* people."

"Well, they are smart. And they talk, *and* they have feelings—"

"Only so they'll have judgment!"

"Isn't that supposed to be why evolution gave humans feelings?"

"That's just my point. Humans got feelings from evolution, and we're free and wild and have our feets. Any feelings a purse has, it got from its designer, just to make it useful, and any feets it has are just trouble."

Dujuv stopped, his weight settling as if he might

strike. "Aren't you forgetting you're talking to a designed breed?"

Jak had, and he felt like a complete gweetz. He drew a deep breath, asking the calm of the Disciplines to run through his mind. "Why is it," he asked, keeping his voice low and neutral, "that whenever we're both toktru scared and nervous about something, I keep picking a fight by saying stupid things? This makes the second time in less than twenty minutes. And you tolerate it!"

Dujuv smiled, his mouth tight and flattened, his eyes still hard. "Oh, no, I don't just tolerate it, I enjoy it. It helps me relax. I find it soothing to think about breaking your neck."

"I bet. Why do I do that?"

"Because you're an idiot. If you'd treat your purse decently, it would tell you." Jak started to laugh, and Dujuv's shoulders relaxed and his bare scalp smoothed like a tugged sheet. "We need to get to the Old China Cafe. Our food is probably ready by now."

They paid the extra for a closed booth so that they would not be interrupted. The waitron delivered the food almost as soon as they had settled in, so now there was nothing to delay getting their results, except their nerves. They used up another five minutes arguing about who should go first, settling on sending in the request simultaneously. "Let's just go ahead and be childish about it," Jak said. "Set up the request on your purse but don't send it yet . . . I'll set it up on mine . . . okay, on three. One, two, three."

The result popped up instantly and Jak stared at it. Everyone knew what it meant when the message began

"We regret to inform you . . ." but Jak read and reread the whole message.

He had missed admission to the PSA by sixty-five points out of ten thousand possible. Assured admission for an unmodified-stock human had been 8529, and his score had been 8464. A few people with lower scores than Jak's had gotten in, but those were people from urgently needed specialty breeds.

"Rat turds," Dujuv said, quietly, looking down at his hand. He looked the way Jak felt.

"You too?"

"Missed it by eleven points. 8166 for a panth to get in and I got 8155."

Jak refrained from considering that with his score, Dujuv would have gotten in; if you went in as a panth, they expected things that were physically impossible for Jak. "I missed by sixty-five," he said.

They sighed, together, loudly. "Well," Jak added, "at least neither of us has to do any pretending."

"Yeah." Duj slammed the table with his hand, making their plates bounce alarmingly. "Weehu. I wonder what we'll end up doing? I thought about it, of course, and I had an in-case plan, but it all seemed very unreal till just this moment. What are you planning to do? Sign on with a general labor brigade?"

Jak shook his head. "Naw. I don't have to go *that* heavy. I'll try the Army. A smart heet like me could make sergeant pretty quick, and from there if you're a good enough sergeant, you can get into one of the officer programs and eventually it's just as if you went to the PSA in the first place. And the next time one of the human settlements gets into something with the Rubahy, or if

Triton tries to secede again, or if we get into another argument about who owns Ceres, we can be out in the dark bouncing around in cryojammies, shooting up the landscape. It's a busy violent world out there, and we can get into all the violence we could ever want. You can't beat that for amusement. Better than a simulation game!"

"You can't get killed in the simulation games. Not literally, anyway. You're not really thinking of going into the Army, are you, Jak? I mean, you just did a great job of describing why not to go in. And you have to be a sergeant for six years to be eligible for officer school. That's like an average of . . . shit, Jak, that's going to be at least two wars. As a sergeant. Which you won't make right away, anyway. Probably three wars before you're a lieutenant."

"Oh, I agree the PSA would have been a better way to go—five years and walk out the door and into the commission. But I'm on entropy's bad side. I didn't get in. I'd still like to be a full citizen and I'd still like to get a good job. The Army looks like the way. And besides, I kind of like the idea of the adventure and the travel."

"Weehu. Fine idea. Adventures like digging foxholes in high gravity, close to absolute zero. And the very first thing you get to do is travel clear to the other side of the Hive. Must be what, two hours on the Pertrans?"

"But after Basic—"

"Oh, toktru, masen? the chance to be a guard on a mining asteroid. Or a ship's B&E on an orbicruiser—four years of cleaning and polishing your stuff and staying in shape, in case they need you for ten minutes of getting killed. Are you totally crazy, or have you just gotten way too far into those intrigue-and-adventure stories you like, or what? At least go into the Spatial, where you can get to fly the ship."

"There's no way for me to do that, Duj, toktru, I've thought about it, and there isn't. The Spatial gets to pick first and there are going to be lots of people ahead of me. I barely have the physap for the Spatial, and I sure don't have the mathap."

"But aren't your mechap and spatiap singing-on? They always need riggers and optimizers."

"They want heets who are top-rate across the board. I looked into this, Duj, toktru, because for some reason after I took that test I specked some bad feelings about the whole thing—pretty well dakked I'd gotten wanged, even before I got the scores. My math scores just toktru *kill* my chances for the Spatial. No, if I want into the Forces, it's the Army. And I'm not going to go through all the hassles of Basic just to hold down a desk or fix a machine, so if I enlist, I'm enlisting to be a dirtkick." The emphasis in his own voice surprised Jak.

Apparently it made an impression on Dujuv too, because he dropped the subject. After the silence had stretched too long, Jak asked, "So what did you have in mind for yourself?"

"I'm going to see if I can get on a professional slam-ball team." Dujuv said, his voice oddly tense. Jak noted that Dujuv's usually relaxed shoulders were hanging high. This was something Duj cared about and was expecting a fight about, so Jak resolved at once that no matter what, he was going to back his tove.

Even though this might be, toktru, the stupidest idea he'd ever heard.

"Well," Jak ventured, "you're a hell of an athlete even

for a panth, and you're a determined sort of a heet, and I think you'll probably make it."

Duj smiled at him. "Thanks."

But Jak couldn't quite stop himself from saying, "It's just that I can't quite believe you were worried about me getting killed in battle if you're planning to play slamball."

"People are not *supposed* to die at slamball."

"But they *do*." Jak knew he should shut up, but he couldn't seem to make himself. Dujuv was too important to him, and he could practically hear his Uncle Sib's often-repeated comment that slamball was something like the ancient Roman arena and something like medieval American television but without the intelligence and compassion of either. "Dujuv, last year was a safety record for the league—they only killed twenty-eight players. Most of those were goalies. And a panth—especially an athlete like you—will be a goalie!"

"Jak, toktru, I did my homework on the subject. Even goalies don't get killed if they're good. There's two hundred teams in pro slamball, and they all have five goalies. It was only sixteen out of a thousand, and at least half of those were heets who should have retired years ago and just stayed in too long. Krayjnean, the Hive National goalie that got killed, was depressed and suicidal about getting too old to play, and he had told people he wanted his league life insurance to pay off to take care of his family—you can't really count that death as an accident. There's usually a couple like that every year, masen? So those shouldn't count. And like I said, if you're good, you don't get killed. See, I did the research."

Jak wanted to argue further but he was already breaking a promise to himself. "Yeah, I dak it's mostly marginal and too-old goalies that get killed. And you're not going to be marginal, ever, and by the time you're getting to be a gwont, with your brains—assuming nobody scrambles 'em for you—you can move into coaching or managing, especially if you have a good record."

"I'm going to have a *great* record." Dujuv's gaze was level and serious. "You and I are not so different. We're both willing to take a little risk to get some travel and adventure. My goal, to start with, is to make it onto Hive National within a couple of years, and volunteer for the travel squad. They go everywhere, even Earth."

"Earth? With all the other opportunities, why do you want to go there? It's a giant collection of pocks in superhigh grav."

"Have you seen the pictures of the beaches around those pocks? And the girls on the beaches? Like say in the pock clusters in North Australia or in Arizona?"

Jak nodded. "I can see your point. If it's not a sore subject, where does Myx fit into this?"

"She'd look light on a beach, toktru, but you can trust me this time: Myxenna Bonxiao and I are completely, totally, utterly, toktru through, masen? Never again. She's not my demmy and I'm not her mekko and we won't be again. All over."

"Weehu, I'm sorry to hear that," Jak said. He did not believe a word of what his tove was saying. After all, it had never been true in all the many times that Dujuv had said it before. But though he didn't believe it, he knew that right now his tove needed sympathy, and Jak had plenty of practice at extending sympathy in the circumstances.

"What happened?" Jak asked. *This time,* he thought.

"Oh, some of it's happened so often that you could almost just say 'the usual,' masen? She just won't leave other heets alone, and she's always very sorry and acts toktru sweet and does outrageously kind and considerate things, afterward, and then I go running back. But I've decided that this time I'm never, never, never going running back. We'll still be friends and be in touch all the time, masen, because we have a long history and I adore the girl and all, and if either of us needs it the other one will be there, that goes without saying, and so forth, of course, but I'm not going running back. It's just too far beneath any reasonable semblance of my dignity.

"But anyway, look, Jak, we were talking about my career choice, and I can tell you're biting your tongue trying to support me, which toktru I appreciate more than I can say, because none of my family and none of my other friends are doing that. So what I can admit to you is what I can't admit to them: I *dak* the odds are rotten, but—I'm ambitious. Furthermore, thanks for the compliment but I'm not very smart, not even for a panth. The genies made me to be an athlete, cop, or soldier, not any kind of great brain. The jobs I could get in the more conventional line would be the Army (and I already told you how I feel about that), or asteroid pioneering (which means being out in the void for most of my life), or being a pokheet—hassling teenagers to keep them from doing stuff that looks like harmless fun to me."

Jak shrugged. "You don't seem crazy to me, Duj."

"Too small a sample for a valid poll!"

The boys started at the sudden voice outside the door.
With a soft ping, the booth door went transparent and
Sesh and Myx were standing there. Jak clicked the un-
lock, the girls slid in beside the boys, and the door
closed, locked, and opaqued again. Sesh grabbed Jak and
kissed him passionately; she was a great kisser, so Jak
stopped thinking about anything else except how good
her tongue felt in his mouth and how nice her body felt
in his hands. When they came up for air, Sesh had that
soft, damp-eyed smile that always made Jak's heart
pound.

Sesh nodded to her left, grinning, and winked at Jak.
Myxenna and Dujuv were kissing, or rather Myxenna
was kissing and Dujuv was pinned to the wall, but she
was doing enough kissing for both of them. Sesh
breathed in Jak's ear, "He's been all jealous and cranky
lately, so she's trying to get him out of it."

"Might be working," he muttered back. "Either that or
he's about to pass out from hypoxia."

While they waited for Dujuv to give in or Myx to give
up, Jak enjoyed looking at Sesh; he couldn't imagine
ever having a demmy he liked better. She was tall and
slender, and at least one of her ancestors must have been
a gracile, for her muscles had the flat, long, strong, chis-
eled look of that breed, and she always moved from her
center, with smooth power, like a natural athlete. She
tan-patterned her light coffee skin, so that her face and
body were marked with a deep brown tiger stripe; she
had deep blue eyes and flame-red hair. Her white one-
piece coverall, short-legged and short-sleeved, fit her
loosely enough to be modest but did not hide the fine-

ness of her body; like everything else about her, it was perfectly chosen and singing-on right for her.

Duj and Myx gave no signs that they were ever going to stop. Sesh shrugged. Loudly, she said, "Ahem, I say, ahem. Myx, let's tell the boys what we came here for."

"I think my boy has a pretty clear idea," she said, sitting back. She was a tiny young woman, with thick, full, black hair, green eyes with blue starring, and pale skin spattered with small freckles. The violet clingsheath she wore fit high on her thigh and she had tugged it higher on one side.

She put on her little puckish smile—the one that had lured Jak, a few times, into things that truly made him appreciate Sesh's tolerance—and said, "Well, we came here to check up on you, and to cheer you up. Once you access your own scores, they become public domain, so we found out what happened to you. Then we called the monitors on your purses, and we saw what your moods were like, and here we are, the Sunshine Squad, to cheer you up."

Duj was obviously precessed. "I thought you and I agreed we wouldn't monitor moods through the purses—"

"That's what we agreed," Myx said, "and we did switch off the monitors on each other's emotions. You seemed to want to do that and it made you so happy when I agreed."

"But then you switched on again!"

"Well, of course. Just because I could make you happy by switching it off, didn't mean I was going to leave it switched off. I wanted to dak what you were feeling. I just didn't want you to dak what I was feeling. That's important to a demmy, Dujy. I'd think you'd know that by now." To avoid looking at him, she made a show of fixing her lipstick.

Sesh sighed. "Duj, if you ever want to be treated as nicely as you deserve, just let me know, and I'll find you someone who will think the world of you and treat you accordingly."

"Mom's already married," he said, gloomily. "So if you two are here to cheer us up, you must have done all right yourselves."

Sesh raised her shoulders and lowered them, a shrug made into a dance, calling attention to her long, beautiful neck. "Myx sailed right through. I told you I didn't feel very much like I did a singing-on job, right after the test. As it happens, I didn't make it—in fact I bombed out. So that's the score for our little crowd—three losers and one winner."

Myxenna spread her hands, as if she were looking for some way to apologize for her success. "I'm still kind of baffled, myself. Toktru, I thought the test was way too hard and I didn't think I did very well. But apparently I guessed right an awful lot of times, or just dakked the overall rhythm somehow, because I got 9241."

"9241 is brilliant," Jak said, swallowing envy as fast as he could.

Dujuv nodded. "So you're in for the PSA, and I guess that means eventually you'll be Prime Minister Myx . . ."

"I think maybe Minister for External Affairs Myx. It's where I'm best qualified."

Dujuv made a little, coughing laugh. "If I'd said that—"

"You'd better not even think it, Dujy. All right, so I'm in public service, and what are you toves going to do?"

"The Army."

"I'm going to try out for pro slamball."

Jak noted with approval that neither of the girls voiced a word of disapproval. "So what are you planning on, Sesh?"

She sighed. "Can you be nonjudgmental?"

"I can try," Jak said, and Myx added, "Of course we can." Dujuv nodded.

"Well, there's a lot of money in my family. I don't think I'll be picking any occupation."

After a painful, dead silence, Myx said, "You can't possibly mean you plan to register S.P."

Sesh nodded. "I do mean that." After an awkward pause, when she seemed to be waiting for one of them to say something, she added, "It's not such a big deal anymore. Toktru it's not. And you can still do lots of interesting things if you're registered S.P. You just can't do anything for money or have any responsibility. That's not a big deal."

S.P. stood for Social Parasite—a person who lived off family money. A registered Social Parasite was a pariah with sharp restrictions on legal rights: S.P.s could own common stock but the government voted it; they had the same free expression rights as anyone else but couldn't vote; they could sue but not speak in court or serve on a jury. Getting your feets back after registering S.P. was painfully difficult, beginning with a mandatory unpaid five-year hitch in the Forces and continuing through four years of re-education and probation. It was a permanent repository for idiot children of the rich, hopelessly eccentric artists, dangerous incompetents, and the incurably annoying. Although people no longer suicided when they were declared S.P., most 350-year-olds, the oldest generation still alive, would rather have been registered as sex criminals than S.P., and even among young people there was still widespread support for sterilizing S.P.s.

"You're really going to do it," Jak said.

"Toktru."

"But, you're not superrich or anything. I mean you don't dress especially well—"

"Thanks."

"I should have said, you don't dress rich. Don't change the subject. I mean I've never seen any evidence that you were rich, and we've been mekko and demmy for more than two years. You don't vacation on the moon or anything."

"Not lately. I've been there, though, on vacation, when I was younger. And I've been to the Aerie many times. And to Mars, and to Earth. It's just that that was all before you knew me. I didn't travel for the last three years because I wanted to finish gen school. Toktru, once I'm registered S.P. and don't have to hide the trust fund from my toves anymore, I'll probably travel much more."

All of them stared at Sesh; none of them had any idea what to say. "Look," she said, "it's not a big deal. I'm not evil. The Wager makes perfect sense if you're smart and ambitious and need to make money because your trust fund isn't big enough. But I'm glib more than smart, my main ambition is nice things and lots of time off, and I can afford all that without any job. And it makes sense to teach the Wager to people so that they're more predictable and easier to get what you want from, but I don't care whether I'm predictable or whether anyone gets what they want from me. The Wager is a great set of values to channel people trying to make it into useful pathways, but I was born with it made, and I have no intention of being useful, which is the first step on the road to being used. I'm not going to wear a skirt that doesn't suit my long legs or go out with a heet that doesn't suit my sarcastic taste in humor, so why should I have values that don't suit my real position?" She sighed. "It's nice to just tell you all this. I'm tired of having to tell you that I won an advertising contest or a sweepstakes or something whenever I want to take you somewhere pricey."

"Oh, no," Myx said. "So you were just—"

"Toktru masen! And I'm doing it again. After all, there's so much money, toktru it doesn't mean anything to me, but my friends mean a lot to me, and fun means a lot to me. I can afford the lightest, usually many times over, and I like taking you all to places that are light. So—no arguments!—I'm financing some fun with my friends, tonight."

"Sesh, no—" Dujuv began.

"I just happen to have four tickets for the closing performance of Y4UB."

There was a dead silence. Those had been sold out for months; if Sesh had gotten four of them legitimately, she had spent a small fortune, and if she'd gotten them from a scalper, it hadn't been small.

It was also the kind of event you fantasized about going to.

"Well," Jak said, " 'Principle 11: Break any principle

except this one and a few others, but expect the consequences.' I hope you two will come along to make sure I don't fall any further into"—he slipped into his best Teacher Fwidya impression—"the *dark swamp* of that *hideous contemporary affliction,* that *cancer* in the *engine* of *society,* that endless font of mixed metaphors, *moral relativism!*"

The girls laughed; Dujuv said, "You'll sound more like him if you use more emphasis."

"Everyone's a critic. But are we going to do this?"

"Oh, sure," Myxenna said. She stretched in a way that seemed to be sort of an anatomy lesson. "It's not like I've always been extra extremely careful about my principles, if you dak me, masen?"

CHAPTER 2

It's Not the Spread,
It's the Score, and You Lost

Jak had summoned Rover, the family private Pertrans car, as soon as he'd gotten up to leave the Old China Cafe, and by the time he had crossed the hundred-meter-wide courtyard between the restaurant and the private-car Pertrans stop, Rover was gliding into a berth there. Rover was a nice-looking car, with the crosshatch in a purple-yellow Mardi Gras retro that was very clash-splash-and-smash; Jak was grateful that Uncle Sib had let him program the car's surface colors, so that the thing didn't embarrass him when he was out with his toves.

As he crossed the courtyard, he glanced up at the high ceiling, seventy meters overhead; Entrepot was located on a series of ring balconies, so that you could always see everything. It wasn't the biggest shopping area in the Hive, and certainly not the trendiest or most expensive, but for Jak and his friends it had been home for a long time, and would be forever—shopping areas paced their demographics, so just as Entrepot catered to teenagers now, in about 180 years, it would be catering to two-hundred-year-olds.

Sesh's revelations had startled him, not just because of what she had said or because she was going S.P., but also because he'd never thought to add together a few facts in his own life. He got into Rover, and, as he always did, said, "Get me home. High-cost tunnels authorized." That cost fifteen times what using the public tunnels did, but he'd never worried about that one way or another.

"Very good, sir," Rover said. As the canopy closed and the Pertrans car pulled out, Jak realized it was one more observation to add to his stack.

Jak lived with Uncle Sibroillo, the only one of his relatives he could recall ever having met, almost the only one he'd ever heard of, and they lived in one of the lightest, most expensive residential districts. They had a private Pertrans car—few people did. And whereas most of Jak's friends had jobs, Sib just gave Jak money whenever he needed it, and though Jak was expected to do all sorts of things (keep up with the Disciplines, learn skills, run errands, keep things neat, maintain some sort of grades), none of it was ever tied to the money.

For the first time, Jak specked that he was probably from a rich family; there was just too much light stuff around to support any other conclusion. Though it had not been kept secret, no attention had been called to it. As the lights flashed by and Rover whipped through the high-cost tunnels, he decided that it didn't make any real difference to him. Probably that was how Uncle Sib wanted him to feel. He was forever discovering that despite his always seeming to have his feets, one way or another his own freely chosen plan, goal, or way of doing things always turned out to be what Uncle Sib had manipulated him into.

Rover decelerated smoothly until Jak could feel that the grav was mostly the grav normal to the deck and not the acceleration of the Pertrans car. The flashes of the windows resolved into brief glimpses of the mostly empty garden corridors of his neighborhood. After a swing off the main track and onto the siding, Rover glided through the suddenly opening door and into the entry room of Uncle Sib's house, a comfortable little lounge that was also the reception area for people who came to see Sib on business, and settled onto the floor. Rover was the only car there, so Sib probably had no visitors.

Jak got out. Turning back to grab his reader, he realized that it wasn't there. He hadn't taken it to school because he hadn't needed it anymore. He might not even need to read for quite a while.

Toktru, between getting his feets, getting rid of school, the prospect of an active life instead of more school, and the Y4UB performance that night—and now the realization that he might not have to read anything for decades to come—Jak felt great, but before he went in to talk it over with his uncle, he tried to put on a solemn face. Uncle Sibroillo would be extremely disappointed about Jak's scores, and Jak needed to look hangdog. The adult world was much kinder to a teenager who appeared contrite.

If Jak appeared ashamed, Sib would feel justified in imposing no penalty and forgiving him instantly; one thing Jak could count on his uncle for was the very best sort of hypocrisy.

Sib was sitting in the chair by the door. "You fell short for the PSA."

"Not by much." Jak looked at the floor and tried to sound like he really felt wanged.

"It's not the spread, it's the score, and you lost, old pizo. Got anything in mind?"

"Kind of."

Sibroillo raised his eyebrows and spread his hands, his gesture for "your turn" or "go ahead."

Jak swallowed; somehow this moment made it real. "Uh, I'm going to enlist. The Army. Probably career, at least start out like it's career. Try for sergeant, maybe a Guards unit or even B&E."

Sib seemed to study the ceiling very seriously. At last he stretched and yawned. "Well, avoiding false modesty, I can honestly say I've done a good job with you. Many of the things I've taught you, and in particular the Disciplines, ought to stand you in very good stead. You're bright, even if not very bookish, and you have good co-ordination, fast reactions, and enough muscle. If you genuinely want to be a sergeant in a B&E battalion, you'll be able to do that. Even the stubbornness and the quick temper can be advantages if you use them properly."

"It sounds like your opinion is founded on something," Jak said, fishing. Any chance to get Sibroillo reminiscing was important; there were big gaps in what Jak knew of himself and his family.

Sibroillo shrugged. "Not much to say. I was a merc a few times, back before you were born. Like most mercs I got my training in a public army. Rather in four of them, across about forty years, off and on, no hitch more

than three years at a time. That's all you're getting out of
me today."

"How about one direct question?"

"Oh, why not? It's not every day you get out of gen
school. One direct nosy question, provided it has no security impact and it's not about my sex life."

"Yuck."

"What do you suppose Gweshira and I do when we go
out, pizo?"

"Double yuck, Uncle Sib, and you're not going to dis-
tract me that easily. Okay, direct question, were you ever
in a B&E unit?"

"For about two years, I was a lieutenant in the Sixth
Rangers, Army of the Hive. Yes, old pizo, I was a beanie
myself for a while."

Jak realized that he had to get out of the room, quickly,
or risk letting Sib see that he was impressed. "And the
Disciplines help?" he asked. "You're not just saying that
to get me to practice?"

"I want you to practice, but I'm not lying or exagger-
ating. The Disciplines help a great deal."

"Then I'd better get to them."

"Please do." But as Jak turned to go, Uncle Sibroillo
leaned forward from his low round chair and caught his
nephew by the elbow. "I'm very pleased that you've
thought about what you're going to do, that your
thoughts are not unreasonable, and that you are ambitious in your plans. It might not be the career I'd have
chosen for you but it is not a bad choice at all. Or if it is,
we're *both* wrong. Now, about this concert or dance or
whatever it is tonight—"

Jak started to laugh. He couldn't help it. Sib spied on

him constantly. "Let me guess how you knew about it. You monitor my friends and their accounts, and you flag entertainment purchases, and Sesh had probably already put my name on a ticket."

"All true, but not the way I used. And besides what you thought of and what I did, there are also four other ways I could have used. If you don't know all six ways, then you probably shouldn't try to get away with anything yet."

"I wouldn't even try."

"You don't lie as well as you should, yet, either." Sib sat on the edge of his chair. "But no matter—time enough for you to learn more tradecraft. Eventually I will stop monitoring you. Either because you'll get good enough to block it, or you'll be out of range. Meanwhile, you have just time to work the Disciplines, spar with me afterward, eat a quick dinner, and still go meet your toves, all showered and pretty. And I do believe you just said you wanted to get on with practicing—"

"I was sucking up," Jak said, "since I knew I'd have to do it anyway. But I guess I might as well get started. Is sucking up another one of those useful skills you've equipped me with?"

"Damn straight, and probably the most useful one of all. Have a good workout; I'll be in to thump you in a while, puppy. Practice your form so I don't hurt you."

"I'll concentrate on my kicking so I don't bruise my foot on your head, you old gwont."

Jak stepped into his sleeping room and changed into his fighting practice suit; the suit on its hook and a large ever-changing VuPostR were the only decorations the room had. (When Jak was not home, he left the VuPostR tuned to the Grand Canyon on Earth; when he was, he tuned it to the Bordello Highlights channel. Not that Uncle Sib would care, but it was better to look like he *thought* Uncle Sib would care.) He noticed that his bed was still unmade from this morning, and pushed the button to make it. He really did have to get his act a bit more together.

The fighting suit flowed into place over his skin, feeling ready and comfortable as always. Down to the gym-and-studio floor of Uncle Sib's house, Jak took the spiral stair by just dropping the eight meters down the center; in this pricey neighborhood, high up near the outer surface of the Hive, gravity was a bit less than twenty percent of full, and Jak enjoyed the slow drift that gradually became a swift descent.

The workout room looked a bit like a padded cell, a comparison that Uncle Sib liked a lot, and a little like a wrestling room in which no one was sure which surface would be the floor. Every half meter on all six surfaces, the soft milky lenses of the projectors, a few centimeters across, stared at him; right now a few of the overhead ones projected soft white light.

As usual, Jak enjoyed the Disciplines. Today he flowed easily into a relaxed, concentrated focus. Almost from the moment that he slipped on the practice helmet in the padded room, the targeting grid that floated in front of his face glowed clear green; his brain waves were showing the clear, attentive no-mind state, free from wandering, daydreaming, worry, doubt, or fussing.

The targets appeared in their familiar order for the first part, the pure katas. First unarmed: hand strikes, foot strikes, knees, elbows, head butting, and shoulder ramming, each a black figure with a small white target zone, closing in on him. In the induced vision from the goggles, Jak's body was also jet-black whenever it moved with perfect speed on the singing-on trajectory; parts that were too low glowed blue, too high yellow, too far right red, and too far left green. The further off his timing was, the brighter they glowed. Each target was presented seven times, for each blow, and then another seven times for Jak's left, off side. The seven positions in which the target was presented marked the center and corners of a hex within which the blow would be appropriate.

First the target glowed on the onrushing figure's face, and Jak hit it with a clean jab. The figure came in up on its toes, left and right, then from the sides farther away, and finally in a slight crouch. Each time Jak hit singing-on, seeing no light or color in his arm. When he had begun the Disciplines, at age four, an absence of lights would have pleased him, and glows would have frustrated him; now it was something he just dakked, without concern of any kind, absorbing it all mentally but having no feeling one way or another about it.

The seven right jabs gave way to seven left jabs, followed by seven spear-fingered thrusts at the larynx, right then left; then hand-heel strikes at the point of the jaw, then hooks and uppercuts. The pace was set to a blow every 1.3 seconds, fast enough to be a workout and to require quick recoveries; Jak's breathing synched into the process, and he was aware that his heart was working at six beats to the breath, just as it should, without caring very much. His body seen through goggles remained perfectly black, and he continued to strike and strike, through crosses, thrusts, and chops.

He finished the first section with the right and left shoulder rams to the straight leg, the front-and-reverse two-leg thrust to the jaw, and the standing clothesline blocks. There had been no glows yet. It was a good day, toktru. His body remained black all through throws, locks, chokes, disarms, short blades, long blades, slug throwers, and beam pistols. Jak burned down his last black attacking figure, drawing a neat line that would have severed the right arm if he had faced a real opponent with a real maser. The score—a personal record—popped up on his helmet, and he pushed the goggles up and took off his helmet. He knelt and let his focus and calm settle deeply, preparing for the second phase, random sparring against the machine, in which it would try to break his concentration. When he felt empty and clear, he reached for the helmet.

He had just touched it when a cord dropped around his neck and tightened, digging into his windpipe and squeezing his carotids so that the dark poured in from all sides toward the center of Jak's field of vision.

His concentration was singing-on today, and although this attack called for action, it did not matter. No start or twitch disturbed his focus. Ignoring the cord for an instant, he reached behind, found pant cuffs, gripped and arched, and backflipped out of his kneeling position, hard work even in the .2 gravity. As they flipped through the air and Jak gained slack in the cord, his attacker tried to put knees against the small of Jak's back, to maintain leverage.

Jak used that motion to twist away, escaping toward

the attacker's feet. He slammed the back of his head into his opponent's crotch as he pulled him over his head. The grip on the cord relaxed for an instant, and Jak got another grip, on his opponent's armpits, and pulled him forward and off as if he were fighting his way out of a frenzied sweater.

The attacker lost one end of the cord, and though it dragged and burned, it flew off Jak's neck. He avoided gasping, and instead expelled his trapped air in a *ki-ai!* as he kicked where the attacker's head should have been, trying to fly backward to get a moment for a good breath. But as Jak kicked, the attacker's foot slipped up the inside of Jak's thigh, using it to guide in until the ball of the opponent's foot slammed into Jak's armored cup.

A bell rang.

Jak went limp for an instant, calmed himself, took that long-delayed breath, then stood and bowed. "So now it's 2030 to 1489 overall."

Sib laughed. "Still obsessed with the score, eh? But most of my wins happened when you were twelve years old and just starting to do this." He held up his hand and spoke into his purse. "What's the score between Jak and me over the last two years, and what do the stats look like in general?"

"477 to 434 across the last two years," the purse said. "Across the last year, 231 to 226. It is projected that within one year, at present rates of change, Jak Jinnaka will surpass you in probability of success. In about eleven years at present rates of change, Jak will surpass you overall."

"Thank you, off," Sib said. "You see, Jak? All a matter of patience. Now we need to get you fed fast enough so you'll have time to get all prettied up for your concert. Let me just okay the food delivery and they should be ready to vac it over. As it happens, I noticed that you went to the Old China Cafe for your after-school meal, so rather than Chinese I'm having Lunar Greek delivered—baked hamster with bechamel on glutles, with mango pastry for dessert—if you can manage to force that down."

It was Jak's favorite takeout, and they both knew it. "I guess I'll have to. Wouldn't want to hurt your feelings."

They had all agreed to meet up at the Genorma Ferry Station, to catch the gripliner over to Centrifuge together; the four of them would take a private compartment together. Jak was the first to arrive, which was typical. He waited in the vast, echoing lobby. Most of the time gripliners ran nearly empty; there were just a few peak-time trips that filled up. Thus most of the time the big space wasn't needed for arriving or departing crowds, and it merely looked like a very large and unattractive abandoned shopping mall with an unusual ceiling display. In the great vaulted ceiling, divided into thousands of meter-wide windows, the eight cables that connected Genorma Station on the Hive with Amroneg Station on the Ring formed silvery lines cutting through the stars; the cables ran to just outside the windows, for the gripliner airlocks were positioned in an octagon around the lobby. As Jak watched, a gripliner was just arriving, a silver cylinder the size of three gymnasiums sliding down the bright line of the linducer cable like a drop of mercury on a wire, as it lost the very last of its speed before slipping into the airlock to dock.

Jak wandered aimlessly around the central shopping area, shuttered now because it was still some hours until First Shift would be getting up and going to work. As he made one trip or another around the cluster of cafes, news-stands, and office supply stores, Dujuv would turn up.

Glancing at his reflection in the shop windows as he passed, Jak thought he was doing a superior job of being conspicuous in a good way—his clothes for the evening were the very model of clash-splash-and-smash; he looked light from head to foot. He had chosen to wear his new singlet with spirals of nonfunctional buttons, over his zebra print coverall, with lace-up red gripslippers with grown-lizard soles. Over the singlet, he wore his lavender cutaway with big, droopy, double-rolled sleeves, popular that year at the Academy and just start-ing to spread down into gen school; he'd have to take that off, of course, for the dancing, but right now it def-initely added. The unattached collar and bowler hat com-pleted the look; he stood out in a way that said he had taste and style, not quite perhaps at the heliopause of fashion, but toktru his orbit was close to tangential to it.

The crowd now coming in for the next gripliner seemed to be mostly families with young children. Jak remembered vaguely that there was a big public play area near Centrifuge, so quite possibly it was just all the Third Shifters who had the day off. The station echoed with screams and shouts; very low gravity is a hard place in which to cope with very small children—when they can leap five meters into the air, and they take ten full seconds to descend from that height, more if they air-swim, little kids rapidly begin exploring whole new di-mensions of misbehavior. Jak quickly lost count of the number of times he heard a parent hissing or growling to a child, "Do that one more time and I'll leash you like a two-year-old."

Not that leashes on two-year-olds were doing much good; the common slang for a two-year-old on a leash was "yoyo," and not merely for the resemblance to the toy. As Jak watched, two leashes, then two tantrums, then two mothers all became hopelessly entangled.

His view through the big viewports in the central dome far over his head was disturbed only by the occasional high-jumping older child. The stars seemed motionless overhead, although the ferry station crawled along the big track that circled the Hive. The Hive itself didn't rotate at all; there was no reason for it to do so, since it got its gravity from the black hole of the power plant at its center, and kept its sunside cool and its darkside warm with an active circulatory system. But gravity was a drawback for many industrial processes and recreation in zero-g was one of the great pleasures to which humanity had become addicted in a millennium and a half of spaceflight. Hence the Ring orbited the Hive at a distance of about 3500 kilometers above its surface decks, a tubular industrial park, playground, port, sports arena, farm, and whatever else it needed to be, less than half a kilometer across but more than 28,000 km long. It was connected by a few hundred ribbons of linducer track running between regularly-spaced gripliner stations on the underside of the Ring and moving stations on the great track that belted the Hive, so that the Hiveside stations followed along, like a toy dog on wheels, under the Ring. Thus the gripliner stations were the only places on the Hive that had regular, predictable days and nights and rising and setting stars.

Just at the moment, the station was rolling around the dark side of the Hive, and the sun was brightly lighting the Ring, which appeared as a thin white streak running all the way across the dome of the sky, with a barely discernible thickness.

Upholding tradition, Dujuv was the next to arrive. He was dressed like Jak but more conservatively, so his clothes clashed rather more, still showing the influence of the hyperbolic clash-splash-and-smash of the last generation. Everything was patterned and all the patterns seemed to vibrate against each other; his cutaway was asymmetric and his bowler had a diffracting surface on which jagged rainbows danced. The eye settled on his clothing less easily than on Jak's, but with his beautiful panth's body, he didn't quite need so much help from his clothes. Still, he could have done a bit better, with a bit more imagination; he was about five percent to the heavy side of Jak.

"You look perfect," Jak lied.

The girls appeared exactly as late as they were supposed to. It was the decade of underwear and slashing, anyway, and in the varying microgravity of Centrifuge, what was under a skirt would matter at least as much as the skirt itself. They both wore cling bodices under frilly camisoles under three filmy layers of slashed sleeveless tops, with everything pulled through; below the waist, they wore open-fronted gozzies cut to a modest mid-thigh (for Sesh) and a millimeter short of arrest (for Myx), beneath which they wore several layers of decorated pants, also all pulled through the slashing. Natu-

rally Sesh wore simple zero-g athletic slippers for dancing, and Myxenna wore red spike-heeled boots for effect. The combination of slashes, openings, and
translucencies made a swirl of flattering color, and the
constantly frustrated expectation of seeing more than
was intended would "draw the cameras, toktru," Jak
said, appreciatively. "You could both end up as motifs."

Dujuv was still gaping.

"Oh, honestly, I just look toktru light," Myx said. "It's
still me, Dujy. Toktru." She grabbed him and kissed him
hard, which seemed to bring him out of that spell, and
plunge him into another.

Once they boarded the gripliner, they had just time to
settle into their compartment, reclining their seats fully
and opening their complimentary drinks, before the
gripliner headed out to the Ring. Linducers like those on
the gripliners and Pertrans produced constant force,
which meant constant acceleration, which was experienced as constant gravity, just as Einstein or Newton
might have explained it. The gripliners shot along their
cables at .9 g, accelerating all the way to flipover at the
midpoint, then, after the five seconds of weightlessness
while the view out the windows rotated 180°, slowed at
the same .9 g for the rest of the way. The trip would take
about twenty-two minutes.

To the four toves, it seemed that they reclined in comfortable chairs, in relatively high gravity, while the Hive
fell away from them; then after eleven minutes, there
was a brief disorienting whirl; and then for eleven more
minutes they reclined as the Ring rose under them and
resolved itself into a great belt of light, then of greenery,
then of streets and homes and workplaces, until finally it

was the ground about to be beneath their feet—but it never quite became that, because the gripliner slowed all the way to dock inside the Ring, joining it in free fall, and once it did, there was no "beneath."

As they emerged from the gripliner, Jak treated himself to a look back at the Hive; he always loved this view. Though they were 3500 km from its surface, the giant space station was eighty times the apparent width of the sun, more than a fifth as wide as the sky itself. The tiny dots of the stations rolling on their tracks ceaselessly around the Hive, the whirling flash of thin silver that was the launch loop at the Hive's North Pole, and the sparkling engine flares of the little Maintefice rockets carrying workers around on the surface all delighted him. There was something about knowing that you lived in the grandest place in the universes.

Centrifuge was only about thirty km from Amroneg Station, where the gripliner docked on the Ring, and the Pertrans took only moments to get them from the station to the club. The club itself was a great windowless steel sphere, a quarter of a kilometer across, encaged in a webwork of steel girders; at the moment it was stationary, and the transparent bridge tube from the Ring to the club was open. The four toves walked up the bridge tube, stars at their feet, over their heads and all around them, to find that as always, Sesh's sense of timing had been singing-on, and they arrived at the back of a short line, just before a long line accumulated behind them.

In the weightless interior of the sphere, they swam away from the bridge entrance, which would be closed when the concert began, and into the vast chamber. At its center, about fifteen meters across, was a transparent sphere that contained the booths, monitors, seats, and control boards that Y4UB was setting up and checking out. Once the slec started, the bridge entrance would be closed and the club would tumble, generating artificial gravity whose direction and force constantly changed, while the central sphere remained motionless and weightless within.

While Y4UB set up and checked out their equipment, a few of the more passionate technogweetzes floated around the central sphere watching them, but everyone else just floated in the immense enclosed space, hanging around and talking to friends. As always, one of the prime topics was whether or not Centrifuge would stay open.

The owners of Centrifuge would no doubt have liked it if they could have gotten continuous use out of the place, like most spaces on the Ring; this was some of the lightest real estate in the solar system. But Centrifuge was really only suitable to slec, and there just wasn't any other use for such a space. Slec had a following big enough so that the revenues were attractive, but it had never quite broken through to a mass audience, probably because its esthetic required people to experience it live and dancing—there would be little point in listening to pure audio recordings of it, and no one, as yet, had specked a way to position and operate cameras for a remote audience to toktru dak the djeste. So each successive team of investors thought that the time for mass market slec had arrived, and each turned out to be wrong, and Centrifuge went on closing and re-opening. "Sooner or later someone will lose patience enough to convert the place to some other use," Myxenna pointed out. "Or they'll come up with whatever else you can do in a microgravity space where the gravity varies in both force and direction at random. It pretty much has to happen. By that time we'll probably be old gwonts and won't care about slec, anyway."

"That's kind of sad," Dujuv said.

"Very sad. So we'd better have fun while it lasts," she said. "I'm going to circulate—it's better to get the *diem carpe*'d while it's still fresh." She tucked, rolled, air-kicked, drifted to the side, and sprang off hard, shooting by the central sphere and arcing to disappear behind it.

"Duj, if you go following after her, you'll look toktru pathetic," Jak said. "She'll come back in a while."

The panth relaxed a moment and then sighed. "But if I don't, I'll wonder what she's up to."

"She's finding a bunch of overmuscled, underclothed heets to flirt with," Sesh said, impatiently. "Now you know. So stick around your toktru toves and relax a little, masen?"

He did, for about ten minutes, until he saw Myx floating in a knot of heets. Then he made the face that meant he knew he was being a gweetz but couldn't help himself. With a sigh, Dujuv pushed off on a trajectory that would allow him to drift gradually into the crowd that floated steadily around Myx as she slowly circled the room, perhaps twenty meters from the great curving burnished-silver wall. As he joined the crowd, Sesh observed, "It's sort of like a solar system. There's Dujuv, orbiting in close, like a planet, and then a flock of heets orbiting further away but trying to get in, like the Kiuper Belt, and then a few girls hanging around at the very outer edges, like the Oort Cloud."

"Except that when one of the comets gets out of the Kuiper Belt and heads in toward the sun, it's Duj that goes hyperbolic," Jak said.

"First one of us that accuses the other of being elliptical gets slapped."

"Toktru."

"Seriously, though," Sesh said, "Myx and Duj. After all this time, I still don't understand it. They're so different, I don't dak how they dak each other." She pulled herself around so that she could float comfortably face-to-face with Jak, legs and arms gently intertwined.

Jak shrugged. "I know what he sees in her. I just don't speck how he can keep seeing it."

"I never get it either." She looked at the crowd, again, and laughed. "I have to admit that she's funny and charming and sexy—"

"And singing-on beautiful."

Sesh nodded eagerly. "Toktru beautiful. But Duj has this weird throwback loyal-monogamy obsession, and Myx can't possibly fit into that anywhere. The strange thing is that he could find more than enough attractive girls, who would love to be his demmy, and they'd really dak what he wanted and give it to him. So I don't know why he's obsessed with getting Myxenna Bonxiao, of all people, to behave contrary to her nature. I mean—when you were with her, what, a few times—"

"Twice."

"You didn't try to get her to be anything other than the way she is."

"The way she is, is what I was interested in," Jak said.

Sesh beamed at him. "That's my tove. And you've always let me have the same feets. But with Duj . . . can you imagine what he's going to be like when he's touring with his slamball team—and knowing him, he'll be getting plenty while he's on the road—and she's at the PSA, with a lot of smart ambitious heets?"

"My tove will be absolutely completely totally insane, toktru. But he's used to that."

Sesh was about to say something, but the great curving walls around them began to move slightly, and a low bass rumble echoed back and forth across Centrifuge; Y4UB was founding their first piece.

Slec, like so many other kinds of contemporary art, was third remove. The first remove had been the solution to problems of technical execution, something that had begun even before spacefaring; today the djeste of the first remove was so complete that only hobbyist-antiquarians bothered to learn to use hand tools like brushes, pencils, or guitars, or to compose sentences or place cameras. The second remove was that of routine creativity: in the last few centuries, AIs had become complex and proficient enough so that if you gave them the outlines of a few "highlight" scenes or a good central image, they could write a Shakespeare play, Kundera novel, or Petrarch sonnet that was singing-on like the real thing; given a photograph, they could paint the scene in a way a human being couldn't distinguish from Leonardo or Van Gogh; given a sequence of a few pitches, they could compose so like Beethoven that Beethoven himself couldn't have heard the difference. And once there were AIs that could do that, the process was instantly industrialized, so that nowadays it produced the background noise or the intellectual wallpaper of civilization.

The third remove was the synesthetic remove, developed just in the last couple of generations. For thousands of years creators had relied on an intuitive sense that some music was "blue" or "red," or that a given curve on a sculpture was "sweet" or that it "sang," or that high comedy is like a soufflé; sufficient time and processing capability had led to machines for which such metaphors were not merely intelligible, but meaningful and machine-processable.

Y4UB was not so much a band of musicians as it was a team of engineer-critics, who could sweep through hundreds of cameras to look for the interesting dance move, the worthwhile facial expression, the pose, the clothes, or the bons mots, sample that, feed it to the synthesizer, and turn it into melody, motif, harmony, or rhythm for the jamming AIs that wove the endless music. Each member of Y4UB was also a proficient phraser, tossing ideas and words into the mix via their microphones, where they sometimes became parts of the light show, sometimes bits of the music, now and then an overall theme, and even, sometimes, lyrics for any of the thousands of synthesized voices that might break from the speakers at any moment.

Slec was dense, swift, heavy-to-light in a moment, yet sustained through a whole evening. If it wasn't possible to really record what happened when a group like Y4UB worked in a space like Centrifuge with a toktru singing-on crowd, that was part of the charm. You genuinely had to be there.

Things always started simply. When the band was founding the first set, they started with a beat, some colored light, a few sounds, and a random pattern of tumbling for the room as a whole; everyone would get up and begin to dance in the air, at first tentatively, and the band would look for some interesting moves or appearances from which to grow the first piece. It was widely believed, anyway, that if you moved with confidence, you were much more likely to attract the attention of the band, and if that happened, the piece would be more about you than about most of the crowd—about as deep a compliment as you could hope for.

Jak was good at slec; everyone said he was one of the lightest dancers. But Sesh was in her own class, toktru superb. She danced like an eagle flies, as if she had been shaped to no other purpose. Jak was athletic and gymnastic, and many people had told him he was very graceful—he privately attributed it to all the practice at the Disciplines—but when he danced with Sesh, he always felt just a tiny bit clumsy, by comparison with her unerring grace; her sheer shining style seemed to rebuke the universe for not being as beautiful as it ought to be. Dancing with her, Jak seemed a little awkward to himself, as if he were having to jerk slightly to stay on her beat, and a little colorless, as if even his best moves were faded, and a little heavy, as if he had somehow slipped out of fashion.

On the other hand, Jak consoled himself, hardly anyone else could keep up with Sesh at all.

Dujuv and Myxenna weren't quite on the same level as dancers that Sesh and Jak were, but they were still a delight to watch; his powerful panth body flowed like a fine martial artist doing katas, and Myx's confident eroticism seemed to say, "Well, yes, of course, I'm the most beautiful person you've ever seen, and of course you want to."

Jak had given up on dancing with Myx for three reasons; first of all, he tended to take on some of the characteristics of his partner, and it was simply more pleasant to take on Sesh's joyful finesse and singing-on style than it was to take on Myxenna's aggressive sexiness. Secondly, when he danced with Myx, it always upset Dujuv, who then had to pretend that he was not upset (something at which he was rarely any good), and it wasn't worth it to Jak to precess his toktru tove. Finally, Jak just hated the jokes Sesh made about "midair optical fucking."

Tonight the mesh between Y4UB and the four friends was singing-on. In the first ten minutes, Y4UB pulled a melody sample off Sesh and a counterpoint bass line from Jak. Shortly after they pulled a color-wash mix off a close pass between Myx and Duj. Then the sampling cameras flew away to look elsewhere, and the four swung into stunts (when they were sampling you, stunts confused the AIs and made it likely that they would just pass over you).

Jak and Sesh clasped hands as their four feet touched surface, hitting the gravity just as it went perpendicular at perhaps .01 g. As they bounced away, the gravity shifted about sixty degrees and decreased by half. They took advantage of that, shooting into a big swing, orbiting each other joined by outstretched arms, and then releasing into one of their signature moves, the double Immelman.

At least that was what Jak thought they were going to do. He arched into the big arc, belly outward, embracing a circle about five meters in diameter, and came around. When he reached over his head, looking up to catch Sesh in a trapeze-grab, there was no one there.

He tucked and spun, precessing, tumbling so that he could look for her. He expected to find that either some oaf had forced Sesh out of her flight path, or some gweetz had tried to cut in (and that Sesh had already given him an educational clop to the chops).

Instead, below and to the side, well away from anywhere Sesh would have gone naturally, he saw her struggling with four men, all of them much too old to be in here. They were dragging her to an emergency exit.

One of them, his back turned toward Jak, had her head locked in his armpit. One was fighting to get her wrists together to bind them, one was just in process of tying her ankles, and the fourth was airswimming a tow line toward the emergency exit.

Jak didn't hesitate; he felt his mind become cool, blank, and alert as it did in the Disciplines, and he tucked and dove, taking advantage of another shift of the great tumbling ball that was Centrifuge. He airswam as fast as he could, building up as much momentum as twenty meters would allow.

They were paying no attention to him, so he went after the one holding Sesh's head. Jak came in on his back, as fast as he could, hitting with the classic sucker block, the way that a defensive back in slamball does when the offside slammer loses track of the defense.

Jak's shoulder rammed against the backs of the man's thighs. He grabbed the back of the man's shirt and spun. The man flipped backward abruptly, and as Jak released him, his face swung into place to be a perfect target for a two-footed kick. With all his strength, Jak drove his heels into the man's cheeks.

The reaction shot Jak out of the fight and into a return loop, while hurling his opponent away in a backward end-for-end spin, probably unconscious. One malph out of the melee, anyway.

As Jak swung around in his return loop, his hands biting air as hard as he could, something bright-colored streaked through his peripheral vision, screaming like a cat on fire. Dujuv was getting into the fight.

Jak finished his loop and closed in on the heet who had been airswimming the line; Duj swooped down on the man tying Sesh's ankles, snagging a grip on his coat to carry the man along, putting him on the outside of a recurved turn, and hurling him away with the split-reed throw, all but instantly. The man was probably not out of the fracas for good but it would take some seconds for him to get back to it.

In the background, Jak could hear someone shouting, "All in *now*! Panth! They have a panth!" Now he was a bare two meters from his opponent. He coiled to attack.

The back of Jak's head seemed to cave in and he started to tumble. The pain was horrible and he could barley focus his eyes. He caught a glimpse of Dujuv tangled in a net, two men holding the lines, a third one whaling away at the bagged panth with a jointed bat. Duj was screaming with rage and thrashing fiercely, but he was helpless.

Jak's tumbling arc brought him up against the outer surface, awkwardly, making his back sting and his head ring even more. He saw Sesh, again, and sprang off the wall, trying to get back into the brawl.

There were now six of them surrounding her. Jak's back was still numb from impact. His head wasn't what it should be after the blow he had taken there. As he closed in, the men airswimming to meet him seemed to move faster than anyone should be able to in microgravity, and there was a wavering about them that he didn't like.

Sesh was tied completely and gagged, and the line was towing her toward the emergency exit, faster than Jak could swim to her. Their eyes met for just a moment; he could see her terror pleading for rescue, in that bare instant before the rotation shifted again, and he lost his orientation as the netting flew around him, grabbed him in a fierce hug, and spun him in a dizzy whirl.

Her final scream, smothered by the gag, felt to Jak like a kick in the stomach. Sesh was dragged out of his field of view. The net yanked brutally, taking Jak, wrapped in it, up against the outer surface just as the gravity shifted that way. He saw boots touching down all around him. Then there was a flurry of fists, feet, and clubs, fading rapidly into terrible pain and utter darkness.

CHAPTER 3

You at Least Understand That
There Are Two Teams

Jak had enjoyed so many intrigue-and-adventure stories whose second or third chapter began with some sentence, image, or experience like "He awoke in a white room" that his first thought, when he awoke in the white room, was that he must be dreaming one of those stories. It seemed likely that he was, actually. Assuming the rules for that type of story were being followed, almost always, the white room would turn out, on further investigation, to be a hospital room. As Jak adjusted to being awake, he specked that he *was* in a hospital room.

On the other hand, he couldn't even remember being in pain at all in a dream, and he was in considerable pain right now. But in the stories, he should have been in pain . . .

He drifted back into dreams that he was sure were dreams.

When his eyes opened again, he saw the same hospital room. At a minimum, this was a recurring dream.

In a story, this is where someone would come by to ex-

plain what's going on, so any moment someone should show up to tell me what happened . . . after . . . The thought seemed incomplete, and he tried to finish it for a while, drifting close again to rejoining the for-sure dreams.

After I got wanged.

It all came back—Sesh, the kidnapping, the fight. Jak really *was* in a hospital room, flat on his back, after a bad wanging. For a while he had been hearing the flat mechanical voice of a monitor repeating "Brain activity shows that the patient is awake." A face moved into Jak's view, and resolved into Uncle Sib.

Still confused and thinking of what happened in stories, Jak asked, "Are you going to say I gave you all a good scare?"

"Actually, you didn't," Sibroillo said, smiling. "No. Not at all. By the time they called me, they knew that you were going to make it, so the question was how fast they could get your neuro repaired, and they could tell me right away that you were not in any real danger. Your friend Dujuv Gonzawara has already been up for more than a day—probably that enhanced healing they build into a panth—and you'll be all done in sixteen hours or so. You'll recover faster, they say, if you're conscious now and then, which is why they're waking you up now, even though the regenerating nerves sting like hell."

"They do," Jak agreed.

"We don't think you're even going to lose much short-term memory. You have a pretty hard head and your brains don't rattle around nearly as much as I would have guessed. We could have awakened you two days ago, in fact, but we waited for major tissue regeneration to finish, so that you would only know in the *abstract* that one of your testicles had been ruptured and one of your eyes had been thumbed out, after you were unconscious. Since you now have new ones as good as the originals, it shouldn't really matter, but—"

"It probably shouldn't," Jak agreed, "but, toktru, it precesses me all the same. Which eye and which nut?"

"The left, for both. But you're good as new now."

"The principle matters," Jak said. "I was already unconscious, so they had no reason to do that."

"Probably just sending you a message," Sib agreed. "They did it after they had already grabbed Sesh Kiroping and the snatch team had escaped with her."

"Sesh! I didn't even think—"

"Of course not, you were unconscious."

"Well, uh, yeah. Okay. But why would anyone kidnap her, anyway? I guess her family is rich—do they still kidnap people for ransom? It seems like something you read about in history books. I never heard of it happening—"

"It still happens, but very rarely. And it's not what happened to Sesh."

"Well, then, does anyone have any idea where she is? Do you know what they wanted with her? Why would anyone kidnap Sesh?"

"That's three forms of the same question, as I've been trying to explain to cops, soldiers, and diplomats for the last four weeks."

"Four weeks! Sesh could be anywhere! They could have done anything to her!"

"Well, no, Jak. Not at all. As I've been trying to explain to all these idiot officials (with very little success,

by the way) we can make a very good guess about where
she is and what is happening to her, and though it is *very*
serious, she is in no personal danger, and we undoubtedly still have plenty of time."

Jak could not believe that Sib was taking this so
calmly. "Her parents must be in a *panic*. They got so
worked up about it whenever I brought her home an hour
late—"

"Her parents? They barely know her and they're much
more concerned with the politics of the situation." Sib
seemed extremely puzzled, as if Jak had brought up the
most irrelevant possible point. Then he laughed. "Oh,
my. You mean Pritararu and Feyxorra. Well, of course,
they're upset, and they are fond of her, but they're also
professionals, and this was a very slick job and no one is
going to hold it against them—"

"Professionals?"

Uncle Sib appeared, if possible, more astonished than
before. "So she didn't tell you at all! We all assumed that
she would eventually—that's part of why we threw the
two of you together, so that she'd have a safe confidant
and one we could watch—goodness! And she never di-
vulged a word of it. Didn't even tell you that those were
her guards, not her parents—damn near perfect security
habits. She's quite a girl! You rarely see anyone like that,
especially not that young. When I was in service to the
Satrap of—"

"Where is she and what is going on?" Jak hissed. He
had never before dakked how maddening it was to need
information from someone that you really wanted to
strangle.

Sibroillo blinked a couple of times, and then said, contritely, "Of course, Sesh means a great deal to you, in a completely nonprofessional way, eh? And here I am talking about her as just part of the job, and you worrying all the time. All right, I'll clear it up a bit.

"Now, to understand where Sesh is, properly, you have to understand who she is, which is not Sesh Kiroping, but Shyf Karrinynya, or more formally, Her Utmost Grace the Princess Shyf, Eleventh of the Karrinynya Dynasty of the Kingdom of Greenworld, by the Blessed Choice of Mother Gaia. And as a matter of practical politics, she's the heir to the throne whenever her father, King Scaboron, retires or dies."

"A princess . . ." Jak let the thought settle slowly into his mind; it didn't fit well or comfortably, and he kept trying to find something that would help him make sense of the idea that his beautiful, funny toktru-tove-and-sex-partner, who he knew as a passionate clothes-horse, gossip, and dancer . . . was supposed to one day rule a kingdom. After struggling for a moment, he managed to blurt out, "No wonder she wasn't worried about finding a job."

Sib grinned. "Toktru! As your friends would put it. No wonder. I can't quite believe she never told you. What an astonishing grasp of security protocol, in a person so young! It seems *very* unfair that she should be kidnapped when she was so extraordinarily good about security practices, now doesn't it? I really *must* insist that you go and get her back from her captors, as soon as you're fit to travel."

"Uncle Sib, you can't possibly mean that we're rich enough to pay a princess's ransom?"

"We have a wealth of information, pizo, and that's

worth more than cash, as a common rule. And I didn't say we were going to pay a ransom, I said you were going to go get her. Different operation entirely. Now, the orange light has come on over your head, which means that you've had about the optimal load of brain stimulation for this time awake, and it's time for you to go back to sleep. So do. Have some confusing dreams filled with pointless anxiety, and when you're awake again, we'll talk some more."

The world seemed reassuringly familiar, probably because Jak was used to being confused, annoyed, and precessed by his uncle. He immediately felt better and slid down toward sleep. "Where is Greenworld, anyway?" he murmured. "Is it that big island on earth where Narssaq Pock is?"

"No," Sib said, "it's in the Aerie, at the tip of the eighth branch. Greenworld is a kingdom low in wealth, middling in size, and huge in importance. The principal products are—"

Some reflexes are so deeply conditioned that nothing overpowers them, not even physical pain, concern for a friend, or anger at having been battered and mutilated. The moment that Sib began to lecture about politics and economics, Jak fell into deep, dreamless, refreshing sleep.

Thirst woke him. He sat up in bed with only minor pain from stiff muscles, and a mechanical arm reached down and extended a black nipple; he sucked a long, cold, delicious draft of icewater.

As soon as he finished the deep, chilling drink, he truly singing-on dakked what he desperately needed.

The toilet stall was only a meter from his bed, and Jak had bounced back into bed, hoping not to get caught in case he wasn't supposed to be up, before he realized how much better he must be, if he could do all that with no difficulty.

That was pleasant, but not as pleasant as the machines asking him if he was hungry and presenting him with a menu. He immediately ordered one of everything, plus an extra one of all the things he especially liked.

Every plate of the main courses was demolished, and at least fifty percent of each dessert was gone as well, before he recalled his conversation with Uncle Sib. He continued eating and contemplated what it all might mean. The djeste of it seemed to be that he was about to get his wish for travel, and quite possibly for adventure. Somehow it all seemed like an intrigue-and-adventure viv, and though Jak was singing-on good at those, he had no illusions that it could have really prepared him for the real thing.

Well, Sib seemed to speck that whatever trouble Sesh was in, Jak could get her out of it. It wasn't much comfort—he kept thinking of her, hurt and scared, and he couldn't imagine what he could do if she was being held against her will. After all, he hadn't been particularly effective at keeping her from being kidnapped in the first place. Nonetheless, if Uncle Sib thought he could do it, very likely it would turn out that he could.

He turned the issue over and over in his head as he continued to eat. The food wasn't bad and there was plenty.

He finally reached the point where one more dessert would be too many, slipped out of bed again to wash his

face and hands, and slid back in, trying to decide between looking for pornography on the hospital's entertainment screens, calling up Dujuv to see if he was doing
anything interesting yet, or just getting more sleep. He
decided that Dujuv would be the most entertaining.

His tove's face on the screen was a little more battered
than it had ever been before, which added some character, but also made Jak think of what a going over the two
of them must have had, to still look like that after so
many days. Duj was grinning. "Hey, tove, you're still
with me. I told'em you were too ugly to kill."

"If that was why I was spared, how did you get hurt at
all?"

They fell silent. For an instant the two forgot to tease
each other, just enjoying both being well and together.
Finally Dujuv looked a little more serious. "So your
uncle must've told you about what's going on with
Sesh."

"Yeah, but not much, just yet."

"Well, good luck to you and to her, old tove. I wish I
could be there to help, but . . . um—"

Myxenna appeared on the screen next to him. "Hi,
Jak, I thought that call was from you." Discreetly she
tugged her top into place and retied it, staying back of
Dujuv's peripheral vision so he wouldn't notice how she
had joined the call. "Dujy, it's okay to brag. This is a big
deal to you and Jak will understand that."

Jak was smiling already. "You must've made the slamball draft."

"Absolutely. Made it and then some. I had already applied and I had my school record, and then there were
pictures of you and me, all over the news, giving a good

fight to a bunch of trained kidnappers, until we finally got beat by sheer numbers. Incredible publicity plus we gave a good account of ourselves. If you were interested, Jak, they'd've drafted you too. I got picked in the fourth round, by Hive National; I'm gonna be playing with their rookie league farm club, Panlucrotic. So I'll be in training starting tomorrow." His face fell in sadness again. "And you're going to be—well, I guess actually Sibroillo wanted to explain that to you himself. I did want to help you out and go along, but everyone says that I wouldn't actually be useful for anything, it's a one-person job. So—"

"So get on with your life and make me proud of you, old tove," Jak said.

They chatted a little longer; because the kidnapping had happened so shortly after the exam results had come out, Jak had not yet heard the gossip about who had gotten in, which scores had been outrageously high and low, and where those who didn't get in were going. Once they caught up, Jak realized that he was starting to tire—apparently rebuilding so much of his body was a lot of work—and Duj and Myx seemed to want to get away, so they all said bye and that they must keep in touch, and closed the call. Jak settled back, thinking that now he'd really like to get some sleep.

Uncle Sib came in with Gweshira.

Gweshira was Uncle Sib's demmy, and had been for so long that Jak thought of her as sort of his aunt. She was short, spare and wiry, with very dark skin and very white hair that fell in loose messy curls. From sparring with her Jak knew that if you didn't beat her with sheer mass in the first five seconds, she'd wang you with her speed and cleverness in the first minute. She taught at his gen school—Jak had avoided taking classes from her, by mutual agreement—and he had often heard other students speak of her in the mixture of devoted love and pure terror that denotes either a great teacher or a sadistic bully. In her case, Jak specked it to both.

Sib was beaming. "Time to get down to business, pizo. The machinery says you're coherent. I told them that you never were before. They said they'd look into it."

Gweshira winced. "I do hope this old scapegrace's corny jokes won't affect your recovery," she said. "He actually was worried about you, not that you can tell, and whatever he might have said. But he's right, there's ground to cover, so let's get started."

"I've been thinking," Jak said, "that to be prudent, we should probably wait a week or two before I leave for wherever Sesh is, just to let me get in some extra practice at the Disciplines."

They both stared at him for a long breath before they burst out laughing. Gweshira in particular seemed to be tickled. "Jak," she said, "I've told Sibroillo for years that he's needlessly obscure around you, all the time, and you've utterly proven my point. I suppose that you thought that what we wanted you to do was go to Fermi—that's where we're nearly certain that Sesh is being held—and then, what? Oh, say, infiltrate the palace guard, scale a sheer wall twenty meters high, locate and rescue Princess Shyf from the chief malph just as he's about to rape her, carry her away half-naked from twenty armed men, shoot your way into the spaceport, and escape in a hijacked warship?"

"Now that you mention it, that does sound toktru silly,

masen? But Uncle Sib said I wouldn't be ransoming her, I'd be going and getting her, so I thought I'd at least be sneaking her out, and if something went wrong—"

"Oh. Well, then, perhaps you weren't quite as silly as you sounded. But in any case, what we need here is not so much heroics as calm common sense, because it's really merely a very ordinary kind of situation in the politics between nations. Princess Shyf was kidnapped as part of an elaborate power struggle, with several different players in the game; we're going to get her back by making someone trade for her. Which that someone will willingly do—because what we have to trade is very valuable.

"Your job is mostly to go to the right person and make the offer. Since you might have to improvise, we're going to give you enough information to be able to improvise reasonably well. So we'll start with discussing who the sides are. What do they tell you about social engineering, in school, these days?"

"Pretty much what they tell us about underage sex and illegal drugs. No one's supposed to do it, officially everyone deplores it, and toktru everyone does it every chance they get."

"You're more socially alert than I ever thought you were—that covers the attitude of society toward social engineering, very thoroughly," Uncle Sib said. "Hypocrisy is the great lubricant of social intercourse. Well, by now you must have realized that I'm not just a retired soldier and businessman."

"Well, I dak that we're rich, or you have a big expense account from somewhere. I noticed that you got me trained early to keep quiet about anything I saw or heard at home. I kind of thought maybe you were a spy. And all those little games you had me playing, about deception and deduction and things like that, and the way you made me work the Disciplines so hard, made me speck maybe I was being groomed for the family business."

"Not a bad guess, but wrong," Sib said. "And now that we're sitting here in a room that is thoroughly bug-swept, and there's reason to tell you, I will. Gweshira and I are members of a social engineering zybot. I had always kind of hoped you'd want to join, later on, and perhaps you will, if you ever manage to acquire any interest in politics, economics, society, culture, or any concern other than clothes, sports, and girls."

"He's healthy, Sib," Gweshira protested, green eyes flashing. "That's what a teenager *should* be interested in. Give him time."

Sib shrugged. "At his age I'd already belonged to a revolutionary underground, been arrested for inciting a riot, joined the secret police, and claimed political asylum on a sunclipper. But I suppose everyone has to get through adolescence in their own way. Anyway, Jak, it so happens that our social engineering zybot has very good reason to intervene on behalf of Princess Shyf—Sesh, I mean, she's no doubt still Sesh to you. You happen to be a logical person for us to use to free her, and so we're going to talk to you about who we are, what we do, and what we need you to do, because you'll need to know all of that. So I want you to at least promise to try to listen and follow what we tell you, because it's vital for Sesh."

"I'll try," Jak said. "Toktru. I will." He felt a sinking sensation; he'd never been any good at paying attention to anything nonathletic, and now that Sesh would have

to depend on him, he was really afraid that his utter in-
eptitude at attention and memory would come shining
through.

Gweshira clicked her tongue impatiently. "Sib, you've
just totally convinced him that no matter what, he's
going to be too bored to concentrate. Let me try, all
right? Jak, I promise I won't try to make you like the
dullest parts by dwelling on them. Want me to try?"

"It's worth a shot," Jak admitted. "And I was kind of
afraid of what Uncle Sib might do. No hard feelings,
please, Uncle Sib, but I think we should let Gweshira
try."

"No hard feelings at all, whatever gets the job done,"
Sib said, plopping himself into a chair to sulk.

"All right," Gweshira said, winking at Jak. "Now, to
begin with, do you know the meaning of the shape and
number designations for the social engineering zybots?"

Jak thought for a moment. Social engineering was
supposed to be a crime—basically conspiring against the
rest of humanity. For hundreds of years, ever since the
Wager had become the dominant religion/philosophy of
the human species, and some of its implications had become clear, it had been theoretically possible that a small
group of people, by using a mixture of every dirty trick
ever invented for social domination, control, and manip-
ulation, might be able to reshape society into whatever
form it chose.

Zybots, as those conspiracies were called, were known
to use all sorts of appalling counter-Wager practices:
propaganda, tailored drugs, assassination, networking,
sabotage, brainwashing, banking, intimidation, market-
ing, charity, lobbying, and public-interest advocacy,

among many others, and most people were willing to suspect them of piracy, slavery, and cannibalism to boot.

That was standard school stuff. But back when Watnek, Redondo, and Riodow had done their pioneering work demonstrating the possibility of true social engineering, they had published everything, hoping that it would forestall the misuse of their discovery. The result was that there was not just one social engineering zybot working behind the scenes, but several hundred, each pushing society toward its particular utopia, each thwarting the others, creating so many second-, third-, and tenth-order effects that Nakaski's Law had set in: "The number of active social engineering zybots converges to the minimum number whose interactions make society too unpredictable to engineer," or as Nakaski had informally put it, "One zybot is a clear and present danger, three are a menace, ten are a pack of annoying assholes, and a hundred are barely a nuisance."

That was as much as Jak could remember; many kids pretended to be loyal to one zybot or another, and would scrawl graffiti—a seven in a square, a one in a triangle, a two in an oval—in places where adults found it obnoxious, but he didn't think they'd ever talked about the shape and number designations in class, or among his peers, and he didn't think most of the kids scrawling the symbols had any idea what they meant.

He realized that social engineering zybots were much more interesting in fiction than they were in school. "You know I love intrigue-and-adventure stories," Jak said after a moment. "Books, holo, flatscreen, viv, I love 'em all. I know that in the stories every zybot—

they're always villains in the stories, there are never any good zybots, I bet that's the censors making it that way?"

"Safe bet," Gweshira said.

"Well, in the stories the zybots always have a name that's a shape and a number, like Square Seven is a gang of malphs trying to take over the whole solar system in *The Terrier Smashers*. And there's a zybot, Rhombus Two, selling an addictive aphrodisiac in *Sex Pirates of Ceres*. But I don't know why they're called those names."

"See, I told you," Sib said, from his chair, not looking up. "The educational bureaucrats—that miserable gaggle of cowardly mousefarts—don't even let the kids know *why* they're supposed to be afraid of social engineering. The idea that even the very worst zybots would ever try for crude raw power like that, let alone—"

"Oh, hush," Gweshira said. "You don't have to worry about the state of his education, anymore, Sib, he's done with that, and think about who we're talking about. If it's up to Jak, he'll never learn anything more for the rest of his life. Anyway, as long as *Jak* knows the truth, we don't have to concern ourselves with how wrong everyone else is, now do we? So turn it down, old pizo, and let me explain things to Jak—it will take half as much time as it will if you help."

She pulled her chair closer to Jak's bed, as if to make sure he had no view of Sib. "All right, beginning once again, the shape and number are a sort of shorthand for how a given zybot wants to see society structured. Sib and I have been members and operatives, for more than a century, of a zybot called Circle Four. Our major opponent is Triangle One. Triangle One organized Princess

Shyf's kidnapping, not because they dislike her or wanted her for any purpose of their own, but to assist the House of Cofinalez in a power struggle, because the Cofinalezes have a close relationship, often a de facto alliance, with Triangle One. Are you with me so far?"

"Circle Four, toves. Triangle One, working for Cofinalez. Cofinalez, malphs. Got it."

"It's more complicated than—"

"Not for him, it isn't, Sib. Now hush up and let me handle this!"

Sibroillo got up and left, closing the door with a heavy thud against its padding. "He'd have slammed it if he could," Jak observed.

"He'll recover. He's a big boy. Sometimes more big and sometimes more boy. Seriously, Jak, you at least understand that there are two teams, and that the Cofinalez people hired the other one?"

"So far. So you—Circle Four, I mean—are willing to help Sesh—Princess Shyf, I mean, this is confusing— because you just oppose anything Triangle One does?"

She sighed. "Well, no, not exactly. We do oppose many things that they do. Every now and then we're allies, and each zybot also does things that don't interest the other at all. But in this case, we have strong reasons to oppose them. That's what I was getting at with the business of the shape and number description. You see, the shape describes how many power centers a zybot is seeking to have in its ideal society, and in what relationship to each other. And the number designates what order of effect each power center should be taking into account in its decision-making."

"Clear as Martian moss soup," Jak said, shaking his head in confusion.

"Well, let's take a simple one. Rhombus Two. They think society should be a balance between law, art, charity, and business, with art and charity working as close allies and law and business kept far apart. So if you diagrammed that, you'd have the four points that define a rhombus, with two in the middle close together—art and charity—and two more distant ones, law and business, far from each other. Is that clear so far?"

Jak shrugged. "Clear-er."

"So that's where they get the rhombus. All right, now, what the two means, is that they think that when, say, an artist does something that affects the law, he should also worry about the second-order effect—how his effect on the law will affect charity, for example."

"What about the two groups I actually have to deal with?"

She smiled grimly. "Patience, patience. Circle Four. A circle has an infinite number of points around a center. Which we think should be a wise, intelligent, democratically controlled government, you see? An infinite number of other powers, all equal in their relation to the state. And a fourth-order effect means, basically, that before the government takes any action about or to Mr. A, it has to think about how Mr. A's reaction will affect Mr. B, how Mr. B's reaction will affect Mr. C, and how Mr. C's reaction to that will affect Mr. D. Where Messers A through D could all be individuals, corporations, zybots, ethnic groups, clubs, unions, the government itself, or the whole social djeste, whatever.

"Now compare that with Triangle One. They want

three power centers—religion (in a single orthodox version of the Wager), the military, and the central bank. And the one means that they think that nobody should worry about feedbacks or secondary effects—you only think about what you do to the other guy, not about what he'll do afterward or how that affects any third parties.

"Basically, zybot names tell you what kind of society they want, and make the programs that they're trying to social-engineer easy to compare. Low numbers like one and two are dictatorships that get things done, and high numbers like seven or ten are democracies paralyzed by having to take so many rights into account. The more axes of symmetry the figure has, the more equal all the contending sides are supposed to be. And the more corners it has, the more groups get to have a say. So that would mean that—"

"So," Jak said, "trying to cut this down to toves and malphs, the Triangle One people want three big power centers that answer to nobody, and you want a democracy that has to think about what it does, and who it affects, but not so much that it can't accomplish anything. Couldn't you have just said that?"

From the way she glared at him, Jak realized, probably not. But after a moment she seemed to relax, and went to get Uncle Sib, to continue their conversation. He came back in with a broad grin. "I told Gweshira that it wouldn't be easy, trying to interest you in politics and economics, when you're so thoroughly distracted."

"She still probably did better than you would have, Uncle Sib. At least I dak the sides, sort of, and I understand enough about Circle Four and Triangle One to know who I'd rather have manipulating my society. If that makes you feel better. Now, what does it all have to do with the House of Cofinalez and, uh, Princess Shyf?"

"Well," Sib said, "Triangle One is always working to get the human race to have a simpler, more power-based and authoritarian structure, more unified under tighter control, that kind of thing. To be fair to them for a moment (something I seldom believe in doing), it's not pure power-worship; they think that the case in Galactic Court is apt to go against humanity, whenever that gets decided in the next few generations, and there's going to be an extermination order against us, and the only alliance we have even a chance of making would be with the Rubahy—who would stab us in the back given a tenth of a chance. So since we might have to fight the whole galaxy, anytime between next week and four hundred years from now, Triangle One wants us organized into sort of a Super-Sparta or Prussia-to-the-Nth, well before that happens, and basically they're always moving to give the human race as a whole a clearer chain of command.

"The way Circle Four sees it, on the other hand, is that if we lose the decision, we won't win the war—we'll be dead anyway—and so we might as well die as our messy, sloppy, disorderly selves, still human, still reaching for the stars and still wallowing in the mud."

"All right," Jak said, "I'm still on your side. What's it got to do with Sesh?"

"Well, do you know who the Cofinalez family is?"

Jak rolled his eyes impatiently. At other times in history, it would have been like asking if you knew who the Borgia, Rockefeller, or Pilaratsaysay families were.

"The family that controls the fissionables monopoly, of course. It's the house that owns the Duchy of Uranium."

"Right, sorry, sometimes you show so little interest that I expect even less of you than you actually achieve, hard though that is to believe. Well, if Triangle One is going to build up their triangle of what's basically church, treasury, and army, they need to get that treasury leg unified—which means helping the great monopolies to grow and strengthen, and then merging them into one vast combine.

"Now, the Duchy of Uranium has always played rougher and been faster and looser about the rules than almost any other monopoly. They *got* their monopoly in the first place by a hundred-year campaign that looked more like organized crime than shrewd business organization, and they did it in clear violation of all of the Wager's social principles—there's no way they should have the sole license for uranium, plutonium, and thorium, everywhere in human space, not to mention having it for all of mining, extraction, synthesis, breeding, recycling, operations, and disposal. And not only did they get that monopoly by illicit force, they maintain it that way. Of all the great monopolies, they have the biggest and best-trained army, and they're the most willing to use it, and of course if you depend on fission for energy, and you annoy the Cofinalezes enough, their beanies will take your fuel rods back—no matter how many bystanders they have to kill, or how much of what gets spilled in the process. So the Cofinalez family is Triangle One's kind of people, and they have a long-running alliance.

"Now, fission is pretty well essential in the upper solar

system—try to use anything else for mobile, high-density power on Triton!—but way down here in the lower system, there are quite a few alternatives, including solar, and for religious reasons that are very confusing and go all the way back to its founding, centuries before the Wager, Greenworld has a religious proscription against nuclear power, and has been a center for the development of solar power. Not just for the technology, although they do make and license some of the very best solar power equipment there is, but also they're major promoters of solar power, and more than that, they regard it as kind of a religious duty to get space habitats switched over to all-the-way solar, so they've always been a thorn in the Cofinalez side. Greenworld and Uranium have been on opposite sides of three declared wars and four unofficial ones in the last two hundred years, in fact, with a nice scattering of atrocities on both sides, some assassinations against both ruling families, everything that people tend to remember for generations after. There's plenty of bad blood between Cofinalez and Karrinynya and deep grudges between their ordinary subjects, *and* a real clash of interests between Greenworld and Uranium, so between all of that, there's not going to be any love lost.

"Now, this quarrel between the Karrinynya Dynasty and the House of Cofinalez would be of only minor interest to Triangle One, just a locus for an occasional favor to an old ally, if it weren't that the last two Karrinynya kings have been extremely influential as minority leaders in the Confederacy of the Aerie. Are your eyes glazing over yet?"

"I'm doing my best, Uncle Sib, but let's see if I can

stay awake if I speck the rest. If I remember right, the majority party in the Aerie is those heets that want to unify it under one system of government, the way we are here in the Hive, but that takes more than a majority to do it—two-thirds?"

"Three-quarters."

"Three-quarters. And the minority has always been much more than a quarter of the Confederacy Assembly, so they have been able to prevent that change, so all the hundreds of little individual habitats that make up the Aerie have stayed independent nations. I can see where Triangle One wouldn't like that much. So what are they going to do, threaten to hurt Sesh—Princess Shyf, I mean—unless her dad, the King, changes the way he votes?"

"Not a bad guess, but, no, it's nothing that crude. The deal is this. If Shyf would consent to marry a Cofinalez in a full marriage-of-lines, then the House of Cofinalez, which is more senior even though all they've got is a duchy and she's in line to be queen, would subordinate the Karrinynya Dynasty, and Greenworld would pass under their control."

Jak felt ill, which was strange. Not long ago he'd have been surprised at the idea of anyone his age getting married, though he knew some people did, particularly in the Tolerated Faiths. Certainly the idea of Sesh getting married would have seemed ridiculous.

But if she was going to marry anyone, then toktru it ought to be Jak. And the idea that it would be part of a property arrangement—"What would Uranium want with Greenworld, if it's so incompatible with what they do? Would they just want to destroy it?" *And would they take my beautiful, wonderful demmy and use her for a marker just so they could wreck one small kingdom?* he thought. Suddenly the world seemed very cruel; he couldn't stop thinking of her smile and her laugh.

"They're not going to succeed at any of it," Gweshira reminded him, firmly. "And anyway even a very small kingdom is too expensive to acquire it just to wreck. But unfortunately, there is *some* method to the madness. They already have quite a few territorial holdings— some on Mars, some on Mercury, many in the Aerie, and of course their big home base in Africa on Earth—so adding Greenworld would expand that territorial base, not to mention adding one of the best middle-sized armies in the solar system to their forces.

"It's their longer-run goal that's really insane. If the Cofinalezes can get Greenworld under their thumb, they'd have an excellent springboard from which to expand their monopoly and eventually take over fusion, gravitational, planetary thermal, and Casimir effect power, and thus eventually, instead of Duke of Uranium, Mun Cofinalez, or more likely (since Mun is old and failing) his son Pukh, could be King of Energy."

"But there's no such thing!"

Sib nodded emphatic agreement. "Nor should there be. It would be like having a Kingdom of Money, or a Kingdom of Information. *Far* too much power in one place. But that's what the House of Cofinalez are driving at, or so we believe. And it starts with getting Princess Shyf to marry a Cofinalez."

"So why didn't they just put a gun to her head, hold the ceremony, and have done with it?"

Gweshira made a face, as if she'd smelled something

bad. "Because we are a *somewhat* more civilized civilization than *that*. Emphasis on the somewhat. No level of marriage below full marriage-of-lines will subordinate one dynasty to another; Shyf can have a consort, or six of them if she wishes (Greenworld has legal polygamy for aristocrats), and it doesn't affect her status—she's queen as soon as her father dies. She can have a hundred term marriages if she wants, and has the energy, without changing a bit of her legal status. But if she goes into a full marriage-of-lines with a line senior to her own, she forfeits the title to Greenworld to her husband. Those are the rules.

"Now, not surprisingly, the aristocrats have surrounded marriages-of-lines with a fence of very strict legal restrictions. And one of the strictest is that consent of both parties has to be verified by a full deep brain scan. That means, among other things, that Shyf has to agree to it without reservation—no detectable coercion. So whichever Cofinalez it is that they want to marry her to, he'll have to win her heart for real. No drugs. No threats. No hypnosis. Not even any lies.

"Princess Shyf knows enough to be pretty hard to persuade. So it's going to take them several years of keeping her in comfortable captivity, during which at least one Cofinalez brother is going to have to exhibit all kinds of charm that his family has never had. That's part of why we're almost sure she's in Fermi—because the most logical person to marry her off to is Psim Cofinalez, since he's second in line for the throne of Uranium, and his father and older brother are both already married, and (for a Cofinalez) he's practically fit company for human beings, and just before Princess Shyf was kidnapped, Psim had a new, beautiful palace grown, with a very high rooftop garden, which is perfect for a prison without bars. Psim's garden palace is in Fermi, which is also where his father's ducal court is, and Psim has been living in that house like a recluse ever since.

"But it will take more than a pretty house to make her forget that she's Crown Princess of Greenworld, or the political realities of the situation. It will probably take at least a year of very gentle persuasion before they can even stop guarding her and keeping her locked in—right now if they leave any escape route open (not likely with the people they have on the job) she'll be out like a greased snake. She's got a cool head with a good brain inside it, and Pritararu and Feyxorra trained her well—give her an instant's opportunity and she'll take it and be on her way.

"They have to honestly change her loyalty, and Psim won't have even begun to make a dent in it yet. Four weeks' delay to get you well was time well spent. Now we just have to get her out of there before her captivity becomes normal and she starts to think she likes the company—which will take quite a while, since most people understandably are apt to hold a grudge about being kidnapped. Actually, having known a Cofinalez cousin or two, I can't imagine that she's ever going to get to like it, but we don't want her stuck there for years, with everyone on our team paralyzed, while reality sinks in for Psim. Now, admittedly, there are rumors that Psim has table manners, brushes his teeth, and often wears matching shoes, which makes him an effete fop next to any other Cofinalez. But still, an elegant, brainy girl like

Princess Shyf must be pretty safe against all the charm he can muster."

"So how are we going to get her out of there?"

Jak had rarely seen such an unpleasant, and yet joyful, smile on anyone before, let alone on Uncle Sib. "We've got something to trade that will get Princess Shyf back to Greenworld, Greenworld back to its rightful place as a leader in the Aerie, the House of Cofinalez into deep shit, and just possibly Triangle One back to square one—where they all belong. Not to mention driving a deep wedge between Triangle One and the Duchy of Uranium."

"If they've got so much at stake, will they just give up? Is the information that good?"

"Well, this whole scheme of theirs is very important to Uranium but it isn't really a priority for Triangle One— they just supplied an expert snatch team, because the Duchy of Uranium didn't have the finesse to do it competently. Now that the princess is in their hands, the operation is all Uranium, except for one Triangle One member—and that person is our target. His name is Bex Riveroma, and he's about as nasty a piece of work as you're going to find, as human beings go. We're going to swap him some old stories in exchange for Princess Shyf—old stories about five very unpleasant events connected with Bex Riveroma, including where and what the evidence for those stories is. Any of that evidence might get him executed, if told in the right part of the solar system.

"Naturally Riveroma would like to see that evidence destroyed. Now, since Riveroma has been placed as the head of security in Psim's new palace, it would follow that if anyone could spring Princess Shyf, he would be the one. How he's going to do it, I couldn't tell you, but the man is a pro—his only good point—and we are offering him the chance to destroy information for which he might be imprisoned or killed at any time. He'll do it well."

"All right, so far I dak where this is going. So I'm going to go to Fermi and—make an offer to Bex Riveroma, I guess—and then when he says yes, give him the information—"

Sib nodded. "Right idea, but it's slightly more complex than that, because Riveroma can't be trusted at all. So you won't be carrying the information, you'll be carrying the address for the information—in a complicated way that means that it will be much easier for them to get that address with your cooperation than against your resistance, so that they have some interest in treating you decently. And you won't give it to him till you get word from us that Shyf is back somewhere safe, with loyal troops between her and recapture. But you did speck the basic idea."

"Why me? I mean, I want to do it, but why me and not a professional courier or a Circle Four member?"

Gweshira nodded at the question, clearly pleased with him. "First reason: because you're a close enough blood relative to one member of Circle Four so that Riveroma will know that if he tries anything, he'll be triggering a blood feud. That makes you safer. Not that he'd always object to a blood feud, mind you, but as I've said before, he's a complete professional, and he won't stand for an unnecessary one. Second reason: because if Riveroma decides he wants to play rough or if he just isn't feeling as professional as he should, he can't get any information about Circle Four out of you, since you don't know it."

"But—he might try."

"Well, certainly. It's always possible that we've miscalculated. Perhaps he's not as afraid of Sib as he ought to be, or perhaps Triangle One will have reasons to accept the risk of outright feud or war. But even if that happens, try not to worry too much. Torture isn't such a big thing in our modern age; generally they do just enough of it to force you to think about any secrets you're keeping, while they have you under deep brain scan, so that they know whether to do a destructive extraction on your brain. Once they confirm that there's nothing in there, you're perfectly safe."

"And I've been saying there's nothing in that brain for a long time," Sib added.

"Shut up, you silly old gwont, Jak's entitled to be worried. Anyway, even if that happens (and it's very unlikely) they might do some bad temporary damage, but it won't be anything worse than what you've just been through."

"Comforting."

"Comparatively, it *is*. Anyway, third reason: if you should, by any chance, happen to find you like the work—or if we discover you're good at it, which probably won't happen because this is a milk run—then we may recruit you into Circle Four.

"Now, we'll be putting a sliver into some vital organ of yours. To retrieve and decode that sliver, Riveroma needs a string of information that will be found coded onto a specific antibody which he will find in your bloodstream. You'll be carrying directions that will tell him why the information he's being led to is valuable, and how to isolate the antibody that will let him retrieve the sliver."

"How did the antibody get there?" Jak asked.

Sib grinned, pulled out a tiny spray bottle, and spritzed Jak in the face. "It'll be there in about three days. Meanwhile, sorry about the sniffles you're going to have."

"So what's in the sliver?"

"A set of locations—mostly safety-deposit boxes, but a couple of vacuum bottles buried here and there, and also some physical locations of high-security computer memory. If Bex Riveroma gets to all those locations before authorities do, he'll obtain the originals, plus all the existing copies, of all the evidence about five different subjects that could each earn him a walk into vacuum or a sleeper bunk in a running reactor."

"What good does knowing the physical location of a high-security memory do you? If it's high security, it's not accessible on the net—"

"But if it's a physical location you can set off an atom bomb there," Sib said. "A lot of spies, mercs, and ops are subtle people, so they tend to value subtlety, but it can be overvalued. Sometimes unsubtle is just what you need, and Riveroma's a pro. Give him those locations and he'll figure out what to do, which is why he'll trade anything in the universe to get those locations. Clear enough?"

"Guess so."

"Now, do you want the sliver in your heart, your liver, your lungs . . . ?"

"Why does it have to be in a vital organ?"

Gweshira explained, "If we put it in your hand or your toe or something, they can just cut that part off, one quick chop when you don't expect it, and search the part at leisure, leaving you with all the hassle of spending a month regenerating. With the sliver in a vital organ, with a limited number of good retrieval paths, they're going to have to follow directions, or else kill you. And Sibroillo Jinnaka is a name that frightens them—they wouldn't kill his nephew for any reason that wasn't really, really important."

"What if they *do* think of something important?"

Gweshira's shrug was not reassuring, nor was Uncle Sib's, and that must have shown on Jak's face. "Cheer up," Uncle Sib said. "Fermi's a great town and chances are you'll spend more time on nightlife than on intrigue. And do you know how many kids never get to travel at all?"

CHAPTER 4

Why Don't We Thrash It Out?

Dujuv did nothing but babble about how exciting and fun it was to be in slamball training camp, and after ten minutes of that Jak was bored—but didn't want to express it. So he begged off quickly, touched the palm of his left hand with his right so that his purse would hang up the call, and turned back to talk to Uncle Sib. "Well, I guess I'm ready to go."

"Your friend seems a bit preoccupied."

Jak shrugged, not wanting to seem childish about it. "He's getting on with his life and career. I guess I envy him that. And I wish he wasn't quite so cheerful when I'm about to go do something really hard."

"Well, friends surprise you. They always do. That's one reason for having them." Sib watched him intently for a moment, but whatever he was looking for apparently wasn't there. "And, you know, you are getting on with your life. Very, very quickly. Two months ago you were an indifferent gen school student with a good income, good friends, and a pretty girlfriend. Now the fate of nations is hanging on you. In fact, let's stop talking about that before it makes *me* nervous. Now, there's time for one more review before boarding. What are you going to do?"

"Get on this ferry, and ride it out to the *Spirit of Singing Port.* Claim my berth. For seventy-eight days, work out, do the Disciplines, and catch the news every single day. Spend no more than my reasonable allowance and watch out for all the hidden charges there tend to be on a sunclipper. Above all else, you said, don't miss the close flyby of Mercury, because it is, and I quote, 'one of the grandest views in the solar system.'"

Sib smiled. "All right, all right. I admit you've listened far more than I ever expected you to. *Now, what will be your procedure after you get to Earth?* Which you know perfectly well is what I was asking you in the first place."

Living with Uncle Sib for all his life, Jak had gotten a lot of practice at smiling innocently. "Oh. That. Well. I'm going to take the ferry to whatever the disembarkation station is, and then a launch down to Fermi, where I will go to the Fermi Hilton, and call you. You'll give me whatever the contact procedure is for meeting Riveroma. When I meet him, I say to him, 'I am carrying information from Sibroillo Jinnaka, and I am authorized to exchange it for a service from you. The information concerns the location of all the extant, court-admissible evidence regarding the Fat Man, the Dagger and Daisy, the business about the burning armchair, the disappearance of *Titan's Dancer,* and KX-126, including all such evidence regarding your involvement. The public key has already been sent to you. The private key, along with the way to retrieve the encoded information, has been coded onto an antigen group in my bloodstream. Here are the specifications for the isolation and decoding of the antigen group, and I will cooperate when you draw a blood sample.' Then I hand him the directions for isolating that, and offer to let him draw a blood sample. Then I say, 'We will proceed no further than that until you agree to perform the service which you will find in the same block of code. When the service is performed, I will cooperate fully with your people so that you can obtain the information, locate the evidence, and destroy it. Should you attempt to obtain the evidence without performing the service, I am authorized to tell you that Circle Four will immediately disclose the location of all the evidence to every relevant police and prosecutorial authority. You may be assured that it will be more than enough to obtain your conviction on serious charges in all five matters in many different jurisdictions.' "

"Then what will happen?"

"Then he'll draw my blood, go read the offer, possibly communicate with you, and one way or another engineer Sesh's escape. While he's doing that he will probably keep me somewhere as a hostage, but he'll keep me in touch with you to make sure that no misunderstandings lead to the evidence being released. When I get the message from you that contains the phrase that we never speak or write, I tell Riveroma to go ahead and get the sliver, and by at least three channels not directly in his control, I notify you that I've done it. His surgeon pulls out the sliver, supposedly painlessly, and I go back to the Hilton. You transfer funds for my ticket home. I catch the next sunclipper.

"Through this entire thing, I stay within budget, avoid

entanglement in anything that isn't part of the mission, and keep my mouth shut and my ears open." Jak smiled. "How did I do?"

"You're letter perfect, which makes me extremely nervous, but too late to worry about that now."

"Attention all passengers. Boarding for the ferry to the *Spirit of Singing Port* commences immediately. Repeat, boarding for the ferry to the *Spirit of Singing Port* commences immediately. Launch in ten minutes. Please advance through the boarding doors at once."

Sib stuck out his hand, Jak shook it, and the two embraced for a moment. Then Sib whispered, "Do good, be lucky." Jak said "Thanks," and he turned and walked through the doors into the ferry, a squat little cylinder barely a quarter the size of a gripliner, studded all around with the heavy tanks and nozzles of a freeflight spacecraft. He had barely strapped in when the tractor platform, on which the ferry rested, began its crawl up toward the North Pole of the Hive, where the launch loop was already spun up to speed—through the viewports, Jak could see little streaks of white, flattened curves or straight lines, blazing brightly across the stars, whenever the sun reflected off the loop. "Your first trip?" an older man beside him said.

"Yeah."

"Thought so. Nobody looks out the window after the first time." The gwont settled into his reading, comfortably sliding a finger into one nostril. "Boring. Lights and streaks in the sky, then an exciting tangle of pipes and tubes and wires. We've got two months of boring ahead of us, and it starts off with the two-hour bore of getting up onto the launch loop. Enjoy the novelty while there is any." Not surreptitiously enough, he checked his finger, and finding nothing, went back to work on his business report and his nose, bent on digging out everything he could.

Jak resolved that he would look at nothing but the viewport until they were safely aboard the *Spirit of Singing Port*.

It was not a hard resolution to keep. The loop at the North Pole of the Hive was about 200 km across, an immense circle of dark superconducting material only three centimeters wide and two millimeters thick, spun up to just over one rpm; the loop surface itself moved at about 40,000 km/hour. In principle Jak might have been nervous about that massive ribbon moving at tremendous speed passing within a few meters of him; if a human in a space suit touched it, the human would be converted instantly to bloody rags on a long orbit around the sun, and indeed that had happened a few times in suicides and in careless accidents during outside climbing. But Jak had never heard of any accident involving a ferry, and despite the fact that it was enclosing a superconducting ribbon moving at rocket speeds, rather than an ordinary powered rail, the linducer grapple, visible on one of the many screens in the cabin, seemed ordinary enough. It fastened around the band soundlessly, and the automated voice said, in a bored tone, "We are grappled and waiting for departure on an optimal window in thirty seconds . . . twenty-five seconds . . ." and so on down to the words familiar and associated with human spaceflight since before Standard had even been a language—"Five, four, three, two, one, boost!"

As the linducer powered up, it became increasingly

magnetically coupled to the band passing through it, transferring an ever-increasing small fraction of the loop's momentum to the ferry. The ferry accelerated along the outside of the loop at about four g, traveling more than three hundred kilometers as it whipped halfway round the loop, crushing the passengers into their seats for about two minutes. "Release in five, four, three, two, one, gone," the mechanical voice said. The linducer grapple opened, the loop fell instantly from camera view, and they were moving in space at five kilometers per second relative to the Hive, in free fall.

Free fall lasted a few seconds, and then the engines cut in for about a minute, putting the ferry on trajectory to intercept the sunclipper. The engine cut out and now they would be in free fall for the next twenty hours.

Jak had seen sunclippers pass the viewports of the Hive many times—the Hive was the busiest port in the solar system, and perhaps three dozen sunclippers passed per year. Since their solar sails were tens of thousands of kilometers across, one could hardly miss them—but they passed at distances of anywhere from a quarter million to a million kilometers, so though their spectacular spread of brightly lit curves, vaults, and bows took up vast parts of the sky for the few hours when they were close by, they had seemed like a comprehensible enough thing, like the pictures of planets from close-in satellites, only a few times bigger than the Earth in the familiar pictures taken from its moon.

But as they neared the *Spirit of Singing Port,* Jak found himself swept away in awe. His seatmate had pulled on sleeping shades and plugged in a skull jack and was now off in some dreamworld. Jak could hardly imagine how anyone could voluntarily miss this. Though the sails were big enough to wrap Venus and the Earth with enough left over for most of Mars, they were only microns thick and hung on monosil cables too thin to be visible to the naked eye; look at a sail edgewise and it vanished, but seen flat on, it was far brighter than the face of Earth's moon.

Yet among all these great planes and gentle curves of white light, it was almost impossible to pick out the tiny bright dot of the ship itself. Barely a kilometer across, the little sphere at the center of the sunclipper was its whole reason for being, the place where several thousand human souls were born, grew up, had children, and died, where all the working and thinking happened, holding the precious tenth of a cubic kilometer that was all the inside cargo space, plus the tight little complex of chambers, corridors, shops, and workrooms for the permanent crew and the passengers—the space given over to human beings was less than what might be found in a giant hotel.

As their angle of approach changed and the sails moved and shifted in the sunlight, the tiny dot of the habitat, like a bright star, moved in and out of sails and shadows, now visible, now concealed. The viewports were filled from edge to edge with sails; the sky was nothing but the great spread of monosil; and yet the habitat itself remained a little dot.

Presently the little ferry began to bounce and bob, brief accelerations of no more than ten seconds each, as it made its arrival approach. Now the *Spirit of Singing Port*'s habitat was a tiny dark circle, with a distinct area, in the center of the vast brilliant expanse of her sails;

they were coming in from the sun side, as ferries always did. The automated systems gradually reduced their relative velocity until they shot across the path of the oncoming sunclipper, about sixty kilometers sunward of the habitat, moving at a few kilometers per second. An instant before they aligned with the sunclipper's loop, it caught the sun in one view camera, and Jak saw the great ribbon, just like the one on the Hive to the naked eye, but if the two had ever been able to be seen together, you'd have known at once that the one on the ship was about a third the size of the one on the Hive.

The linducer grapple closed on the track in a camera closeup. Everyone's life, at that instant, depended on the machines successfully managing speeds measured in kilometers per second, at distances measured in millimeters. Jak toktru wished he had been nicer to his purse.

The grapple did what it was supposed to. They were slammed by over two g of weight as the linducer grapple pulled against the loop, which carried them around in a great arc, bringing their velocity to zero relative to the ship as they glided soundlessly into the receiving dock. "Everyone on board will deboard *now*," the voice of the ferry said. "Relaunch is in nine minutes four seconds, repeat nine minutes four seconds, from *now*. Everyone off *now*." Because so many people had napped through most of the trip, it flashed the lights and made a variety of annoying noises.

Jak knew that his meager bags were supposed to be waiting for him in his compartment on board, and he hadn't taken anything out of his pockets or his jumpie, so he just slung his jumpie on and swam forward to the hatch, which led to a flextunnel, and from there into the ship's receiving bay, a big airlock where a DNA reader took a small skin scraping to confirm that he was the person who owned the ticket. With eight terminals and fewer than twenty passengers, the process took less than ten minutes.

Now there was just the matter of seventy-eight days to fill. The two greatest concentrations of human population in the solar system, the Hive and the Aerie, are in the Earth's orbit, at the stable L4 and L5 Lagrange libration points—the places where the balance of gravitational force between the Earth and the sun on any object is such that if it drifts out of position, it will be pulled back into it—hence the cheapest place to be located, since fuel need not be expended for station-keeping. The L4 and L5 points form equilateral triangles with the planet and sun, so that L4, where the Aerie is, is 149 million kilometers—or just about two months—ahead of the Earth in orbit, and L5, where the Hive is, is the same distance behind.

Though this saves energy and therefore money for the great majority of the human race that just wants to stay where they are, it complicates matters a great deal for the few travelers; there are few cheap or easy trajectories for going between L4, L5, and Earth. The problem would be much worse if it were not for Mercury; almost always, the cheapest way involved making a flyby of one of the libration points, using the solar sails to drop down into a low fast orbit, intercepting Mercury, then using a gravity assist, and the extra force light sails get close to the sun, to send the ship upward on a close pass by either the other libration point or the Earth, with enough momentum to continue on up into the farther reaches of the solar system. On this particular trip, they would be dropping within Mercury's orbit and overtaking that planet, making a flyby there, before shooting up past the Earth, where Jak would leave on the ferry, seventy-eight days after getting onto the sunclipper, having been all the way round the sun (a fact that was endlessly belabored in travel ads touting the glories of vacations on Earth or the moon or in the Aerie—"and every time you travel, you put another year into your life.") Sunclippers never stopped except for overhauls or damage; as Jak left her, the *Spirit of Singing Port* would be upward bound to the Jovian system.

Jak spent ten minutes trying to speck the ship map, and then just spent the util to have a sprite guide him to his stateroom. The little dot of light, like a stage Tinkerbell, danced down the corridor in front of him. At the moment this part of the ship was in microgravity, so it was easier to airswim and leap than to try to walk for a while, until they descended into the outer rings.

After several turns and descents in a few hundred meters, Jak found himself walking the main corridor of the heavy or "dirtpig" ring of cabins. It had seemed strange to him at first that whereas the expensive neighborhoods in the Hive were the light ones, the expensive cabins on the ship were heavy. It made sense if you realized that people like one-tenth gravity or so—the lightest available in the Hive, and the heaviest shipboard—and pretty much by definition, rich people are the people who get what everyone would like.

The sprite bounded and looped down the corridor. It settled on a door in front of him, making the mad figure eight that indicated it had reached its destination. The door popped open.

Jak's first thought was that he had been delivered to a closet or perhaps a toilet. His "stateroom" was a little rectangular box with a built-in seat at the back, big for a coffin, small for a study carrel.

A white placard on the side wall was titled "Directions for Use of Single Stateroom." On the front of the seat was a handle that he could lift and pull, after bracing himself against the walls with both feet, since otherwise he tended to slip around in the .1 g. A door opened from under the seat, and a compartment swung open, revealing Jak's bags. He threw his jumpie in with them, and, following the directions, rotated the compartment farther, so that it carried his bags away under the seat.

Another handle appeared on the new surface he had pulled out, so he pulled on that. The structure underneath extended, taking up almost half the remaining stateroom space. He reached over the new surface, gripped the edge of a cushion, and flipped it forward. Small legs popped out and gripped slots in the floor. Jak faced a bed that left him just room enough for his shins between the edge of the mattress and the door.

He folded the bed back and continued to follow the directions; this was amusing, in a horrifying sort of way.

The surprising height of the little room—enough for a tall man to stand upright—was explained by the fact that this was a premier-class stateroom, "with full private bath." With the bed folded back into the seat, pushing on the handle caused the seat to slide into the wall and an inverted suction toilet to emerge from the wall above it. The toilet then rotated down to floor level. Simultaneously, a shower head emerged from the ceiling. According to the directions, one could either use the toilet for its regular purpose "having particular care to seal the unit before re-storing it," or one could use it as the drain for the shower, allowing the toilet to suck the water out of the room, "again having particular care to seal the unit before re-storing it." Jak thought the repetition was probably warranted considering the consequences of forgetting to do that.

Jak resealed the toilet and folded it back in. The placard had said that there "might be some noise, due to automatic flushing and cleaning, after re-storing toilet." The "some noise" sounded very much like sticking one's head in a running rocket engine.

With his "stateroom" completely explored, Jak set out to see the rest of the areas where passengers were permitted in the ship. Each of the six counterrotating rings of cabins, except the outer "dirtpig" ring where cabin space was priced too light to waste on common areas, had some attraction or other, supposedly. He quickly got the hang of using the scoops to get from ring to ring; the door into the scoop space would not open unless you had at least a half minute to get into the lift box. Once you did, and the door closed behind you, the scoop from the next level, a long gradual slide, would come in under the lift box and carry it up until you matched the next ring for height and speed. It felt like a combination of a slow elevator with a particularly sickening amusement ride.

On each level, Jak discovered that the supposed amusements were the same sort of semantic travesty that "stateroom" had been. The "four pools" on the level just above him were two pairs of individual-sized flowpools on opposite sides of a big rotating drum; you could swim (assuming you didn't become hopelessly disoriented by the Coriolis and the rush of water from the front to the back of the pool), but realistically what they were was high-grav power bathtubs. The "casino" on the next deck was a six-screen gambling machine arcade. Each of the "eleven 24-hour restaurants" on the third deck was two tables with a food dispenser whose ethnicity vaguely matched the painted decorations. The second deck's viv rooms were so small that signs warned against trying to play any game in other than solo seated mode; the "24-hour dance club" on the light deck was an ovoid about five meters on its long axis, with recorded music, a drink dispenser, and some flashing colored lights. Jak had been in at least one jail cell with better atmosphere.

After that tour of the "ultimate in luxury facilities," to quote the sales copy, Jak checked the time and discovered he had used up about forty-five minutes since his arrival. Only seventy-eight days to go.

The viv is the traditional refuge of the truly entertainment-starved, so Jak went to the second deck. But he was used to viv games in big rooms with full contact suits and dozens of people playing, coming and going all the time; these little solitary games were hardly worthy of the name. After an hour of shooting it out with bad guys and whipping it out for bad girls, Jak was tired, irritable, and bored.

He still wasn't hungry and anyway dinner would probably not consume an hour. For a few dreadful seconds he considered plugging into some eduviv and studying some subject or other. When he realized he was actually contemplating voluntarily getting more schooling, he wondered how close you could come to going mad in just a couple of hours.

Finally he had a thought that made him laugh out loud, startling the morose man who was eating chow fong at the other table in the Ristorante Italiano, where Jak had been idly toying with a cup of espresso. Jak made some gesture of apology, got up, and went down to his stateroom to change, still chuckling.

He had thought that Uncle Sib had been moralizing as usual, along the lines of "always brush your teeth after meals," when he had said, "You will want to work through the full Disciplines at least twice per day, maybe more." Now Jak finally dakked that Sib had merely been making an accurate prediction. That *was* what Jak would want to do, at least until he acquired some shipboard toves. There was hardly any better way to kill many hours than in the no-time of the Disciplines, and he could always use more practice.

After he dressed, he checked the room screen and found that passengers who wanted a full-g workout could use the centrifuged practice rooms in the crew gym. He might as well work out there, considering that he was going to the place that defined full-g; besides, it would help to tire him and make him more likely to sleep. He booked one of the practice rooms immediately and called up a sprite to show him the way.

He had just climbed through the hub and down the ladder into the practice room, and had barely begun to warm up in earnest, when a ping overhead announced someone at the door. Glad for any source of distraction, Jak pushed the come-in without checking to see who it was.

The ladder extended from the door in the ceiling down to the floor. The shutters slid open. The heet who climbed down was about Jak's age and wearing a baby-blue crew coverall. "I was watching you through the viewer," he said. "When you do Stroke the High Table, do you always do it with your middle finger split from your ring finger?"

"You had to drop in to check my form?"

"I had to come up with some way to open a conversation." The heet dropped the last few rungs to touch down gracefully on the padded floor. His skin was deep, warm brown, his eyes set wide with long epicanthal folds. He was squat, built like a wrestler, half a head shorter than Jak, probably heavier, with no fat. "I'm Piaro Fears-the-Stars. Astrogator Clade, but studying to be a master rigger."

"I'm Jak Jinnaka."

"Do you want to work out together? You were about to start the Disciplines when I interrupted you—do you have anything scheduled that you have to do soon?"

"Not a thing, till dinner, which is four hours from now for my seating," Jak said.

"Well, I have three hours till my mess call. Why don't we do the Disciplines together? Then we can have at least an hour and a half to spar. There's only ten or so other crewies who do the Disciplines that are even close to my age and level, so I know everyone's tricks and they know all of mine. I love it when a passenger who does the Disciplines comes along—it's a chance for some variety, maybe to get surprised, to try things out in a situation that isn't predictable."

"Sure, let's."

They set up in opposite corners of the centrifuged workout room, more or less admitting that they would be studying each other's style while working through the first, formal part of the Disciplines. In the quiet back of his mind, as Jak flowed from strike to strike against one dark attacker after another, he took his notes.

Piaro did almost every possible move with a closed hand, rarely dividing or extending fingers. That made sense—blows were better than grips if you spent most of your time in microgravity, with nothing to amplify the force of a throw or a grapple. On the other hand, there seemed to be no reason at all for Piaro to favor inside foot sweeps more than outside—Jak's style was the reverse—except taste. Blade forms were very different, with edge and point, forehand and backhand, used in very different mixtures and contexts. Projectile hand weapon forms were nearly identical—using a slug thrower is mostly a matter of pointing it in the right direction and holding it steady. With beam weapons, the difference again seemed to be in environment—Jak had been taught the more reliable burn-and-seek technique, Piaro the more precise aim-and-flash, which made sense if you considered what was apt to be behind or around the target in their respective expected environments.

When they finished the Disciplines, Piaro said, "Well, I saw plenty of differences."

"Me too. Of course, since we're going to spar, the question is, does the winner win because he's innately better or because his system is better?"

Piaro stood, stretched, and grinned. "Why don't we thrash that out?"

"By finding out who gets thrashed? Sure. Freestyle, catch-as-can?"

"Sure. Ship rules are all weapons simulated, tap out, monitors work on probable."

"Makes sense. They probably can't afford to have you laid up very often."

"No armor, except your cup, though."

"Good. I mean, good, it'll be faster, and good, I feel a lot better with the cup! Point a round, dub to escalate, trip to stick?"

"Yeah."

Freestyle, or "catch-as-can," is intended to train people for real fighting, and so it is fought until one opponent or the other, in a real fight, would be dead or disabled. How close "would be" gets to "actual" is determined by local custom; the ship's rules were gentle, with the expectation that if the other person got a clear advantage, you would double tap to acknowledge it, and that the artificial intelligences monitoring the fight would be relatively liberal with decisions, declaring whoever gained the first clear irreversible advantage to be the winner of the round.

Rounds start with bare hands; the first person to escalate to a knife or gun has an obvious advantage, so if you escalate and your opponent wins, your opponent gets two points for the round. If you escalate and your opponent wins without counterescalating, your opponent picks up three points.

Jak won the first round on a one-time trick. He made the guess that anyone who swept inside as much as Piaro did must be used to fighting someone with a too-narrow stance. So Jak deliberately stood narrow and rocked slightly forward onto the balls of his feet. A split second later, as the expected sweep came in, Jak continued his motion into a spin and lunge, thrusting his left hand against Piaro's head and pivoting his torso for a body drop that put Piaro flat on his back at Jak's feet. As Jak's hands flared into the butterfly entry to the carotid grip, Piaro tapped out and the monitor said, "First round, Jinnaka. One to zero."

Piaro laughed, got up, and said, "Well, if that was a lucky break, we should do this more so I can even things up. And if it was skill, we should do this more so I can learn your way."

"What if it's talent?"

"Then we need to do it more so that *you* can find out that, talented as you are, I have even more talent."

The next round was different. Jak wasn't going to try the same sucker trick twice in a row—Piaro was too good for that and besides it was a point of honor.

This time, Piaro had a way of doing a split stance that drew Jak forward to his weak side, letting Piaro slip in an inside sweep that didn't quite dump Jak, but put him off balance and slowed him. When he reached for a grip to counter, his hand suddenly flew sideways as Piaro's counterpunch rang his head.

He staggered back one step, and as his back foot came down, Piaro kicked Jak squarely on his armored cup. Jak was startled more than hurt, but as he instinctively bent around his groin, he felt the pulled-but-firm touch of the edge of Piaro's hand on the back of his neck, just as Piaro's knee flew straight up, stopping just as it lightly brushed Jak's face. Jak double tapped just before the monitor said, "Second round, Fears-the-Stars. One all."

The next half-dozen rounds established that though their styles were very different, they were fairly evenly matched, so sparring was going to stay fun for a long time. Even better than the matchup of skills was the matching attitudes and approaches: they tapped out when beaten, they didn't block their way into mutual stalling, and when either of them was taken by a trick he hadn't seen before, after the round, they took a few minutes to share and work through it together. (As Uncle Sib was too fond of saying, quoting some past master or other, "Getting surprised once is educational, surprising anyone with the same trick more than once is sadism.")

After twenty-four rounds, it was Jak thirteen, Piaro eleven, and it could just as easily have been the other way. By mutual agreement, they sat down to pant and stretch. "Toktru, I like the way that you're serious," Piaro said. "If you spar with most of the heets on the *Spirit*, you'll find that mostly their objective is just to keep the round going. Twenty-four rounds in an hour and a half seems about right."

Jak nodded, drawing a deep breath to speak comfortably. He specked that back on the Hive he had been neglecting his full-grav workouts pretty badly—he was more tired and sore than he should be. He could feel a dozen bruises forming on his legs and arms, the muscles between his shoulder blades ached, one cheek stung where Piaro's foot had slapped him harder than intended, his heart was thundering, and there didn't seem to be enough air in the universe no matter how he gulped it. It was wonderful.

"Well, my Uncle Sib says he hates people who just keep a round going. He says that the point is to train for serious fighting, and if a fight is serious, it rarely lasts more than a minute. The three rules he gave me about sparring were no dancers, no nubbies, and always catch-as-can."

"Huh. I can see why no dancers, and always catch-as-can—practicing formal styles of combat might lead to passing up opportunities in the real thing, masen? But what's a nubby?"

"A heet who really loves to win at sparring, so he trains himself, and/or gets illegal modifications, to be able to accept tremendous amounts of pain and still be fully functional. Then he adds insane quantities of strength training and muscle-building drugs to the mix, and he always tries to fight with minimum monitoring, even with no monitoring if you're stupid enough to agree to it. Then he just ignores the damage you do and comes in and gets you with those gorilla muscles. Most of them are real proud of all that damage they've taken, so they only get functional repairs, not cosmetic ones, afterward, and they always make sure you can see their scars.

"Of course like any kid I ignored Uncle Sib's advice a couple of times, and toktru, I paid. I got *wanged* once by this giant heet *after* I broke his arm and blinded him, for real, I mean, no tap-out about it, one of the malph's eyes was out of the socket and the monitor still didn't stop the fight. He just closed in and crushed my windpipe. I pulled four days in the hospital, he pulled twenty-three, but officially he won and that was what mattered to him. And he sent me a thank-you note because I'd broken his nose in a way that he thought looked real light."

Piaro shuddered. "Anybody who cares that much about wanging me that way can have all the honor he wants, in exchange for not doing it." He stretched forward over his crossed legs, working out soreness from his lower back. "You know you're not required to eat at your dinner seating. And passenger food is the same as crew food."

"So . . . ?"

"At your seating, you'll discover that every other passenger on board is at least fifteen years older than you are. Most of them will be trying to impress each other with how bored they are to be here, how many times they've done this before, and how much they didn't want to travel but it was just too important so they had to make this inconvenient, wretched trip even though they would so much rather just stay home. So I thought maybe you might want to join me at mess, as my guest, and meet some crewies around our age?"

"Sure. Toktru sure."

There were about thirty heets in the Bachelors' Mess, ranging in age from about fifteen to about twenty-five, but the noise and confusion seemed more like a hundred. Piaro ate at the middle table, so Jak was right in the center.

Dining at a twentieth of a g, one-quarter of what he was used to at home, made Jak into the evening's entertainment. His new messmates, used to very low grav from infancy, could drink from an open-topped cup and eat soup with a spoon without missing a drop; Jak could only envy them as he supplied the table with a good deal more amusement than he supplied himself with nutrition. His most amusing performance, everyone agreed later, was when he inadvertently hit himself in the face with a quarter of a cup of orange juice; the part that didn't quite go into his left ear sailed over his shoulder and headed for the older bachelors' table. A big heet with orange hair and very dark skin, laughing as if it were the funniest thing he'd ever seen, caught the whole arcing flow in an empty cup, receiving a round of applause from the room.

"Well," Piaro said, "my record is intact—I've brought someone to disgrace the table again." But his eyes twinkled as he said it.

The big man nodded, bowed, and gently handed the cup to Jak. "At least your drink is aerated. No flat taste. Don't take this too personally. Without passenger guests, half our dinner-table conversation would vanish."

Clevis, sitting on Jak's right, who seemed to be the oldest one in the middle bachelors' table, said, "Toktru." He sliced a chunk of pressed protein that appeared to be only slightly smaller than his head, and swallowed it with what seemed to be only a little chewing for form's sake. "Piaro has been well known for bringing passengers to mess since about the time that we were all having strained carrots together. We like to argue about whether it's his friendly way to be sadistic or vice versa. But we're all glad he does it. Younger passengers, stuck on the ship alone, get really bored and miserable, so it's good to give them a social life. And we all know each other way too well, so it's good to make us mix with new people. So welcome, and don't worry much—within about two days you'll have control of liquids. Assuming you did back when you lived in higher gravity, anyway."

Jak nodded politely, and the uproar around him resumed.

After a while, he asked Piaro, "Mind if I ask you a question that might be personal? If it's offensive, please excuse my ignorance."

"Principle 201," Piaro said, smiling, referring to the one that said, "Always excuse ignorance and punish malice; only a malicious person is ignorant of the difference."

"Well, all right then. Your family name is Fears-the-Stars?"

"I know it's not in the Nakasen form, if that's what you're getting at. We practice a very different form of the Wager on the ships than you do in the Hive."

"I knew that," said Jak, who had been warned all his life that it was heresy, "but what I meant was it seems like a strange name for anyone who's going to spend the rest of his life in a spaceship."

"Not really. Most of the spaceborn have names that refer to fear, caution, or distrust. Usually of the family specialty. It's a compliment, in its way. A crewie that isn't afraid of what he works with is too dumb to trust. It's a good thing for an astrogator to fear the stars, because the stars can be deceptive, and if you get fooled, you can end up on a course that leaves you bankrupt or starved. So they teach us fear from the start, any way they can, even on your first day on a job on your fifth birthday."

"On your fifth birthday—what do they assign you to do? Make your own bed, tie your shoes? How do they teach you to be afraid of a job a five-year-old can do?"

From Jak's left, Clevis explained, "Oh, people do *that* stuff as soon as they can, mostly by the time they're four. No, five-year-olds trim sails, watch scopes to back up the software, keep an eye on the reactor, now and then mind the helm. That's how you acquire fear."

"I can see that. I'm afraid already. A little kid in a job like that—do they even have the ability, at that age, to dak what happens if they screw up?"

Piaro shrugged. "Oh, we don't just assign them a job and give them their feets. There's always somebody who's at least twelve standing over you when you're little. To take control if you stop paying attention, and to supply that sense of danger."

"You stand there and remind the little kid?"

"No, the real danger, to a little kid, is that if you do it wrong, or stop doing it, you get whacked on the back of your head."

Jak was stunned; hadn't Paj Nakasen specifically forbidden striking a child in the *Teachings*? (Or had it only been in the *Suggestions Concerning the Teachings*?) He was so startled, in fact, that he very nearly violated two of the Principles himself, just thinking for so long—134, "Do not reveal your thoughts to anyone whose power over you is unknown," and 86, "When it is necessary to dissemble, do it quickly." So Jak said, "You know adults never hit a kid on the Hive? Or, when they do, it's a criminal offense."

"People say that about most places," Pabrino said. He was tall, thin, pale-skinned, and very dark-haired, probably the youngest heet at the middle table. "I always wonder how anyone can learn anything in school if there's no incentive."

"Well, I learned as little as I possibly could, so you might have a point at that. But even if there's not as much inside my head, the back of it is definitely happier."

Clevis nodded. "I've known many passengers, including quite a few wasps, and I'd have to say that's one way we're really different from you. Crewies don't worry so much about being happy, or any other emotional state. I didn't like getting hit, but I always knew that it wasn't because somebody was enjoying it or working off his frustrations or anything. We say crewie kids should get hit like bolts get tightened—that is, you don't tighten a bolt because you like tightening, or because it's a bad bolt or you hate the bolt, you tighten it because it's better when it's tight."

Jak shuddered. "I can't imagine."

Piaro grinned. "Well, I had some trouble imagining, myself, when I heard about how they have sex on Venus."

"Yeah, but that's *fun* to imagine."

It was too much of a cliché to be a good joke, but it gave the whole table something to share a laugh about.

"So why are you traveling?" Piaro asked. "And are you getting off at Mercury?"

"I guess you could say I'm a diplomatic courier," Jak said, just as he'd been instructed to say. "Headed for Earth, the stop after." He had a cover story he was supposed to spill at every opportunity, and this was the story that was supposed to eventually give him a chance to spill his cover story.

"Weehu! No wonder you're starting the Disciplines on your first day aboard. We carry a lot of diplomatic couriers, and it looks like it's the dullest job in the world, except for, what, a few minutes a year when someone's trying to take the pouch? I had no idea anyone started at that career so young. Most of the ones we see are in their thirties at least."

Jak sighed. "They tell me it's more like a few seconds of excitement a year. Anyway, I *am* getting an early start. I'm sort of an irregular—I have a relative in the business and this is my entrée to it."

"Well, it's good that you're getting a start," Clevis said, gulping a big mouthful of a sticky red-orange pudding. "It's certainly much more exciting than what most wasps end up doing with their lives."

Jak knew that Hive citizens were commonly called wasps, and that the term could be friendly, hostile, or anything between, but this was the first time he'd heard it used with complete neutrality—just the name of the thing. "I'm afraid you've dakked it singing-on," he said. "The Hive is rich and safe, so if you want excitement you have to look elsewhere. People complain, all the time, about that."

Piaro said, "Now that's one way crewies are toktru *not* different. On the ship, people complain, all the time, about always being worried."

"We even name our families after our anxieties," Pabrino pointed out, and the conversation drifted back to crewie naming customs.

At the end of dinner, Jak was happy to find he was invited to the Bachelors' Mess on a permanent basis; furthermore, besides Piaro, two more heets who practiced the Disciplines wanted to spar with him, Brill wanted to play chess, and Pabrino wanted to play Maniples, although they would have to carefully work out when the possible time was since a Maniples match was more interesting and challenging if it was continuous, playing one took a double shift, and double shifts off were rare. But Clevis and Brill had some control over scheduling, and would be happy to create the block of time for Pabrino to play against Jak—"After all," Brill explained, "we're all going to bet on it."

Jak returned to his stateroom feeling that this voyage wasn't going to be nearly so long as it had seemed just a few hours before.

CHAPTER 5

They Weren't Trying to Trick You, Exactly

In the next few days, Jak could hardly help noticing that while he really liked his newfound toves, they had things to do and he didn't. Piaro, Pabrino, Clevis, and Brill were all toktru toves, but games, conversations, workouts, and sparring all ended the same way—whoever Jak was with had to go work.

Jak didn't resent his new toves for having to work—after all, they would all be on the *Spirit* for the rest of their lives and it only made sense for them to contribute to it. What bothered him was that he had nothing to go and do; neither his outward nor his secret missions required him to do anything other than enjoy the ride as best he might. It made him feel nonfunctional, probably the way an S.P. felt all the time, and that made him think of Sesh . . . he realized that he missed her very badly, perhaps because shipboard rules were set up so that normally you could only see crewies of the gender you weren't attracted to, so he hadn't seen anyone female, distant glimpses and one elderly passenger excepted, since coming aboard.

He didn't know it at the time, but he was already working on that problem. He had let his secondary cover story spill just as Uncle Sib had told him to do, and was happy to see that Sib apparently knew his craft. Unlike on the Hive, onboard a ship, adult and teenage crewies talked and gossiped all the time, instead of keeping to their own social circles. Consequently, Jak's story of being an apprentice diplomatic courier could not possibly hold up with adults; real diplomatic couriers were older, well-trained specialists, and routine corporate couriers weren't paid enough to travel interplanetary. Besides, shipment by stealthed drop capsule was normally more secure—"You can intercept anyone, somewhere, because they have to travel with a big heat source and something to make air and food, at low accelerations, and all that usually gives you a way in," Uncle Sib had explained, "but a black surface-chilled radar-transparent sphere the size of a volleyball, traveling cold and ballistic, along any of an infinite number of orbits millions of miles long, is a real interception problem."

Jak's claim to be an apprentice in a family business (in an industry in which there were no family businesses) was the "secondary cover"—the story designed to be blown in order to make the primary cover more believable.

The primary cover lay slightly closer to the truth. It was that Jak was infatuated with Princess Shyf after his long relationship with her (very nearly true); that he was carrying a message from the King of Greenworld to

Psim Cofinalez, demanding that he release the Crown Princess (in the neighborhood of the truth); that doing this was extremely risky (mildly risky—Psim was thought to have relatively little of the celebrated Cofinalez personality made up of equal parts of rage, impetuousness, and aggression); that Jak had volunteered to do it (true) because everyone else was afraid to (false); and that Jak was therefore risking his life for love while professional diplomats cowered at home (absolutely false). Supposedly Jak would be taking a ransom offer to the second son of the Duke of Uranium, who, it was hoped, would then release Princess Shyf instead of holding her prisoner (vaguely like the truth); the offer was all that Greenworld could afford but most likely not enough (false); and once Psim refused, Jak was to deliver an ultimatum that would begin a war between Greenworld and Uranium (false) and was therefore facing imprisonment and probably torture himself (completely false) all for love (again, vaguely like the truth).

Sib's instructions had been to appear confused when people asked questions about the secondary, and then to divulge the primary to anyone who seemed to be friendly and trying to win his trust. "Don't even think about the real story," Sib had said, "always keep reasserting the secondary cover even in front of people who already know the primary, and gabble like an idiot about the primary."

Within a mere few days, therefore, as Piaro, Pabrino, and Brill had successively become close enough friends, Jak had leaked the story to them. Since they had sworn to maintain absolute secrecy, they had told only a few toves, who had each told only a few toves, until in less than a week the whole ship had heard the story.

Because Jak was pleasant and friendly and delivered the story with the same wide-eyed sincerity he usually used when lying to Uncle Sib about some illegal, stupid, or immoral thing at which the authorities had nearly caught him, most people felt deep sympathy for the brave young man in a hopeless quest to rescue the princess who was far above him socially. Jak would explain, "I probably won't even get to see her, or any part of Earth except the spaceport, a couple of palaces, and a jail. But it's something I can do for her, and I get to feel like I *tried.*"

What neither Jak nor Sib had reckoned on was that aside from being a *good* story, Jak's primary cover was also a good *story*, and although the custom was for crewies to avoid passengers that they might be attracted to, reducing expensive exogamic crew loss, communication within the crew was very free, so the younger female crewies heard about it quickly. Soon Jak was madly popular with a dozen girls who had never seen him (nor he them).

When Jak did become aware of it, it changed his life forever—and afterward, he could never decide whether that was for the better or not.

He had finally gotten to play Maniples with Pabrino. When he had agreed he had had no idea how big a deal this would be; his first clue was that they not only had to find a suitable double break in Pabrino's schedule, they also had to find a break in which most of the middle cohort of bachelors could watch the contest, and the contest was carried live on shipboard viv, with probably a third of the crew experiencing it in real time and many of those who had to work recording it for later.

The crewies were excited because as far as they were concerned, the match meant something. Pabrino was the youngest ship's champion ever at Maniples, good enough to have defeated champions from four other ships during co-orbits and co-approaches over the years, the first when he was just eleven. In fact, Pabrino had never been beaten in intership play. Jak was a worthy opponent—he had played second singles for his gen school team and been ranked around number ten for gen school seniors in the Hive—and because ship and Hive players played each other rarely, it was difficult to learn much about their relative strengths by comparing their records. This made the whole match much more uncertain, and crewies like to gamble—numerous desserts, cleaning shifts, graveyard watches, and outside rec times were at stake. But it also meant a chance to find out how Pabrino might do out in the wider world, and that was even more exciting; was he just "pretty good for spaceborn" or was he just possibly one of the rare masters?

Everyone said that Maniples was loosely based on chess, but they might as reasonably have said it was based on real warfare, or on intrigue-and-adventure fiction, or on scissors-paper-stone. There were two sides, Green and Black, each with a small fleet of warcraft and a small force of B&Es. Their home bases, armed with enormous numbers of bomb and beam weapons, were armed, slowly-mobile space stations in synchronous orbit around a planet, beginning at a point 180 degrees away from each other, so that neither base could see the other at the start. A great deal of the micro-game consisted in trying to move forces through the always-shifting Dispu-Zone visible to both bases. The planet was always arbitrarily created just a half hour before play began; it would be the size of Mars, but much warmer, fully habitable, with the surface exactly fifty percent ocean and the land divided into prairie, forest, desert, polar caps, mountains, swamps, permafrost, and jungle according to the arbitrary generating program.

The objective of the game was to get a fast missile targeted and locked in on the enemy base, at which point the enemy would be forced to surrender. If the bases were moved far enough to become visible to each other, immediate mutual annihilation ensued, officially a draw.

Each side had one big heavily armed sunclipper, with nearly the firepower of the base, capable of escape velocity (but vulnerable to fire from the base, slow to accelerate, extremely visible because of its size); three low-to-high-orbit space-only orbicruisers, with much better acceleration than the sunclipper but smaller and fewer weapons, stealthed but visible every time their engines ran; nine lightly armed surface-to-low-orbit warshuttles, with high acceleration in short bursts, stealthed to be visible only during their brief engine firings; twenty-seven submersible aircraft; and eighty-one B&Es, each equipped with a single-seat helicopter/hovercraft capable of carrying his personal gear and either one small fission bomb/mine, or one base-wrecking missile—not both. During the half hour of studying the planet before battle began, in the area where its own base was visible from the surface, each side was allowed to place thirty-six landing fields, any of which could handle its whole surface-capable fleet, and all with plentiful spare parts, fuel, and ammunition.

Stealth was deliberately imperfect; it reduced the distance at which radar or light rendered a thing visible, but never to zero.

When one piece attacked another, combat was resolved by simulator duels. Your coordination, reflexes, and training played a role as much as your strategic abilities.

Uncle Sib thought Maniples was important, and even though Jak never listened to him, he had absorbed that attitude. Jak had many times endured an Uncle Sib monologue something like "There are just six forces at work in the present epoch, three positive and three negative, which unite humanity; remove any two of them and we would fall apart into anarchy. Two are traditional and internal, both positive: the desire to copulate with strangers and the drive to get rich. Two are external, both negative: the risk of more wars with the Rubahy, and the risk that when the Galactic Court have finally heard all the evidence and arguments and done all the mysterious things they keep doing, they will issue the Extermination Order and try to put an end to the human race. And two are internal and relatively new, one positive and one negative: Maniples and slamball. All right, I'll stop, I know you've heard it before, just eat and get out of here."

Some people, especially on Mars where the public passion for it was very great, devoted their lives to Maniples. "Great games" anthologies, in which you could

experience what had come through the goggles, head-
phones, and vivsuits of the masters as they played each
other, were consistent best-sellers as entertainment. Like
chess, go, bridge, or belludi, it seemed arbitrarily simple,
yet its possibilities were inexhaustible.

Almost everyone started to play Maniples around age
six. Most people found they had no talent and played it
little or not at all after adolescence; many continued as
hobbyists; some few brilliant ones became professional
and began ascending the ranks of Masters; the very few
who became Greater Masters or above could live in just
about any human settlement in the solar system as the
most welcome and honored of guests. To study for one
year with any of the half-dozen Greatest Masters still
living, who had all passed their three hundredth birth-
days, cost half a terautil, as much as a large sunclipper, a
patent of economic nobility for a noncritical resource, or
a private preserve a kilometer square on the lightest deck
in the Hive.

So the heavily intermarried, mutually dependent families that were the crew of the *Spirit of Singing Port* were
fascinated with the possibility that in their midst, far
from any of the luxuries, competition, support, or importance of the great cities of space or the planets, just
possibly they might have a genius at one of humanity's
great pastimes. This didn't mean that they took it easy on
Pabrino or coddled him. If anything, they expected more
of him. But it did mean that when Pabrino played anyone new, in real time and not via simulation, it was
watched by just about the entire crew.

Jak was relieved to discover that Pabrino was superb—so much better than Jak that he could form no real

estimate. If Jak had been the person who revealed Pabrino's limitations (if any), he might have suffered the traditional fate of the bearer of bad news, socially if not literally.

Not that Jak didn't try his best to give a good account of himself. But Pabrino was better at the great majority of things that mattered. A B&E controlled by Jak usually won against a B&E controlled by Pabrino in single combat, and they were about even with surface-to-space warshuttles, but in all other kinds of combat Pabrino excelled him, and in strategy Jak was very far out of his depth.

Though the match took over six hours, Jak knew perfectly well how it would end ten minutes after it started, when a ground shot he'd never have thought possible came out of an area he had thought was secure, and Jak lost a Black orbicruiser moving to high orbit. Jak counterattacked the Green B&Es who had done it, killing all three of them, but lost two Black aircraft in the exchange.

In the ensuing hours the disparity in material only became worse, as Jak was forced into one unfavorable sacrifice after another. When what appeared to be a final mass wave attack by Green came crashing at him, he had barely deployed his few remaining Black forces into the DispuZone when Green B&Es seized four of his landing fields. As he whirled to meet that threat, a Green warshuttle popped up over a stretch of horizon that lack of material had forced Jak to leave unguarded. Its missile locked on the Black base, and that was the end of the game.

Pabrino's potential as the player who would inscribe

the *Spirit of Singing Port*'s name in history was once again confirmed. Jak was certain that Pabrino was better than the best gen school players in the Hive, maybe a great deal better, and said so as they emerged from their vivsuits, damp and acrid with sweat.

Both laughing with relief, they gulped the fruit drinks that Piaro held out to them. The other bachelors crowded around to shake hands, thump backs, and generally celebrate a day when they all did something unusual. "I'd like to play you a few more times," Jak said, "but I don't speck anyone will bet on me again."

"Just having a new opponent is great," Pabrino said, pushing a damp mess of black hair off his forehead. "Fewer predictable tricks. Best fight I've had in more than a year. It would be *great* to do this a couple more times."

Brill handed them each a wet towel, and they mopped their faces and exposed skin with it. "This is a good start but I sure hope there's time for a real shower before dinner," Jak said.

Piaro nodded. "More time than you'd think. This happens to be one of the scheduled days for families to eat together. And by request of my family—I tried to warn them, really I did, but they wouldn't listen—you're eating with mine. That's in about an hour and a half, so grab your kit, go get showered and presentable, and I'll come by your stateroom and pick you up."

"You've never even talked about your family," Jak said.

"Well, a lot of times, on shipboard, you don't. Most ways your workmates and your messmates have a bigger impact on your life. But family counts for something, and as it happens I've got one. The regulation one mother and one father, plus a twin sister who would have murdered me if I hadn't brought you to dinner. She has this idea that you're going to be interesting."

Jak grinned. "What if I am?"

"Then my sister is even dumber than I've always thought. This is someone who—well, never mind. If I start telling stories about her, she'll start telling them about me, and though mine about her are the absolute and completely humiliating truth, hers about me are a tiny grain of truth wrapped in such a thick shroud of exaggeration and fabrication that . . . oh, well. Best not to start. So, anyway, Phrysaba wants to meet you, and you're coming, tove. I promise somehow I'll make it up to you."

Jak couldn't imagine what was so interesting about himself, but he went off to the stateroom whistling anyway, and made sure he smelled and looked good. After all, female attention is flattering regardless of the female, he reasoned to himself, and it had been a while since he'd had any, and even though Piaro apparently didn't get along with his sister, all the same she was probably no worse than a bit on the plain side, or maybe whiny or rude, and Piaro was a good tove and Jak could be charming and pleasant, to help out a friend.

Jak was about as unprepared for Phrysaba as it was possible to be, because it had never occurred to him that a brother might be so biased against his sister, and so he had thought Piaro's account must be somewhere in the neighborhood of reality, at least. With the wide array of opportunities on the Hive, and the very early opportunities to have one's own life and explore one's own interests, sibling rivalry is rare and mild there. But on shipboard, with every position up for grabs and life tightly controlled, jockeying for position within the family is as natural as scratching an itch, and about as hard to learn not to do in public. So Piaro had been anything but an objective reporter.

Later, Jak thought that perhaps he should have guessed anyway. Piaro was a good-looking heet; how terrible could his sister be? Ship's companies are almost uniformly brainy due to the combination of self-selection, genetic modification, early stimulation, and constant social pressure; Phrysaba was competing, in that smart aggressive pool, for a post as an astrogator. As a future rigging chief, Piaro had the native perfect manners that are a necessity for people who live in close quarters and meet strangers often; Phrysaba added an upper-class, officer's polish to them.

But although in hindsight Jak realized he should have expected Phrysaba to be a remarkable and interesting person, and quite likely beautiful, in fact the revelation hit him like a dark meteor from a high orbit. About three minutes after politely meeting Dolegan Fears-the-Stars, Piaro's father, who shook Jak's hand and said a word or two of welcome before pulling up a ship's financial records screen at the table, and less than a minute after meeting Laris Fears-the-Stars, Piaro's mother, who appeared to be bored and was doing something on her screen all through dinner, Jak found himself gazing into Phrysaba's eyes, feeling what he always did when his heart was grabbed—simultaneously like the luckiest heet alive and like the biggest gweetz the human race had ever produced.

She was slim and taller than average; she had the sort of sharp, clear features that seem to express every passing feeling. Her skin was a slightly deeper brown than Piaro's, her eyes a little less wideset, but the family jaw and eyebrows were unmistakable, and they graced her as if some wise genie had chosen them specially. She laughed only when things were funny, smiled as if the world were constantly singing-on the way she wanted it to be, and asked the sort of question that quickly converted Jak from feeling like a babbling gweetz to the discovery that he was a more interesting fellow than he'd ever thought he could be.

Toward the end of dinner, Phrysaba turned to Piaro and said, "You're right, he'll do just fine."

Piaro sighed. "He'd better, you have him hypnotized by now, Sis."

Jak was trying to frame the question when Piaro explained, "It's the time of year for the Exchange Dance. Basically because there's so few of us on the ships, people tend to get paired up and stay that way even though they may not be crazy about each other. So at the Exchange Dance you go and dance with everyone except your date—old-style ballroom dancing, so that everyone gets to talk. The idea is that it provides a relatively painless way for people to get out of arrangements that might no longer suit them, but that they've been in for years. Well, as it happens, Phrysaba doesn't have a mekko and never has, and the ship is short of heets her age, so she needs someone to go to a dance with her and not dance with her, so that she can see about stealing someone else's mekko."

"That is *not* the purpose. I just want to go and it's bad form to go without a date and everyone else in my class has a date and is going and—"

Piaro raised his hands as if being held at gunpoint. "You see what happens. I try to help her social life and she gets violent—"

"The only way you'd ever help my social life would be if you spread the rumor that you were adopted!"

Jak watched the two of them bicker for several minutes; he was starting to dak that this was how the twins were affectionate with each other. Probably anyone who was silly enough to harm one of them would be dead at the hands of the other, almost instantly.

"Uh, by the way, the answer is yes," Jak said, when he judged that their score was about even; she had just told Piaro that looking at him made her wonder why Mother hadn't eaten her young, and he'd indignantly replied that undoubtedly she'd thought about eating Phrysaba, but refrained for fear of being poisoned.

The two of them stopped and stared at Jak.

"The answer is yes," he said. "You were leading up to the idea of my escorting Phrysaba to the Exchange Dance, masen? So I was saying yes."

"*You're* supposed to ask *her,* tove," Piaro said. "And then she has to consider."

Jak shrugged. Sib had thumped it into him any number of times that customs were not a matter of making or not-making sense; they were a matter of playing the game or not. After all, which "makes more sense"—only touching the ball with your hands in basketball, or never touching the ball with your hands in soccer? "Well, then," Jak said, "give me some help and guidance here. Is there a formal way to ask? Anything I have to do while asking?"

Phrysaba got a strange gleam in her eye. "Well, it's customary to stand on one foot with your hands over your ears and all the pockets on your coverall turned inside out. And the family likes to have a picture of that—"

"Sis!"

"Okay. Okay. Just thinking of the fun we could have. Actually, no, you just ask."

"Not quite. You also have to pay her one or two really flowery compliments," Piaro said. She glared at him. "And that's not a prank."

"No, but it's embarrassing. I was hoping to skip it."

Without looking up from her computer screen or raising her voice, Laris said, "Go all the way around the orbit or don't even chart it, Phrysaba. If you want to be asked according to custom, then be asked according to custom. If you want to skip over parts, then let the young man make up his own way and don't hold him to custom. No picking and choosing."

"Yes, Mother," Phrysaba looked down as if she'd been bawled out.

After an awkward pause, Jak said, "Well, then, Phrysaba, you are so beautiful that I can barely think at all when I'm looking at you, and you have completely fascinated and charmed me the whole time we've been talking, and I would be deeply honored if I could escort you to the Exchange Dance."

She seemed to choke up—he hoped from the extravagance of the compliment, and not some gaffe he'd made—and said, "I will have to consider. I'll have my brother carry word of my decision to you."

"Did it, Sis, did it! Just like a regular person! Anyone who didn't know you would never know what a gweetz you are, toktru!" Piaro exclaimed.

Even their parents laughed. Somehow that broke the ice. Within a few minutes, Jak was once again completely enthralled by Phrysaba.

Afterward he knew that he must have eaten the rest of dinner only because he was full, that Piaro was there only because the two of them went to one of the canteens for coffee and conversation after, that he had said good night to Phrysaba because he remembered her warm sad smile. And he knew he had a problem. He was supposed to be rescuing Sesh, not falling in love with another girl.

Two days later, he was playing dodec handball with Piaro, a game at which they were very evenly matched, and both of them were beginning to pant and to shake off sweat that hung in the air for many seconds thanks to the microgravity. "I feel like I'm breathing liquid me," Piaro said. "Like to take a break, or better yet just quit?"

"Toktru, yeah, one or the other, and I'm starting to like quitting." Jak pulled up his shirt to wipe his drenched face; when he dropped the shirt back it was soaking. "If nothing else this trip is getting me into the best shape of my life, which is going to be handy if I end up spending months under house arrest on Earth."

"Yeah. Given what a full gravity feels like, and what it does to your joints and muscles, no wonder people moved off the Earth as soon as they could." Piaro stretched and said, "I'd say a warm soak and some cold juice?"

Jak nodded. "Sounds good."

Passengers rarely used the ship's Public Baths. Those from the Hive, the richer parts of the Aerie, and the mining colonies generally had strong privacy taboos, and people from planets and larger moons got seasick in the sloshing of the warm low-gravity tanks. Jak had discovered, the first time Brill and Clevis had invited him, that his psyche was apparently missing the modesty component of his home culture, and the slow, gentle rocking of the big warm tank of water worked miracles on tired, sore muscles. Now he preferred the Public Baths to the awkward shower in his stateroom.

The two toves left their clothes on a bench and wandered among the dwarf trees that surrounded the bathing pool; generations of developing the perfect graft host had brought about tree trunks straight as a post, on which grew branches of a dozen fruits. After picking and paying for an apple, a peach, and a mango, Jak tossed them into the juicer, selected the temperature, and threw the switch. After a brief shriek of machinery, his pitcher of ice-cold juice emerged.

As he settled into the bathing pool beside Piaro, he said, "You live a fine life on the ships. I'm starting to wish I had the mathap to join the Spatial; this has to be better than push-ups and rifle cleaning."

Piaro shrugged. "Spatial ships are tighter, more rules and more enforcement and all, than free merchants like us, but supposedly they have better amenities. As long as you don't count not getting blown up as amenity."

He took a sip of his own banana-orange mix and said, "And actually, in kind of a roundabout way, we might be able to help you with getting into the Spatial, along with resolving an awkward social problem." He stretched again and said, "Oh, that's good on the shoulders."

For a long while, the two stretched and scrubbed, till at last Piaro said, "It so happens that my sister found three separate occasions to talk to me yesterday."

"That's unusual?"

"Three in a month would be unusual. *This* was bi*zarre*. We're better friends than we let on but we're headed for different roles in life and we don't have much to talk about. Furthermore, all three conversations were about trivial matters. Further-furthermore, each trivial matter then led around to a single topic, which was *you,* old pizo. Don't ask me why, there's no accounting for taste, but I think Phrysaba toktru likes you. And she seems to also really like the fact that you're off to heroically rescue that princess, too—she won't let me make jokes about 'heroic house arrest' or you being a 'heroic errand boy' anymore—and to me, anyway, it makes no sense, because if she has a crush on you, that's more than problem enough, and if you add in that you're obligated to this other girl, it makes everything completely impossible. But somehow you've made a big impression, and Phrysaba's never been really strongly interested in any particular heet before. And I bet you know that that's going to be trouble if anyone older than us notices it."

Jak didn't quite know what to do or say. His friend dakked it singing-on that this was going to be trouble. And he had no business getting involved with a girl on this trip, especially not when the whole point of it was to rescue Sesh, who was probably languishing in a prison cell right now, or at least being forced to hang around in a garden with a heet she didn't like, which, for Sesh, was practically the same thing. So the entire situation was a disaster, and he had to hope Piaro had thought of a way out.

On the other hand, his heart was leaping up for pure happiness. What could *that* mean?

"Well," Piaro said, "the last I knew you were planning on joining the Hive Army—assuming that for the next few years your occupation isn't 'prisoner' or 'hostage'— but as far as I know nobody prefers the Army to the Spatial if they can get into the Spatial, masen? So you don't have one of the aps. Well, did you know that if you earn United Association of Spacecrew points, that gives you a leg up for joining the Spatial?"

"Yeah, but the UAS is even harder to get into than the Spatial. It's considerably harder to get into than the Hive's PSA, which I didn't get into, which is where all the trouble started in the first place."

"It's harder to get into if you walk into the UAS office in the Hive, or connect via net, and apply. But UAS wants everyone who works in space to have a union card. And on every union ship, if anyone wants to work, there's always work, and there's always training available. So if you applied to work on general labor for the *Spirit of Singing Port*, you'd be able to get both work and training—about as much of both as you wanted— and work is good for UAS points and training is good for *lots* of UAS points. You'd need about six voyages before you could join as a full-ranked voting member, but any points at all count very strongly toward your application to the Spatial, and if you worked this voyage and the one back to the Hive, especially if that's a long one, my guess is you'd be pretty nearly certain of getting into the Spatial. Or if you didn't want to do that but you found out you liked sunsailing, well, with a provo membership and that many points, you could probably ship out from the Hive within a year or so—they give some extra consideration to anyone trying to earn his permanent card."

"Toktru? To tell you the truth, even with all you toves being so nice and inviting me for all the rec and games stuff, I'm pretty bored, and it would be great to have more to do."

"Don't mention that around the ship's shrink when you interview with him—they don't let insane people work. But I suppose in the abstract I can kind of understand how you might feel that way." Piaro drank again, stretched, and said, "I assume you see that besides maybe helping you get into the Spatial, there's the other advantage, which applies right now. It gets you and Phrysaba out of all kinds of trouble. Anything between a passenger and a crewie is frowned on, even just a social friendship. But if it looked like you intended to be a crewie someday . . . then you and Phrysaba could spend time together, and I don't speck people would disapprove. Better for my family, better for you, even better for my sister."

"But if she's already, um, infatuated, and especially if you think it's not going to work out—"

"I have faith in both of you, Jak. You're about the most unromantic heet I've ever seen, and she's about as romantic as they make'em. Two weeks of being mekko and demmy and the two of you won't be able to stand the sight of each other. Just be nice about it if you decide to dump her; I know she'll be kind if she dumps you. Want to towel off and drift toward mess?"

After dinner, Jak was at loose ends; all the crew his own age happened to be working that shift. He wasn't going to make a complex situation worse by trying to contact Phrysaba. After admitting to himself that there wasn't much that was fun to do, just now, he went back to his stateroom, got into his pajamas, and rummaged around in his bag. He found his purse wadded up in the bottom, where he'd tossed it the first chance he got, and pulled it on to his left hand, making sure his fingers moved freely and that it felt comfortable on his palm, fastening the straps around his wrist, flexing to wake it up. He darkened the room, and said, "Bring up news access."

"Now you tell me," the purse said. "You haven't wanted that in years. I'll have to get all kinds of modules that I deleted years ago, and reorganize memory. This is going to take a full minute and you'll probably reprimand me for it. Great."

Jak fingered the pain button, just above his wrist, significantly.

"All right, all right, all right. I'm getting it. I was just telling you it would take some time," the purse said. "You're just very hard to predict. I've almost got it. And will you want it all projected on the wall?"

"Yeah."

"And will you need this more in the near future?"

"Toktru."

"All right. Then I have to do a couple more things with

memory before I can get started. Please don't zap me. I'll get it as fast as I can."

"Do it." Jak wondered idly if a purse that liked you, like Dujuv's, was better than this, or even worse for chattering.

The news access brought a shock. Uncle Sib had told him not to expect to find much, because after all Sesh was being held in secret and probably word would not leak out for a long time, if ever. But to his surprise, he found ninety-two stories immediately, most of them referencing an initial story by Mreek Sinda, who had been at Centrifuge, working on a fashion-and-art piece about Y4UB, when her cameras and microphones had picked up Sesh's kidnapping. Across the following weeks, she'd done a commendable job of digging up the rest of the story—that Princess Shyf had been living as Sesh Kiroping, who the friends who tried to rescue her were, and so forth. And now half a dozen rivals of Mreek Sinda were also doing followups.

Jak sat scratching his head. It was funny how news reporting could change what everything meant, even when it did get the facts singing-on. If he hadn't known it was himself and Duj, he'd have thought they were a couple of heroic toves, toktru. On the other hand, he winced when he saw the malphs hold himself and Duj, unconscious and spread-eagled, and swiftly and efficiently do the damage that had put him into a regeneration ward. There are many good things to be said for style and mastery of craft, but they don't apply to all crafts.

Furthermore, Mreek Sinda had eventually established that he was on his way to Earth and that he was probably carrying a secret back-channel message from Greenworld to Uranium. So she had managed to penetrate to several different places where Uncle Sib had planted the primary cover.

Her most recent stories, and those of her competitors, focused on the reaction in Greenworld—Jak noted that Sesh really did resemble King Scaboron. Mostly the news from Greenworld consisted of diplomats saying that the situation was grave, that Uranium had behaved badly or at the least that one of its ducal house had, that the whole situation had to be watched carefully and that this was the most serious kind of matter in diplomacy, and that simultaneously there was nothing to worry about, everything was being taken care of, it would all turn out fine, and any speculation about a diplomatic rupture, let alone a military intervention, most especially let alone a war, would be completely irresponsible and had no basis in reality.

Well, at least this explained some of the hero-worship he was getting from Phrysaba; if he'd tried to look her up and found something like this, he'd have been impressed too.

It didn't seem to him that it would affect his mission much; after all, when he arrived at Fermi, he was supposed to try to contact Psim Cofinalez's household, as well as the public affairs office of the Palace of Uranium, and proceed as if he really were mainly concerned with delivering his message. And it was kind of flattering as long as he remembered not to believe it—Mreek Sinda's reporting made him sound like someone interesting.

Of course, with tens of thousands of news sources and millions of different-interest readers, most people would never know about him, but a few tens of thousands of people around the solar system might be impressed, and you never knew, one of them might be able to do him some good.

He decided to give Uncle Sib a call and see what he thought of the idea of applying to work on the *Spirit of Singing Port*. It would beat being continually bored, but maybe there was some aspect Jak was overlooking.

Sib's reaction was straightforward. "Old pizo, you are being had. But it's really good for you and I think you should go along with it."

"What do you mean, had?" No such thought had occurred to Jak; he drummed his fingers impatiently on the communications desk while he waited for Uncle Sib's image to go from a still picture to motion again.

"—ship's crews always have gender balance problems," Sib said, after the radio lag. The detector that took it back to motion when you spoke never seemed to work quite perfectly, so half of the initial "sh" had been cut off. "It's an effect of having a small population. They don't want to lose ship-raised people, who are far too valuable, so they have to find potential mates for them who might want to move shipboard. And they very often recruit passengers. They're going to offer you a position as a cupvy, and I strongly suggest that you take it. First of all, your friend is telling you the truth—it's your way into the Spatial, which is worlds better than being stuck in the Army. The Hive Spatial is just about eighty percent union anyway, so you can even get more union points during your hitch. You could end up as a crewie, which, as you've noticed, is not a bad life, and besides it might be a good place to be if you decide to join that social club your aunt and I belong to. And you did want to travel. Okay, now you ask questions." An instant later his face froze into a still photo.

Jak had the odd thought that Uncle Sib might be doing anything right now during the radio lag, but after all, just nine days into the voyage, the lag was still less than a minute. Probably Sib was only scratching or sipping his coffee.

Jak shook himself out of his reverie and asked, "What's a cupvy? And if it's such a good deal, why are they trying to trick me into it?"

About ten long seconds later, the time for the radio message to get back and forth, Uncle Sib's face moved again. "—C-U-P-V, Crew, Unpaid, Passenger, Volunteer. They'll tease you about it and there are dozens of CUPV jokes you'll hear, but half the space crew families on the sunclippers started out that way, and you'll be fine if you just take it in a good spirit. It's basically affectionate; crewies think theirs is the best life in the solar system (they do have a case) and they only invite people they like into it.

"And that's the answer to your other question. They weren't trying to trick you, exactly. They're just aware that because they lead highly regulated lives, and most people who can afford to travel in space as passengers *don't* lead highly regulated lives, their way of life might seem very strange and unpleasant to you. So they try to give you the chance to see what you might like about it, but they're nervous about the subject because they know that so many noncrewie people have neither the sense of responsibility nor the dedication to really learn the lifestyle, you see? But you might. You haven't been raised as a spoiled brat, like most people with your advantages. I've tried to make sure that you know about doing what needs doing when it needs to be done. So you should have more than enough self-discipline to fit into their culture, if that's what you want." Sib looked down and licked his upper lip; for a moment Jak thought he was about to ask for more questions, but then he realized it was the way Sib always looked when he was about to ask something awkward. "Uh, just to check here . . . I suppose I'm just kind of wondering if things have changed at all . . . by any chance is there a really lovely, intelligent, charming young woman involved in this process?" His image froze; Jak's turn to talk.

Jak couldn't help laughing, and immediately told Sib all about Phrysaba. "So she's just bait for acquiring new crewies? She and her brother seemed like such toktru toves!" Jak said to the motionless image of his uncle's face.

After the long lag, Sib looked precessed. "Not at all! As I said, it's not a trick! They wouldn't be doing this if they didn't really like you and want to share their way of life with you. You really should feel flattered, honored, and welcome, and it's absolutely a friendly thing they're doing—you're not being shanghaied or press-ganged, honestly!

"I was about to point out one more advantage, was all. After all, once you get Princess Shyf out of her predicament, you must realize that she can hardly come back to the Hive for a while—her cover here is blown, and anyway agents of Uranium might well try another kidnapping. So she's going to have to spend at least a long time, until things cool down or agreements are worked out, back at the family palace in Greenworld. It was kind of time for that anyway—she needed to get much more acquainted with her family, and the politics, and the court traditions. And I do know how fond of her you really are and that no matter what, even if she were to decide she wanted you as one of her consorts and you were to accept, it's going to be a few years. So I was sort of hoping that . . . well, you're a healthy young man, and you know, pizo, there's one thing that always helps a broken heart recover—"

Jak grinned. "Uncle Sib," he said, "you've sold me on the advantages, toktru, but having you worry about my love life is far too weird. All right, I speck you've told me everything I needed to know." They chatted for a few minutes; Sib gave him the gossip from home, and Jak talked about the strangeness of being a minor star of the news.

When they disconnected, Jak immediately called up the appropriate screens and signed on as a CUPV. Before he went to sleep that night, he had already been issued two old coveralls that didn't quite fit right, each with "CUPV" printed on the chest and back, in the large block letters that Jak associated with convicts, plus a UAS Points Log to clip to the breast pocket, and a schedule of shifts. The next morning, when he rose to go to his first shift, he found that he had a message from Phrysaba, inviting him for coffee that night. It felt like the world was falling into place.

CHAPTER 6

There's Always Gold in Mercury

Within an hour of reporting for work, Jak was bounding down an auxiliary propulsion tube about three meters across, pulling out panels that had detectable rough spots and replacing them with new, smooth panels. The interesting technical part of it was that you were only supposed to touch the sides on panels that had been identified as rough and were about to be replaced.

In the abstract, Jak was well aware that if it had not been him, it would have been some shipborn ten-year-old, who would no doubt have been much less awkward and much quicker, not to mention also not spoiling two smooth panels early on by slipping and missing. But having to stay in the moment to get it done felt great. The rush of trying to drop a quarter kilometer in .02 g, in a very precise pattern aiming to hit the eight points where sprites danced on the surface, all the while carrying the ultralightweight replacement panel with him, challenged and exhilarated him. After one initial bad drop that spoiled a panel—the shift chief, Lewo Treadora, seemed almost to expect it, and was not the least bit unkind about it—Jak enjoyed the complexity and precision of the task, the way in which his own skill developed, and perhaps most of all the thought that he was doing something that might matter.

After Jak put the last panel before break in place, he felt like he'd finally done a singing-on job. Lewo said, "All right, nice work. The truth is, that's some of the best I've seen from a CUPV, and it's just your first day, so by the end of the voyage, I think we ought to be able to make a moderately clumsy, not-too-dangerous rigger out of you."

Jak took that as the compliment it was and asked, "If you could, do you suppose you could tell me why I was doing that?"

"Well, really it was to let me see whether you had the coordination, the aptitude, and most of all the willingness to learn. A certain number of CUPVs don't want to do jobs that are tedious, or take concentration, or aren't glamorous or demanding or exciting enough. If you're not willing to do what one of our children has been doing for years, and try to become as automatically good at it as one of the children, then I need to know that so I can shunt you off to harmless and trivial things. And so far, anyway, you pass that aspect of the test with your screen solid green; I'm going to feel pretty confident about putting you into jobs that matter that aren't necessarily the most fun but are where you can learn the craft fastest."

Jak nodded. "Thank you, but what I meant was—why do we replace panels for being rough?"

Lewo laughed. "And I thought it was a philosophical matter. I was just about to give you my whole philosophy of education." He laughed again. "Do you know what an auxiliary propulsion tube does?"

"Propels auxiliaries?"

"Not a bad guess, which is what I say when you're completely wrong but I'm not going to make fun of you about it. When we need extra thrust, we open the tube to vacuum at one end or the other, point it in some direction, squirt in some charged propulsion particles (high-energy protons, fission electrons from the ship's reactor, sometimes hard alpha), put a like charge on the walls of the tube, and pump current through the big coil that surrounds this tube on the outside, to set up a magnetic field running through the tube parallel to the walls. Basically it's one of about two hundred nozzles for the ion rocket. Very small errors in the surface can create turbulence in the flow, which can rob us of a big percentage of the power, which is bad. Panels get rough from chemical processes, dust, all sorts of things, but it's so cheap for the nanos to make more that we just replace and recycle constantly. So you made two kids' day, today, two of my nine-year-olds, because they do this every day all day long."

Jak looked at the shift clock. "So, making a wild guess, I bet there are some more tubes I'm supposed to do?"

Lewo beamed at him. "I see budding executive material already."

After the third tube that day, the job might have gotten dull, but Jak tried to focus on doing it well. Besides, once Lewo mentioned that the nine-year-olds could do a tube in less than half an hour, whereas it was taking Jak about an hour and ten minutes, it gave him something to shoot for. As Jak finished his last, fourth tube for the day, and signaled the robot to haul him up the center, he was pleased to see that he had finally done one in less than an hour. "Do you happen to know," he asked Lewo, "if this is what I'll be assigned to again tomorrow? I'm kind of hoping so, because I'd like to get good at it."

"Eh?" Lewo looked startled, and then suddenly grinned. "I can't quite believe you asked that. Oh my, pizo, you are a rare breed."

"I'm sorry, did I ask—"

"Not at all. The other, hidden part of the work assignments I give is that they help most passengers find out that being a crewie on shift is dull hard work, for the most part. Probably three-quarters of CUPVs they send me quit after the first day, pretty much all after the second. The usual question is about how soon they can steer the ship or something silly like that. So, all right then. You're on tube duty for a while, till you're good at it." From the way Lewo smiled and shook his head as he made the entry, Jak had to conclude that somehow, what he had said must be singing-on what he ought to have said.

He went to his offshift workouts—Disciplines sparring with Clevis, who was weak at it but a good sport and much better than just working out against the machine—feeling a little tired, with his muscles just not quite what they usually were due to the unaccustomed ways of using them. It felt good, and the Public Baths after were really lovely. Jak wasn't sure that he'd want to be a crewie for the rest of his life, but he was finding the possibility hard to dismiss.

Also, he wasn't sure, but it felt like the atmosphere in the Bachelors' Mess was subtly different; word gets around fast in a small community, and perhaps Lewo had said something or other that had indicated how pleased he was with Jak's work. Or then again, perhaps Jak had just felt a little guilty before about doing no work when everyone else did, and now he didn't, and therefore the difference was in him and not in his messmates. Whatever the reason, he felt more accepted, more like someone who belonged there and less like a guest, and he liked that feeling, as he tried to explain to Phrysaba over coffee that evening.

"It's strange," she said, "how some problems can be invisible till you get to see them in other people. All of us here have been accepted our whole lives—I mean, not necessarily *liked*, there are some pretty bitter feelings here and there—but I've never had to feel like I wasn't part of the *Spirit*, or if I quarreled with someone, I'd never hear from them." She ran a hand through her short hair and said, "So how did you end up with a princess, again?"

"I told you, she didn't seem that different from anyone else. Smarter and prettier than any other girl I know, of course, kindhearted and loyal, and she had the good taste to be interested in me—"

One reason why Jak felt less guilt about his situation was that Sesh was one of Phrysaba's favorite subjects of conversation. Her other favorites, in no particular order, were the complexity of optimizing a course for maximum revenue, what to wear for the Exchange Dance, how nice it was to talk with someone who cared about her feelings, the failings of her brother as a human being, and what an absolute pain projective geometry in which you brought seven dimensions down to the usual four was; unlike Piaro, she still had some years of academic study ahead of her.

Piaro had told him that his sister was generally quite shy and reserved, but Jak noticed after a while that he was having a hard time getting a word in; well, very likely a part of his attraction to her was that he was willing to listen. Or at least to look into her eyes in a way that almost anyone would mistake for listening. The last time he had been paying attention, she had been talking about the difficulty of an exercise she was working through in numerical simulations training; now the subject seemed to have switched to whether, in the much-less-fashionable world of the *Spirit of Singing Port*, it was time yet to introduce the asymmetric fashions that had been common in the Hive for the better part of a decade, and especially whether she could possibly be the first girl on board to get away with wearing gozzies.

Jak went to his bunk that night a little less enamored and a little more confused; he really didn't know what to make of Phrysaba.

A few days later, after their shifts and after a dozen or so rounds of Disciplines sparring, Piaro and Jak were catching their breaths and contemplating whether or not they wanted to go any more rounds. "How's the work going?" Piaro asked. "Lewo specks you're doing all right."

"That's what he tells me, too, so either he's maintaining a consistent story, or I'm doing all right. I'm off propulsion tubes and out in an evasuit, now, defouling lines. It's scarier but the challenge is nice."

"Yeah, we lost a seven-year-old a couple of years ago doing that. Brill's cousin, I don't remember his name. Poor kid never did take to being swatted, and he was trying to jolt one of the mountings up and down, just throwing the lever back and forth—which they tell you to only do in emergencies—because it was late in his shift, and I suppose he didn't want to take the car a hundred or two hundred kilometers up toward the sails to free up a fuse point so he could replace the lines."

The monosil lines that connected the sunclipper to its array of continent-sized shrouds were astonishing for their ratio of strength to weight, but over time they tended to lose the one-atom-thick coat of hydrogen atoms that kept them from sticking to each other. Once enough hydrogen atoms were lost, when two lines bumped, they fused, with a strength far greater than anyone could separate, and left to themselves, all the lines would eventually have ended up as a tangled mass of fused spaghetti, collapsing the sails and leaving the sunclipper helpless in space. A typical fuse point would grow from a centimeter to a few kilometers long within an hour, so they were not something to neglect, and had to be dealt with immediately. Hence, whenever two lines fused, it was necessary to go out to where they had joined, fuse two long patching pieces onto the lines somewhere on the sunclipper side of the fuse point, go over the fusion to where the lines separated again on the sail side, fuse the ends of the repair pieces to the lines there, and finally cut away the ruined piece of monosil, winding it onto a spool for recycling.

In an emergency, it was sometimes possible, by yanking on the two lines, to cause the fused lines to break apart, usually leaving one of them functional and the other dangling, and to fix the latter with a simpler, easier procedure that didn't involve going out. It made for a sloppy joint, left a weak spot in one line, and sometimes simply didn't work, and you weren't supposed to do that.

"So what happened to him?"

"Oh. Well, it was nasty. He got caught jouncing, so he was about to take a whack on the head, when he unclipped from the safety lines and tried to run away. But, you know, on a cable platform—maybe three dozen monosil cables under tension—and being unclipped, and panicking, he kicked kind of hard, and he sailed right across a monosil cable."

"Errggh." Jak felt sick. Monosil cables weren't much thicker than a dozen strands of DNA; they would go through metal like a cheese slicer through butter.

"It must've been pretty quick. He was cut in half probably before he knew it, and out in the vacuum, the explosive decompression from all those open organs and blood vessels would have made sure he was unconscious an instant later. It also propelled him away from the ship—so as far as anyone knows, he's still out there in a cometary orbit, on his way to somewhere up beyond Pluto, coming back into the lower system in a few hundred years."

"I still can't believe you have little kids doing that kind of work."

Piaro shrugged. "Most of them learn. Practically all. But for every environment, there are people who can't or won't function in it—or at least observably don't. This kid was always in trouble from the moment he could talk and move; he always acted like he thought the rules were there because adults were mean, like people hit him for fun or because they didn't like him, like if he just whined about it then everything would change to the way he wanted it to be. I have no idea how he came to be that way. He wasn't raised any different from any other kid." Piaro paused to stretch and said, "Wow, you really got a good shot into my ribs last time; I think you didn't pull it as much as you might have."

"Sorry, my mistake," Jak said, "I just plain misjudged. I hope you're not hurt."

"Not badly. You pulled it most of the way. And at least after the Exchange Dance, when everyone's sneaking into corners, I can offer to show someone my celebrity bruises." He breathed deeply a couple more times. "What the hell was that poor little gweetz's name? I can't remember. Anyway, I had to watch him a few times, and as far as I could tell he really did think the whole world was some weird game that we were all playing to exclude and hurt him, and he seemed to think that all of us could just change it for him, but we were refusing out of pure nastiness.

"I don't think he ever dakked that his environment was dangerous—and that's the sort of problem that the environment is really good at fixing, unfortunately." He bent forward over his crossed legs, pushing down to stretch his back and hamstrings, and added, "And if nothing else it makes a good story to tell to other kids and to CUPVs. We might lose a crew member every other year to accidental death, and we get a serious injury more often than that, just due to people being on entropy's bad side, and that's bad enough, without adding stupidity and mulishness to the mix."

"I wouldn't think that people who were so careful would worry about getting caught on the bad side of entropy."

"Oh, there is such a thing as pure bad luck and unfortunate coincidence and all that. But, if we thought or talked about it too much we'd all be too afraid to work, masen? Pabrino's dad got killed when a hidden defect in a propulsion tube gave him a burst of ultrahard alpha. No way anyone could have known that would happen. It's just that mostly what luck you have, you make, and that's important to remember, so that you keep making it."

"Just now I don't think I could forget." Jak shook his head. "You know, I realize it was for good reasons, but you all probably really did dislike that poor kid, after a while, since he fit in so badly."

"I suppose we did. And he might have sensed that. But we were also trying to keep him from dying the way he did. Look, I didn't mean to bring up anything so gloomy; I just wanted to make sure you don't get too enthusiastic and become careless. Since you seem to really like working shipboard, Lewo deputized me to talk with you about it. Really, he's doing it because he's impressed, and because he specks you might stick with it and become a crewie, and you need to be a good one."

"I appreciate that, but I haven't been careless yet, I don't think—at least he hasn't said a word about it—"

"I guess he was looking through your vita and he found the thing about you climbing the light shaft, and started to think maybe you were more reckless than you looked."

"Well, I have to admit it was pretty stupid of me to get involved in that, so I can understand his concern." Jak smiled, hoping to get the subject changed; he had a feeling that the light shaft incident would be with him for a long time. "All the same, I have to say that dangers and gloominess and all, I like being a CUPV. It's better than just being a passenger—I don't know what I'd have done with all that time if you and your friends hadn't gotten me into this."

Piaro seemed to hesitate for a moment and then said, "I should probably confess. There's something I didn't tell you about because I was afraid of scaring you off. Nothing awful, we all live with it regularly, but in all fairness you should have known before you decided to sign up, and I guess now, as we've gotten to be better friends, I'm starting to think you probably do have a right to know, right now, while there's still plenty of time to just go back to being a passenger. Have you heard everyone grumbling about the cargo switch at Mercury?"

"Once or twice. Since there seemed to be need for general labor, and since I don't have anything like enough points to stay out of the pool for the jobs nobody wants, I just signed up for GL for that whole period. Lewo says I'll really learn what being a crewie is all about."

"Oh, no! Well, you'll certainly learn *that*. But I didn't tell you, and I should have, and now you're going to hate me."

"How *much* am I going to hate you?" Jak was thinking that he could always suggest that they do some more sparring, depending on just what he was about to hear.

Piaro sighed. "It's just that when we do cargo switch at Mercury, we do it on the loop. It takes the whole crew working to do it—about twenty-four hours to set up, three hours of pure screaming madness for the switch, and then another four hours for safe shutdown. Mercury needs *everything* and they export stuff that everyone needs, and the ship only earns money when stuff transfers, so at Mercury we practically empty the hold and refill it. Most of the crew gets very little sleep and only occasional meals during that time, but the GLs—like you're going to be—usually get no sleep at all and never eat when they aren't in motion. It's about the most exhausting thing you can do. In fact, it's such a strain on ship's resources that we generally just lock the passenger side of the *Spirit* down, keep the passengers all in their cabins with food delivered, tell'em that unless it's the air we aren't fixing anything, until it's all over. They all get cranky and complain constantly, but it's the only way we ever make cargo switch on schedule."

Jak shrugged. "So if I weren't doing GL as a CUPV, I'd be sitting alone in my stateroom with my thumb up wherever, with everything locked down so that even what amusements you have wouldn't be available. I'd be wondering what was going on, and trying to see things on the onboard cameras and having no idea what they were. Whereas, as a CUPV, I might be overworked and precessed and so on, but I do get to work."

Piaro laughed. "Oh, do you get to work. Oh, oh, do you."

As the days went by, Jak found that he liked his life as a CUPV more and more. It took away the need to pass the time, and gave him toves, and something to talk about with them. Once Lewo and the other supervisors realized that he wasn't just trying it out, but would actually be working for the rest of the voyage, they put more effort and attention into training him, and held him to a higher standard, and so it became more interesting and challenging.

He occasionally wondered why Duj hadn't written, but maybe writing was just not a male thing, or maybe it wasn't a panth thing. He saw Phrysaba almost daily and their romance, friendship, or whatever it was settled into a comfortable routine—something he had never had with Sesh, and wouldn't have wanted for the rest of his life, but for the voyage, it was pleasant. They saw recorded plays and movies together, played viv games (shipboard morals being what they were, they stayed away from the ones that involved sex—Jak was quietly amused that he had acquired a demmy that he had yet even to kiss, and that they hadn't even checked each other out on viv), and played mixed doubles at various sports with other people their age.

Once, when they were having coffee together in the evening, Phrysaba was saying, "I don't know, it seems like I've been everywhere but I've never visited anywhere. I mean, I've seen all the inhabited worlds up close at least once, most of them twice, and the busy lower ones like Earth and Mars more times than I can count. I've seen them all from orbit and picked out the features and seen the cities glowing on their night sides, but you know, I've never once put foot down on any of them. Now partly that's because they're stricter with girls than they are with boys, but most of the boys here never want to get off the ship, either."

Jak nodded. "I've always dreamed of traveling. It just seems to me that with four planets, two big stations, dozens of inhabited moons around the gas giants and hundreds of inhabited asteroids, and all the rest of it, there's too much to see to get it all seen in one lifetime, and it would be so *light* to just get started, masen?"

"Once," Phrysaba said, "when Piaro and I were nine years old, we dropped off a load of cargo at Pluto. And I got to be on helm during part of the close approach. That was about the most exotic thing I've done—and it was all from the cockpit of the ship, anyway."

"It would've been kind of hard to have taken surface leave there, even if you'd been old enough."

"Not that hard. There is a little human settlement there, Ultima, to service the Rubahy trade. Most ships unload stuff to the humans in Ultima, and then the Ultimans are the ones who deal with the Rubahy. It tends to make everyone else comfortable and the Ultimans rich. So there are humans there, and there's a human settlement available to live in. But I don't know if you can even get surface leave there—the Rubahy try to restrict the number of humans coming in or out of Ultima, for security reasons I think."

"Hah. I thought Pluto and Charon were still officially ours, even if the Rubahy have been squatting on them for a thousand years. We ought to be able to make regular inspections, the way a landlord can. After all, we won the war. Wanged them, toktru. That should count for something."

Phrysaba shrugged. "That was a thousand years ago. Besides, the Rubahy, and the Ultimans, were nice enough to the ship—all the communications were models of courtesy—and they paid huge bonuses all around. And like everyone always says, it's possible that someday we're going to need them. If the decision in Galactic Court goes against us both, it'll be us against the galaxy, and we'll need anything that will fight on our side. And say anything else about them, they're fighters."

Jak was about to make the standard retort that since, if Galactic Court ruled against the two species, the odds were terrible no matter what, one might as well die in good human company, except that he remembered what Uncle Sib had told him about the views of Triangle One, and it seemed uncomfortably like that. "Well," Jak said, "I guess there's some truth in all that, and I can dak the idea that we're in the same capsule and breathing the same air so it's better not to fart. But after all they're the ones that put us in our present predicament, and they're vicious and evil and gross to look at. I wouldn't use the word 'terrier' around one, because I'm not that kind of rude, and if it comes down to humans and Rubahy against the galaxy then I guess I'll fight side by side with them, but I don't have to like them. Have you ever seen one? It's a sight to turn your stomach."

She shook her head. "We haven't carried a Rubahy passenger in my lifetime. I've seen pictures, of course."

Jak nodded. "The pictures are accurate enough but somehow they don't give you the feeling of how terrifying it is to dak that something that looks like that is alive—let alone that it's looking back at you. Anyway, because the traveling section of the Galactic Court meets in the Hive, and because so much of the trade with the Rubahy goes through the big corporations that tend to have headquarters on the Hive, around the Hive we always have a lot of Rubahy on board—though 'a lot' means 'around three thousand,' which isn't all that many to compare with the billion-plus humans.

"Sometimes, for some reason or other, they invite the Rubahy to come out and speak to school classes. That's where I've seen them. The thing is, there's not any great number of things to talk about—it's a very simple story. They tried to conquer us. It didn't work out. They smashed up a lot of our home system. We made Alpha Draconis flare up and baked their home system. Suddenly, in the middle of all that, a galactic authority that neither civilization knew even existed ran in blowing a whistle and handing out penalties to both sides. That's all there is, and repeating it doesn't make it more complicated, or interesting, and toktru it doesn't make either side like the other one better or dak the other point of view. We have excellent reasons to hate each other, and they're so alien that we can't even be sure that they have the concept of hate."

Phrysaba looked straight into his eyes and said, "I just can't believe hate is a good thing, ever."

"Well, I can dak that much." Jak sighed. "Anyway, since the history took two minutes or less to cover, and it was inflammatory, they'd usually just say 'Any questions for our guest?' and then we'd ask our questions, and after each question, the Rubahy guests would explain why the question was meaningless in their culture, and then they'd try to explain what would be meaningful, and we wouldn't get it.

"So like for example we'd ask, 'What's a Rubahy family like?' and, in this weird whistling tone, but pretty good Standard if you listened carefully, he'd say, 'We don't have families, we have . . .' and then he'd make a strange noise. Which would turn out to translate as the 'oath-sworn uncles club,' or some such. We're just never going to dak them, not ever, nor they us."

Phrysaba shrugged and said, "Well, I suppose if you take in enough anti-Rubahy prejudice when you're growing up—and the Hive is really the place to get a big dose of it—then what you're saying probably all specks singing-on. But out here, we know that Rubahy traders trade fair, and we know that if you're in trouble in the upper system and send a help call, like as not it'll be a Rubahy ship that answers and they'll do whatever it takes to help you. And a lot of us, human and Rubahy spaceborn alike, speck it won't be for a war that we'll need the Rubahy. We'll need them for the getaway."

"The getaway?"

"Well, despite the school you went to and the way you went through it—"

"Hey, we had championships in six sports and one viv program rated us 'most promiscuous.' Don't knock my school."

"Despite, as I was saying, the school you went to—I do suppose you've heard about the possibility of the Extermination Order?"

"Yeah, people are always using it as an excuse to be nice to the Rubahy, because if the Galactic Court does issue an Extermination Order, it's possible that both species will be ordered exterminated, and if that happens we'll need allies—especially since it will be us and the Rubahy against the galaxy. But that won't happen. First of all, we're a nice species and they're not. And secondly, given what kind of armed forces the Galactic Court probably has behind it, anyway the war will be over and everyone, human and Rubahy, will be dead, before the different presidents and kings can even phone each other."

"If you're talking about fighting, and you're talking about the space stations, you might be right. But human and Rubahy crewies see things differently. We aren't looking for allies to fight beside us because none of us are planning to fight. Free merchants aren't fighters, to begin with, and our ships are so vulnerable that they might as well have bull's-eyes painted on them. We can't contribute a thing to the war, which probably will be about as long as you say. But nobody knows how an Extermination Order would be carried out, and maybe they can't hit everyone everywhere all at once. Maybe they hit the planets and the big stations first, masen? That would make sense.

"Now, space is big, and all sunclippers can be self-sufficient indefinitely. If suddenly there are bright flashes all over the solar system, from where the settlements used to be, and nothing on the radio but static, then human and Rubahy alike, we'll all furl sails, run black, coast up into the dark away from Sol, and then set out for Canaan."

"Canaan? Where's that?"

"I think every crewie knows the story; since you're turning crewie, you might as well hear it, too. Somewhere out there, within fifty light-years, supposedly, there's a solar system that would work as a new home for us and the Rubahy, though everyone seems to know, somehow, that the only habitable zone planet is pretty nasty and desolate. At least that's the news that came back on *Titan's Dancer*—are you all right?"

"You just startled me. I'd heard of it before."

"Well, of course, you've heard of it, silly. Even a completely illiterate gweetz who never follows the news will have heard of *Titan's Dancer*. It was the biggest thing in the news when it happened, and even though it was half a generation before we were born, people are still talking about it all the time. It was practically made to order for vid and viv dramatizations, masen? A ship missing for centuries radio-hailed Earth, came in for its approach, matched orbits with Singing Port, millions of people saw it with their own eyes and radar recorded it, and then it vanished completely in a time interval too short to measure. Having heard of *Titan's Dancer* is like having heard of Atlantis, the Bermuda Triangle, the Sea of Crises Flood, or Captain Breeko's Gate."

Jak had no idea what any of those were, though he was pretty sure someone had mentioned something about them in school. He had recognized *Titan's Dancer* only from what he was supposed to say to Bex Riveroma. He didn't like to admit it, but he was beginning to see that the way the crewies took their schooling seriously was probably a help to them—it gave them something to talk about when life was really boring. Oh, well, he'd just have to avoid boring situations.

Phrysaba was still talking, he realized, and he had not been paying attention, and once again missing his chance to learn something. "—seven or eight senior captains, so we'd meet up at some point in empty space and go from there. It has lots of names, Canaan, Shangri-la, Over Jordan, Mount BRC, New Masada, Ghostworld, Prestojon, but it's all the same story."

Jak specked that if ever the Galactic Court gave the extermination order, he'd either be on a sunclipper, which would go to Canaan, whatever that was, or he'd be killed here in the solar system, so there was no special reason to ask her to repeat anything, and reveal that mostly he'd been thinking about how much he hated school, how nice Phrysaba looked, what a waste of time history was, and how much he'd like to get Phrysaba alone and naked. No doubt Uncle Sib was right, and any attempt to educate him was a waste.

Before the Exchange Dance, he got a thorough briefing from Piaro about every aspect of the tradition. Like most traditions ranging from funerals to Christmas, it had evolved until it largely attacked what it was supposed to support; rather than mixing up the couples, it tended to confirm them by requiring everyone, always, to get permission from the other member of the couple before any contact of any kind. Jak graciously granted permission all night for Phrysaba to dance and talk with everyone; she did the same. But except during their brief dances with others, they were seldom more than a meter apart all night.

Not that Jak minded. Phrysaba had chosen a very conservative asymmetrical dress, off the shoulder on the left with a raked hem high on the right, in a solid burgundy, that, for all its stodginess to Jak's eyes, did reveal that she had a very fine figure. When he walked her back to Unmarried Women's Quarters, they stole a minute in the corridor, between couples and cameras and all, to kiss and touch; Jak discovered that there was at least one way in which she wasn't shy at all.

After a few more kisses, she led him quietly to an unused, dark utility space, and whispered that she wanted to "try the whole thing."

When they had finished with Phrysaba's introduction to the whole thing, and both were feeling comfortable and happy, Jak said, "I suppose I should feel guilty about Sesh, but it's not easy to; I probably won't even get to see her again, probably not ever. And they *have* to keep her physically comfortable, no matter what the idiots on the viv and the vid are saying."

Phrysaba rolled against him, her small firm breasts pressing on his chest, and gave him a long deep kiss. "There. That may help you forget."

"Well, you don't have the skill level yet—"

They practiced some more, but weren't quite inclined to continue again; he was a little tired, she was a little sore, and both just enjoyed the contact with each other too much to want to interrupt it.

"So," she said, "since tomorrow afternoon is when the ship starts prepping for the cargo switch at Mercury, we probably won't have another time like this till after that—probably a couple of days afterward, allowing for recovery time. I have a feeling that this is best when you're well rested and in a good mood."

"Your feeling is singing-on. Everyone seems to be either anticipating or dreading the cargo switch—why? I mean, if it's so awful, why do ships do it, or if it's such a great thing, why all the bitching?"

She sighed. "About a week from now you won't have to ask at all; you'll dak it as well as you dak anything. The great thing and the terrible thing about the cargo switch at Mercury is that it's a short time of unbelievably intense work and the whole future of the ship rides on it. I had a literature teacher who said it's kind of like how groundside farmers used to feel about harvest, or retailers feel about Christmas—either it works or it doesn't, and if it doesn't, you're scrogged. Mercury is the thing that keeps most of the sunclippers flying and making what little profit we do; they're really the heavy-metals industrial center of the solar system, so they need everything biological, informational, pretty much anything you don't make out of metal, and they export stuff that everyone else needs—pretty much everything you make out of metal.

"Plus they're located way down the solar gravity well but also where there's the most sunlight and solar wind to catch in the sails and scoops. So no matter what you picked up in the upper system, if you can just drop in for a fast swing around Mercury, you can sell the whole cargo and get a whole new one that will be in demand, and usually pick up enough momentum to have a fast, straight shot to your next destination. That's why there's the old saying among crewies that 'There's always gold in Mercury.'

"But on the other side of things—well, first of all, unloading almost all of the cargo and replacing it with another cargo is quite a job. The stuff comes aboard in mixed lot containers and then goes into containers routed to everywhere on Mercury, so we have to get it from all its various storage places, repack it for Mercury, loop launch it, get it onto Mercury's loop—which means that everyone who can fly a longshore capsule gets to play a frantic game of tag in space for hours— and fit all that into the window of a brief pass at the planet.

"And then, too, it's dangerous. That much cargo handling always is, and the sails are more dangerous when there's a loop deployed, and around Mercury you're always coping with substorms."

"What's a substorm?"

"Mercury has a pretty strong magnetic field for its size—not like Earth or Jupiter, but plenty more than most other planets—and particles from solar storms get trapped and sometimes pile up in one place or another, so that you get these very intense local events, which can make the sails do weird things because part of how they're controlled is by manipulating electrostatic charge on them, and they can suddenly pick up a charge ten or twenty times what we use to control them, just at random.

"Coming into the Jovian system or the Earth system it's no big problem, because those planets are big enough and their fields are strong enough so that usually when you're dealing with a substorm, you're fairly far out in space, with lots of time to recover. Mercury's field is weaker, and Mercury is airless and small, so you can literally have substorms touch down on the surface—that's why they have so many deep shelters all over the planet. So you can be just a few thousand kilometers away from the surface, with a million square kilometers of sail spread, a short distance from Mercury's launch loop and with your own loop deployed, when all of a sudden the sails start buckling, or waving, or collapsing, or pushing apart from each other. It scares the hell out of everyone, and rightly so.

"And that," she said, "is everything I know about why we all hate Mercury and love Mercury. Because we have to go there to keep going, financially (we'd never make it financially if we didn't), and because once we do it's miserable hard dangerous work. How do you feel about rescuing this princess of yours?"

"I guess it's kind of the same," Jak said. "I have to, but I'm scared, but I really want to . . . Well, shall I take you back to your quarters, or do you want to work on forgetting all about it for a while longer?" He stroked the inside of her thigh, letting his fingertips just reach onto her buttocks.

"Hmmm. Forget the cargo switch, or forget the princess?"

"Bet if we try we can forget both," Jak said, and kissed her deeply, again.

When he finally got to his bunk, before he drifted off to sleep, Jak thought about how quickly everything with Phrysaba had happened, but still it seemed very much in character from what he had learned of crewie ways. The spaceborn are not sentimental. They tend to make a firm, considered decision, one way or another, and then implement it with complete commitment. The djeste of it all specked to Jak, when he thought about it. People who spend much of their lives making close passes at objects moving at orbital speeds, and are forever making irrevocable decisions that will determine what happens to them many months hence, are people who act more than they worry. It was another reason to think he might want to stay in this world—after he rescued Sesh, of course. Everything came after that.

Jak had gone to bed early enough to make sure of getting an extra hour of sleep, because everyone had warned him about how exhausting cargo switch would be.

It took about eighteen hours to spin up the loop. Thus they always started the loop when they were a bit more than twenty-four hours from transfer time, so that they had a generous allowance of extra time and so that the most likely problems would still leave them time for another try. Ideally there would be eighteen hours of spinning the loop up and shifting freight in the hold into containers to be taken over; an hour and a half to fly all the containers to the Mercurial loop; an hour and a half to fly back the new containers; and then three hours of moving containers and catching and re-storing the longshore capsules. If anything went wrong, it could be much longer. A few "lucky" workers—and Jak had volunteered to be one of them—would be working at top speed for very nearly the whole time.

Because rotation made everything more difficult, for the last day and a half before the cargo switch, the concentric rotating rings of the ship were very gradually braked to a halt, until finally the only remaining gravity was the fraction of one percent of a g from the solar-sail acceleration. When Jak awoke, he found a pen and a pair of earrings, which he had left on the little extensible night table, bouncing slowly around the room. He checked to make sure nothing else had wandered, caught his belongings, stowed them, and folded his bed. He pulled on his crew coverall and swam through the now all-but-gravityless corridors toward the central area where removable walls had been pulled to form a giant commons.

The sound of the big early breakfast was loud and sharp, with the nervousness of those who had done the planning, the boisterousness of those who would be working hard and long, and most of all the awareness that today they would be doing something unusual. Jak filled up quickly on the squeeze bottles of coffee and the pastries filled with textured protein; the stuff had been engineered to get more than a day's worth of calories into everyone quickly, without stuffing their stomachs, and as far as Jak could tell from the heavy acid feeling in his gut, it was working.

His first assignment was in the holds; nearly all the boxed cargo in the hold would be getting off at this stop, and it had to go into the big cargo containers in a particular order. As he moved each container into place and locked it down, its sides glowed with the numbers of the containers that must be parked next to it—get it wrong and a warning bell sounded, not to mention the supervisor glaring in a very disturbing way. Only the smallest children got it wrong, and even they learned quickly because their friends and older sibs made fun of them when they made mistakes. Of course, autodollies did most of the moving and large parts of the lifting, but human hands and eyes were still the quickest, and the ability to look into a cargo container a hundred meters long by twenty square and see dozens of numbers, then recall where they might be, was surprisingly important even when the machines were keeping accurate track of the location of most of the cargo most of the time. It takes a human eye, attached to a human body that might get some extra rest if things work out, to guess ahead and cause the sort of result commonly called luck.

All the while, Jak was walking back and forth beside autodollies, or carrying a box around a corner or through an opening too small for the autodolly, or helping to carry boxes because the autodollies were all in use and this could speed up the loading process, or rechecking what an autodolly thought it should do next and changing that to something better.

After six hours, with only a minute or two now and then for a drink of water or a quick piss, Jak was beginning to see why Piaro had thought he ought to be warned about what this would be like. He was tired and sore, and he'd bumped himself now and then just often enough so that a part of him was already looking forward to the big party in the Public Baths that traditionally followed cargo switch. Furthermore, though he and the many others had already loaded an impressive number of containers, the pile of containers waiting to be activated and opened was still at least two-thirds of what it had been when they had started, and the vast stack of loaded containers did not look nearly as impressive as the many, many rows and heaps of yet-to-be-packed cargo.

Then Lewo came by and tagged him on the shoulder.

"Old pizo, union promotion rules say I need to add a few untrained workers for the spin-up crew, and you're thoroughly untrained—I should know, I failed to train you myself. Report to the loop room in twenty minutes. On your way there, hit a bathroom and wash up, then hit a canteen and get at least two sandwiches and two cups of coffee in you. You're overworking and underresting."

Jak managed to exceed orders by one sandwich and two cups of coffee and still get to the loop room a minute early. Where the cargo packing had been a matter of adding human judgment to large-muscle activity, the loop room was a place that relied on the human brain's ability to multitask and to absorb and interpret large amounts of information quickly. Uncle Sib had always said that every task at which humans excelled machines made use of some ability that had been useful back in the caves. Rethinking cargo packing on the fly was using the same parts of the brain that had evolved to make decisions when a hunted animal didn't do what it was supposed to. What he was doing in the loop room was using the part of the brain that, fifty thousand years before, had been good for hitting a bird with a thrown stone.

A loop is a closed ribbon of superstrong superconductor, moving at very high speeds, yanked through a superconducting magnetic coil like a plunger through a solenoid and kept open by its own centrifugal force, so that it forms a giant circle. When fully deployed it is tens or hundreds of kilometers across and moves at several kilometers per second; any craft with a variable magnetic drag linducer can be accelerated up to the speed of the loop, and if it has the power reserves to run the linducer for forward propulsion it can even accelerate beyond loop speed, so that the amount of fuel a shuttle or package must carry is drastically reduced.

Outgoing cargo carries a small fraction of the loop's energy away with it; incoming cargo adds energy to the loop. When the loop is braked and coiled for storage, almost all of the energy is recovered into the brakes, so very little energy is wasted, and in fact if a ship or station happens to be receiving more than it is sending, very often it ends up with a net energy gain (for which, of course, it is expected to pay).

Phrysaba had explained that to Jak; since they were dropping off an unusually large and heavy lot of cargo at Mercury, they would be deliberately coming in on a trajectory that would require the highest delta-v permissible, to produce an exaggerated net energy difference and thus slightly increase profits. This meant having the biggest possible loop at the highest possible velocity; it made the *Spirit of Singing Port* harder to handle, but they had done this many times before, and it had always worked out.

On an immense station like the Hive, almost as big as Earth's moon, where spaceships of all kinds come and go constantly, a loop is simply left up and running, but because of its enormous angular momentum, a loop is also a very effective gyroscope, and on a sunclipper, which must move and maneuver, having a loop running for more than two or three days is a major nuisance. Thus when approaching a big station, an asteroid, or an airless world that has a loop up and running, a sunclipper deploys its loop as late as possible before closest approach, aiming to have loop speeds and directions at the outer edges match as nearly as possible during a critical period of no more than about five hours, and then furls its loop as soon as possible after cargo and passengers are transferred. While the loop is deployed, the ship is almost unmaneuverable, locked into its course until it can recover the energy from the loop.

Deploying a loop is like spinning up a lariat big enough to lasso New Jersey, fast enough to orbit the Earth, while running it through a croquet wicket. Many thousands of parallel processors run faster-than-realtime simulations to decide when to attach another piece and when to cut it open to expand the loop. But although machines have superb reflexes, they are not noted for their perception. Machines can calculate what is about to happen, and calculate what will happen if you change something, and they can draw it on the screen, but they cannot tell a harmless wobble from a disastrous snarl nearly as well as a human being.

So the job Jak and his many co-workers were doing was to supply judgment for the massively parallel processor system that ran the loop. He had a scale from red to green, with yellow between, and a movable pointer, on his screen; the machine showed him possibilities a few seconds into the future, and he marked them as anything from harmless to disastrous on that scale. Each evaluator saw a dozen possibilities per minute or so; every possibility was evaluated by three different evaluators, and only those which received three full greens were considered for actual implementation. The result was that with 250 evaluators working, the system could consider about a thousand possibilities per minute, which gave it an effective accurate reaction time many times that of a human being, and yet with an almost human level of judgment.

The most dangerous period was the middle period of the spin-up. When the loop was still small, just a kilometer or two across, it had relatively little momentum and any accidental waves or wobbles could be fixed by drawing energy back; when it was all the way out to sixty kilometers across, it had so much momentum that the last increments of loop material and kinetic energy could make relatively little difference. But between about five kilometers' diameter and about thirty, it was still possible to jolt the loop enough to make it misbehave from mere normal increments of energy and material, and it was no longer possible to trust that the available forces would suffice to keep it controlled and out of various forms of dangerous behavior—sinusoidal waves that could cause it to brush the coil with explosively disastrous results, twists that could make it begin to fold in with equally catastrophic potential, and so forth. Thus, where a small number of technicians sufficed at the start and the finish, the middle required everyone who could be taught to recognize the basic pattern of trouble and move the slider quickly enough.

Outside the loop whirled at about five kilometers per second; at the end of the coil, new pieces were fed on, each ten meters or so long, folded so that both ends were attached to a welding clip. The clip grabbed the loop and welded both ends of the new piece to it, just a half centimeter apart, then snipped the loop between the two new attachment points, fast enough for the new, welded-in length to clear the entrance to the coil about a second later, as the loop came back around. Second by second, dekameter by dekameter, the loop grew and circularized into space on the sunside of the sunclipper, a mere kilometer from the thousands of monosil lines that could cut it instantly. Making the whole job harder, the angular momentum of the loop locked and held the ship in a single orientation that constantly threatened to collapse the sails, so that the sailing crew was triple its usual number and working like mad; fusions were constant, and riggers were out cutting and splicing all the time, as well. The whole process, from the three mainsails each twice the size of Africa to the city-sized habitat to the immense racing loop behind it, stretched across six thousand kilometers of a sky, a barely controlled disaster that was always less than a second from going out of control.

A distant corner of Jak's mind was grateful to be as busy as he was with the screens and images; if he had thought about what was happening, he might have frozen in sheer terror.

When Jak's relief tagged him and sent him to the foot of the relief line, the process of swimming out of his chair disoriented Jak.

He gratefully gulped the icewater and more coffee that the kids serving the line brought to him, swallowed the nutrition supplement they handed him, and washed it down with yet one more round of coffee and icewater. He breathed, stretched, and focused as the line of other workers taking a break moved ahead of him. Everyone around him was also stretching, yawning, trying to work out the kinks. The line snaked into a rest room and Jak got a welcome moment's relief.

Less than twenty minutes after being relieved, Jak was

at the head of the line. A light pinged on over the terminal operated by a woman of about forty; Jak swam over and relieved her, and within moments he was back into his screen, in that curious state of focused meditation, deciding between harmlessness and disaster. It was the tenth hour of the approach; they were far less than halfway through the process.

CHAPTER 7

On the Bad Side of Entropy

The hours went by in a blur; watching the screens was like sparring, dancing, or playing some of the more intense viv games—you couldn't afford an instant to speck about what you had just done or what might be coming next, all of your concentration had to be on doing the right thing in the present. Jak kept his focus, aiming for that singing-on state familiar from the Disciplines, and kept working. When he had his next relief, the loop had grown from about ten kilometers' diameter to almost thirty, and was becoming steadily better behaved.

The line of people taking relief breaks was longer now, as more people had been brought up from cargo packing, which was mostly complete. That meant everyone got a perhaps-five-minutes-longer break. The hold was now jammed to all surfaces with packed containers, and the outside of the ship was beginning to bristle with containers tied to longshore capsules, waiting to slide up the tracks onto the loop when the time came. Probably a third of the ship's crew was working outside at the moment, lining up the containers for loop launch and keeping the rigging from fouling.

People taking a break could look directly out through a big viewport at the planet Mercury itself. They were overtaking Mercury in its orbit, moving six km per second faster than the planet itself, only about 25,000 kilometers now from their closest approach, so Mercury loomed into the space beside the outer sail, fifteen times as big as the moon from the Earth and far brighter. The straight lines of the great ore roads were visible on the daylight side; on the night side they continued as strings of lights cutting across a curve blacker than the illuminated dust around it, like a photograph cut and pasted to its own negative.

The immense Caloris Basin, one of the larger impact craters in the solar system, was about two-thirds in daylight; the third that was in dark was widely scattered with bright lights, for the processes that had shaped Caloris had provided vast, rich deposits of many kinds of ores close to the surface, and there were mines everywhere. Within the dark part of the Caloris Basin, a little sprawl of bright dots, looking as if some giant had glued the Pleiades down on the face of the planet, marked Chaudville, and north and to its left Bigpile was a cross-shaped patch of bright lights; those and the roads were the only man-made features that Jak could definitely identify.

A soft, melodic ringing from the public address system announced that it was important to listen to the next message. Everyone in line, and at every station, was silent at once. "Mercury ground control indicates that we have a substorm in our path," the voice of the captain said. "No possibility of a course correction unless we abort. Storm is rated as slight-to-moderate in risk. I'm going to ask all personnel to come inside within ten—"

A strange, undeniable sensation grabbed Jak's attention; he realized later that it was the subtle shift in direction of acceleration, felt inside as if the gravity had shifted. At the instant he felt it, he knew only that it was something he didn't want to feel, something *wrong*.

Through the viewport, he saw an odd, folded curve that had not been there a moment ago.

One mainsail had collapsed, and was fouling several other sails; as random fusions spread up the lines, the simple, beautiful curves of the sails were becoming a tangle like a wadded bedsheet.

The crewies spinning up the loop stayed at their posts and kept working, but even they kept stealing glimpses at the big viewport. Then, as suddenly as the shadow of a bird passing overhead, tangled sails dropped past the viewport. A terrible groan ran through the ship as the unaccustomed forces yanked at its structural members; there was a noise like a great explosion, and then nothing but the usual background noise of the life-support systems. At all the terminals, the loop workers sat back, as if stunned by a rock that had flown out of the screen at them.

"This is the captain. People, we're on the bad side of entropy. The boom you heard was the jettison of the loop coil, taking the loop with it—along with about a quarter of our total sail area. Preliminary radar result shows that we will at least not have to pay damages for collisions or unauthorized landings; it will probably go into a salvageable solar orbit. Cargo switched is *scrubbed,* repeat, scrubbed. Financial consequences will be assessed as soon as possible for crew debate and vote. Astrogation assures me that we have enough of a gravity assist so that with remaining sail we can reach Earth in about thirty-six days, just eight days behind schedule, and once there we will be docking wherever the insurers tell us to, for an overhaul and a decision. I'm terribly sorry to say, however, that at the moment we have a complete failure to function as an effective business." There was a long pause. "I now ask that all personnel, including those inside, run a pizo check. We are receiving no transponder signals from the debris, so there is no one alive trapped in it; we need to know if everyone is still here. Please remain quiet and orderly until pizo check is completed. If you don't have a pizo, please use your purse; call 8888 and type in 444 at the cue to let us know that you are all right. Cue in five, four, three, two, one."

At the bell tone, Jak logged in. He didn't have a pizo because he was not yet officially a member of the ship's company.

One of the many ways in which this had happened at the worst possible time was that your pizo was normally a co-worker with whom you shared shifts, and ideally interests as well, so that you were in a good position to check on them at once. During cargo switch, though, everyone worked everywhere, as needed, and often one pizo had been working outside on sails while another was inside on container loading. Mostly, they found each other through their purses immediately, but the few remaining cases were an anxious matter.

After about a half hour, the tall girl behind Jak in line said, "This is bad. If everything was fine, it would have finished by now." She wiped her eyes. "I'm just glad that Krea was on my purse two seconds after the captain announced pizo check."

Jak had been about to say he hoped that it would be someone that neither he nor she knew, but luckily before he spoke he realized how stupid that was. In the little world of the ship, there was no such thing as a person you didn't know.

"So, since I'm new, do you mind telling me what's going on? What are they doing right now?"

"Following up on pizo check, rechecking all their missing ones, just to make sure it's not the one in a million chance of a purse being damaged and the owner being okay, or some gweetz who took off his purse while working, or anything like that. Or it could be that they've got some noncalls, which always take longer to check back on. That was a big scary accident. There could be more than one person . . . lost . . . and if both pizos in a pair are lost, that takes a while longer to detect. Then once they rerun the pizo check on the missing people, they'll start looking for the moment-to-moment record, and see if they can find what happened where the missing person last was. But once it's been this long, the news is never good."

Jak looked from face to face of all the people around him. Every one of them was nodding; apparently everything the girl was saying was toktru. He and the girl floated there, treading air to station-keep in the microgravity that shifted quickly because they were so close to both the sun and Mercury. They had nothing to say, but they did have a terrible need for company. Ten more minutes crawled by. In all the huge space, with everyone floating idly, there was hardly a word spoken; many people were quietly staring at some surface near themselves, breathing deeply, getting ready for the news.

Jak worried that he wouldn't respond right, would interfere with their grief by not feeling or expressing it in the way the spaceborn did. He wasn't afraid of being rude—Uncle Sib had schooled him too well for that—but he did fear that he would intrude, would just not fit in, because it would be obvious that he couldn't grieve for someone he didn't know.

As it turned out, that worry was pointless; the reason it had taken so long was that two pizos had been lost together. Brill and Clevis had been outside, trimming sail, when the *Spirit* had run onto the substorm, and were still trying to get back to the ship in the little two-person line car when the sails had collapsed and enfolded them, sweeping down past the ship and into the loop.

With so much sharp monomolecular material around and so much energy in the loop, whatever had happened to them had been quick. A directed microwave signal had found and turned on their purses in the wreckage, and the recovered records showed immediate cessation of vital signs in each of them, less than a second apart, less than three seconds after the loop coil was jettisoned.

In the next few days, the *Spirit of Singing Port* felt as if its every hold were crammed with sadness. The memorial services were attended by everyone, and Jak discovered that what everyone said was true—crewies were thorough about their emotions. He had been to two funerals on the Hive, and in both of those people had appeared to be more embarrassed than anything else about the fact that a friend was dead. Here, people wailed and screamed and shouted, and faces were drenched. Jak didn't quite feel like doing that himself, but it was comforting to be able to cry openly for Clevis and Brill. They had been two toktru toves, and Jak had never lost anyone before.

The funerals had released some feelings, but only time would heal them. For many days the Bachelors' Mess, which had always seemed about to explode with lively energy, was a place where people ate quickly, most leaving as soon as they were done, a few sitting silently with coffee for hours afterward. Often Jak was one of the ones who sat quietly, with Pabrino and Piaro, sometimes talking about their toves, more often just being company for each other. Jak and Phrysaba sometimes had coffee or played some game, but the energy seemed to have gone out of that too.

The *Spirit of Singing Port* limped upward to Earth like a beaten dog, as if the ship itself understood how defeated they were. The captain, the CEO, and the officers spent long hours in conference with the insurers, and returned to their families to say that everyone was being polite, everyone was being nice, and nobody was being specific.

Insurance would not cover a full re-outfit. Insurers did not do that. They wrote riders onto the contracts to make sure a crew didn't carry supplemental insurance, because a ship in a bad corner, obligated to the insurers, was more profitable than any premium that any free ship could hope to pay; to a great extent the purpose of insuring free merchants was to capture them into the short-haul trade.

Some bank in the insurers' pocket would be happy to offer them a short-term loan at ruinous interest to cover re-outfitting the ship, as long as they signed away all control over their own operations. Then the *Spirit of Singing Port* would pay it back by doing a hundred or so of the lucrative runs of the sinusoid trade—Hive to Mercury to Aerie to Mercury to Earth to Mercury and back to the Hive, with contractual obligation to make no ventures out into the dark beyond Mars until the loan was paid off. It would be a harsh way to live—a full cargo switch at every port, port flybys not more than three months apart—but ships had gotten out from under such obligations before, and Phrysaba and Piaro might not yet be fifty at the time the debt was paid off and they could resume free-trading. (Of course, by then they would have to retrain the whole crew.)

Or perhaps something high risk and high profit could be found, "Just a shot at an OBS," Phrysaba said, as she and Jak sat holding hands and looking out a viewport at the steady tumble of the stars in their slow eternal corkscrew around the ship. "We could pay for the sails and lines practically out of petty cash, and the loop isn't that much, but it takes a fortune to cover what we're being charged for delivering our cargo at least five months late, which is what's happening—a bit over a month to Earth, a month to refit, a month to work up to Earth escape velocity, and two months back to Mercury. Not to mention that we'll probably end up with an extra week here and there in refit, and an extra week here and there waiting for a window. The *Spirit* is pretty well trapped, and it could be a century—think about that, a third of our lives—before we're all the way back to normal free operations."

"What's an OBS?" Jak asked.

"It's another one of our legends, I suppose. One Big Score. Taking a load of a cargo so valuable to someone who wants it so much that we can name our own price. Plutonium to the Rubahy, for example."

"You'd *do* that? You'd sell something you can make atom bombs out of to the terriers?"

She winced at "terriers," but she just said, very mildly and reasonably, "Only about half of the thousands of nations have signed that treaty, and we don't belong to any nation anyway, and besides the ban is just a political gesture, Jak. The Rubahy have to have fissionables, for their power reactors—they're living on Pluto and Charon, for Nakasen's sake, they can't use solar power, the sun just looks like a star out there, and do you want them getting Casimir power?—besides the Rubahy *do* get fissionables, one way and another. Human politicians like to strike postures about the subject, but you can't expect an intelligent species to agree to starve and freeze just to make our voters happy. And there are a half-dozen other cargos that would work if you don't like the idea of fissionables to the Rubahy. Slaves from Earth to some of the mining settlements. Three or four different drugs I could name. Certain necessary parts for Casimir bombs to Triton, or maybe just a few hundred mercs under cover, enough to overrun the occupying forces.

"Helping another rebellion on Triton get going might actually be the best we could do, financially, actually. Every time they rebel, the Tritonians always set up a hard-cash government that pays in gold or fissionables, so you always get something you can spend.

"So if we want to save the ship's feets, do or die, here's what we'd do: pick up four hundred mercs and four hundred slaves on Earth. Swing by a mining settlement somewhere in the main belt. Dump the slaves, pick up Casimir melters, which convert to bombs very nicely. Out to Triton to sell the melters and deliver the mercs. Go into Neptune orbit till the rebels win and can pay us—that wouldn't take long. They pay in plutonium, and we take the nine-year haul to Pluto, sell the plutonium to the Rubahy, fill our holds there, and bring tons and tons of platinum and *xleeth* back on Earth. Actually just enough platinum to provide a plausible cover for trafficking in *xleeth,* and we'd probably offload that to a smuggler rather than bring it in."

Jak stared at her. "You'd actually—"

"Just trying to give you a context. Our regular bank would probably do a nudge-nudge wink-wink arrangement with us to just take plutonium to the Rubahy on a straight shot. And unlike the drugs, slaves, mercs, or Casimir bombs, the plutonium wouldn't get used for anything bad; let's face it, the Rubahy are *not* going to jump us all. They've built an impressive little civilization out there, and individually they're great fighters, but they aren't a military power and a few hundred tons of fissionables won't make them one."

"So is that what you're going to do?"

"I suspect that the captain, her pizo, and the senior officers are looking at every possible thing, including some that are dirtier than what I mentioned. We'll do whatever we can, or whatever we have to. But so will the other side, and insurers would really prefer it if every single ship were on a routine back-and-forth milk run, with the outer dark reserved for old ships that couldn't make a dime. Left to themselves, the insurers would starve half the settlements in the solar system. So now they've got us tied down on the bed, and it might be that the only way we get untied is to be cooperative and keep telling them how much we really like it, and just hope that they'll get careless and trust us and we can suddenly take their balls off."

"That's a vivid way to put it."

She shrugged. "The *Spirit of Singing Port* was a free ship the day she was born and her company has been free for two hundred fifty years. Every irritating little rule and reg on board, every long-term policy, every goal, everything we dream about and every frustration we make for ourselves, is our own, made by us, for reasons we dak. And some of our reasons have to do with getting stuff to where it's going, and doing our part for humanity, and all that, and some of them have to do with necessities like profit, but there's also coming around Neptune to see the sun's dim light washing over its cold face, and looking at the Aerie from a distance and knowing that that monstrous tangled mishmash of metal and glass, big as a Jovian moon, over four hundred independent nations, or just making the long drop from an upper world down to Mercury and knowing that you're warm and safe and cozy with your toves but you're also streaking like a comet through the solar system. Without the way we feel about things, this all might as well just be a job."

*   *   *

For the first time in generations, the *Spirit of Singing Port* was in Singing Port, at the great shipyards where she had been built, waiting for negotiations to finish so that her re-outfitting could begin. Her power was on trickle, her remaining sails furled, and to all appearances she was no more than a pod attached to the inside of that huge metal cavern, twenty by ten kilometers, open to the vacuum via the great open doors above and below.

Through the viewport in the passenger area of the *Spirit*, Jak could see through the Earthside entrance to the shipyard; fifteen hundred years of spaceflight had not made the view less spectacular. Between the bands and whorls of cloud, the plains of Asia spread out in the noon sun, dotted everywhere with the little circular lakes that marked the pocks, the impact points from the Rubahy bombardment.

Coming straight from Alpha Draconis, the projectiles had pounded Earth's northernmost reaches hardest; wherever the Dragon's Eye had gazed steadily, as it did north of the twenty-first parallel, pocks were strewn thick across the Earth's face. Where the Rubahy's home system had risen and set, between the north and south twenty-first parallels, the pocks thinned until there were hardly any at 21° S. Below that, Earth had sheltered her children, and Antarctica, southern Australia, and large parts of South America remained untouched, except by the terrible tsunami that had pounded the coasts of the whole planet during the Bombardment.

Jak tried to visualize what the view must have been like from orbit, a thousand years ago when a projectile had hit every half hour or so. He remembered the recordings from school: bright flashes on the night-dark ocean, the dark silvery waves spreading out in concentric circles; brighter flashes and visible dust clouds as the projectiles tore into the land. Arriving at 99.99 percent of light speed, the little projectiles, each a sphere of quartz smaller than your fist, had blasted holes a kilometer and a half wide in the Earth's crust, the equivalent of a good-sized fusion bomb, and they had struck the Earth and the other inner worlds at a rate of about fifty a day for more than fifty years, until the system of defense devised by Ralph Smith (or had it been Julius Caesar? Jak always had trouble remembering ancient names) had put an end to the attack.

What remained now was beautiful—all of the northern and much of the southern hemispheres were dotted with clear, shining circular lakes, and when you crossed the noon line, the ones more or less directly under you all reflected the sun back into space, forming thousands of bright dots of lights wherever you looked. From here in geosynchronous orbit, each was just barely big enough to have a distinguishable shape, like a period in tiny print.

The biggest problem with saying good-bye is that you always want a few more minutes of it, and you never have anything to say if you suddenly get them. Jak had shaken hands with Lewo, Pabrino, and Piaro, and hugged Phrysaba any number of times; they had all said "Well" and agreed that they must keep in touch. They had all agreed that there was no good reason for any of them to come visit him in Fermi, especially since he would probably be spending his time there under house arrest. They had all agreed that if the fates delivered the *Spirit of Singing Port* back into free-trading, Jak would be a very welcome applicant for a company member. Phrysaba had whispered, "I'll miss you," in his ear several times, and he in hers.

Unfortunately, the descent launch that was forever about to come by and pick him up kept getting more pickups added on the way, and getting delayed. It was now about an hour past time, so they had all done all their good-byes thoroughly with some extra good-byes thrown in.

This was perhaps a good thing after all, because when the descent launch, a small, old thirty-seater called the *Vespertilio Tartari,* finally appeared, the pilot only called Jak about twenty seconds before it nosed into the construction docks and pulled up to the passenger pickup. The launch was shaped like the lid of a teapot glued to the top of a shallow bowl, with its wings already tucked for descent forming an A shape over three battered old fins. The pilot's cabin in the top cupola bore, for some inexplicable reason, the ancient "Batman" emblem. The way it scraped the airlock suggested that its pilot was inexpert, its microcontrols needed adjusting, or very likely both.

Jak hugged Phrysaba with one arm, Piaro with the other, and contented himself with a wave to everyone else as he scrambled to get in the airlock door, towing his net bag full of luggage and his jumpie behind him. He had no sooner gotten into the *Vespertilio Tartari,* tied down his bags, and taken his seat, than the automatic voice announced that departure for their next pickup would be in "three-two-one-now," giving each count much less than a full second.

A hard shove of the cold jets, resonating in the old

launch like snot going down a bad drain, cleared them
from the construction docks at Singing Port. The launch
shook for a few moments after the jet stopped firing.
Since his ticket to the surface only specified first available transport, and no one else looked worried, Jak did
his best to convince himself that this really was how
things always were, but he was suddenly painfully aware
of the way his crewie toves used "orbital" and "short
hauler" as pejoratives.

Jak looked around. Mostly the other passengers were
bored business people in coveralls with corporate logos,
with a scattering of kids in their early teens trying to look
bored and usually succeeding; there were three elderly
passengers who were chatting loudly with each other
about all the things they'd seen on their trip, and Jak
gathered that they had just returned from the Big Cir-
cuit—that once-in-a-lifetime twenty-year voyage around
all the major human settlements in the solar system that
rich people took to celebrate their two hundredth birthday. All of them had descendants who were teenagers
and who, they kept assuring each other, would be *so*
thrilled to meet their far-voyaging adventurous ancestors, and to see all the photos, holos, vid, and viv that
they had recorded. Jak imagined being one of those kids.
He thought about Uncle Sib and how he had been everywhere but didn't like to talk about it. He realized how
much he appreciated the old gwont.

The only empty seat remaining was next to Jak; apparently it would be filled from somewhere else in the
docks, because the little craft was maneuvering over toward other ranks of ships. At first Jak didn't speck what
it must mean when the metal shape that grew large in the

viewport in front of him was made up of strange, inhuman curves and angles; really, he didn't realize until the hatch opened and the Rubahy came in and sat down next to him.

Well, after all, this would only be for an hour and a half, and they wouldn't even need to speak. Jak concentrated on the viewport, and the Rubahy made no effort to start a conversation.

They drifted out of the shipyard bays on inertia, continuing through the huge opening with just occasional spurts and rumbles from the cold jets.

Jak was sitting very near the nose, if you defined the nose as the part farthest from the rudder; the wallowing old *Vespertilio Tartari* was smoothly streamlined, as any space-to-atmosphere craft must be, but even new she hardly looked dashing or aggressive; if most launches in the intrigue-and-adventure stories Jak liked were described as "slim and deadly," then the *Vespertilio Tartari* would have to be described as "fat and harmless." This did, however, give her a great front window, and since it was Jak's first really good look at Earth, he was enjoying it. The reentry-surfaced belly of the launch was still pointed out into space, and they were flying backward, with the thrusters pointed toward their direction of motion. They would be for quite some time—from geosynchronous orbit, it was about a forty-five-minute flight down to the atmosphere, using the "direct drop" flight path.

The hot jets cut in with a tremendous roar, starting the long drop, and they flashed past the shredded cablehead that had once joined Singing Port to the surface, in the pre-Bombardment days when skyhooks were practical because human beings thought they were the only species in the interstellar neighborhood. Supposedly from orbit you could still see the long straight scar, two kilometers wide and a half kilometer deep, that the cut cable had laid across the face of Africa and North America. In the first weeks of the bombardment, the cablehead on the ground had been destroyed, along with the first twenty kilometers of cable, and as Singing Port had begun to drift dangerously, the mayor had made a bold decision to drop the cable and maneuver back to geosynchronous position rather than evacuate her city. She had spoken the famous words, "Nothing will stop that cable from falling eventually. When it's us-and-them—or them—it's them," which Paj Nakasen had later accepted as Principle 38.

It was one of the bits of history that Jak remembered vividly, because it had been one of the best scenes in *No Truce with Terriers!*, a terrific viv that he had played through several times before Uncle Sib had confiscated it. It had been so interesting that he had gone so far as to ask Teacher Fwidya about it, and been assured that "that or something enough like that to make no difference is what happened, or at least is widely believed to have happened." Which was as close as Fwidya ever got to saying "yes."

Jak glanced to the side and forced himself to set aside the feeling of *wrongness* that was always his first reaction to the Rubahy. The bend in their legs, the short fluffy-feathered tail like a duster, the smallish floppy scent-gatherers that looked like ears, most of all the big round eyes and square jaw had all given them the name "terrier," but no one could have called them that name in any seriousness. Their coat of fine pin-feathers could be blotchy in white, black, and brown in any number of ways, some of which indicated hereditary castes; this one had the large brown spot of the warrior stretching over his right shoulder, running most of the way down his back. Confirming that, his jaws protruded slightly to make room for the extra slicers and fewer molars of that caste.

Presently, the launch flat-spun end for end, hitting its timing singing-on according to the setback monitor. The Earth stayed in the front window, and Jak concentrated on that. He might not like Rubahy but it was rude to stare at anyone. The blue and white whorls of the Pacific passed below, and the great glaciers of Alaska; Jak tried to imagine the world during the later part of the Bombardment, when the planet froze under a pall of dust and water vapor, and thought again how little you could see from any window; after all, to look at the Hive from this distance, it would seem nothing but a big, thin-tired, spinning spoked wheel with a very thick hub. The clouds over the Pacific today were very ordinary clouds; if there had been many more of them and they had lasted a much longer time, and dropped much more snow on high elevations, the world would be utterly different, but Jak could not have perceived the difference from orbit.

The Earth grew bigger and closer steadily; they were making a fast descent, something launches almost always had to do, being routed through literally millions of satellites, short haulers, and debris, so that the launch had to stay very close to its appointed point in its reentry track or risk the explosive results of a collision at orbital velocities.

North America, the terminator line just reaching for its western coast, loomed huge in the window, taking up almost all of it, when Jak saw the bright flash in the ocean from somewhere just off California.

Half a minute later, the window became pitch-black and it was too dark to see inside the cabin. A many-g force rammed him against his seat belt.

In the darkness, shrieking people sailed over Jak's head and made a flurry of horrible thuds against the forward window.

The darkness cleared as suddenly as it had appeared; it had been no more than two seconds all told. Jak saw the tangle of bodies along the bulkhead under the forward window; more than half the passengers had not been wearing their belts.

Through the strangely unclear, as if dirty, window, he saw the Earth loop madly away and return from the other side—the launch was rolling and pitching.

Jak looked up and behind him to see what the pilot was doing, and saw that the automatic emergency hatch to the pilot's cupola was sealed; beside the emergency hatch, the windows that provided a view of the outside of the cupola were dirty like the front window, but he could see clearly enough—the pilot's cupola was gone, leaving only some bits and pieces of metal like crumpled, shredded aluminum foil.

He looked down to find he was looking into the eyes of the Rubahy warrior. "A sandgun," the Rubahy said, his voice a piercing whistle over the wails and moaning of the other passengers. He said it as calmly as if he were announcing the lunch menu. "Someone or something caused the Los Angeles sandgun to fire on us. I wonder if there's enough automatic control left to bring us to a safe landing? It would be a very good thing if there were, I do think."

The Earth rolled by again, no more slowly than the last time. "I don't know either," Jak said, "but if the automatics are going to try to land us, I wish they'd get started."

The Rubahy made a strange, burbling noise, like bubbles rising in a very deep metal bucket, which Jak remembered from school was supposed to be the sound of laughter. "Just so," he said, "just so. Well, if it happens it will be good, and if not, I am in the company of a fine humorist, one with such a kidney of quartz that I must say I am certain I am in company honorable enough to die in, so there is not a thing to worry about."

The Earth crossed the window again; now they were looking down into night over North America. Jak wished he could be quite that sure that there was nothing to worry about.

The Rubahy made the bucket-bubble noise again, harder this time. "I must remember that to tell my friends, if I should survive. 'I wish they'd get started.'" He continued to make the laugh-noise off and on as the Earth rolled past the window again and again; all around, other passengers wept and prayed.

"You see what happens when you don't wear your seat belt?" a bored voice said.

CHAPTER 8

Thank You for the
Honor of Your Company

After a long instant, during which there was an audible hum from the speakers in the cabin, a voice said, "Please, everyone, make sure you are belted in. High-acceleration maneuvers are about to begin, in seconds ten nine eight . . ."

Jak realized after an instant that the voice was not really bored—it was merely the mechanical voice of the ship's automatic recovery system, and doubtless it had been programmed to issue reminders about safety precautions, but not to have any judgment about human context. Still, he had to admit, he was making sure his belts were snug, looking at the heap of shattered bodies along the forward bulkhead. Mostly they seemed to be in business coveralls—probably frequent travelers who had heard all the announcements one too many times and didn't see any reason to bother with administrative nonsense anymore.

The acceleration was abrupt and severe; in a series of bursts, the launch whipped around to get headed down into the atmosphere at as steep an attitude of attack as it could stand. Probably, Jak thought, its priorities were simply to get everyone safely to the ground as soon as possible, and let all the niceties sort out later. The view through the front window was once again nothing but the black of space. Jak's chair rotated under him to support his back directly against the acceleration, and the terrible force became greater and greater until the dark ring began to close around his vision and he felt himself drifting away; the glare on the window blacked out the stars, so that it might as well have been a painted black wall.

Through the center of the dark ring, where he still had some perception, he became aware of glaring flames dancing across the window; they must be coming into the middle part of the reentry. Or since he'd never been here before, was it just "entry"? He felt like the question was a very interesting one to consider in the abstract but he couldn't seem to give it the emotional focus it demanded.

The crushing acceleration lessened, and he drew big gasps of air, unaware until that moment that he had been having trouble breathing. The flames across the front window vanished. The sky was now a very deep blue. They had made it through what was supposed to be the worst part—though given how badly damaged the launch was, that could be no more than a guess.

The sky gradually lightened. The launch fired cold jets a couple of times, coming around to flying nose forward rather than falling belly forward. The Earth below still showed a distinct curvature, but far off in the distance; as Jak watched, the glaring white glaciers of Europe and the deep green of Africa rolled up into his field of vision.

They were still far above the Earth, streaking along at many times the speed of sound, but nowhere near the orbital velocity and altitude they'd begun with; if they weren't safe yet, they were at least safer.

The sky became the bright blue that Jak had seen in pictures, and the Earth lost its curvature, and still they raced on. Horrible as the accident had been—or was it an accident? Jak had never heard of a sandgun firing by accident; they were part of the old defense system for Earth, put in back during the Bombardment, left in place ever since in case of war or attack, but he couldn't imagine that they fired automatically often, surely not into the busiest space in the solar system.

The launch was now racing in from the sea to cross the northwest coast of Africa, and Jak could see the whole landscape dotted with pocks; the Bombardment-induced changes in the weather had poured water upon the old Sahara, and the nightland below Jak was dark and lush with plant life, spattered everywhere with little, almost perfectly circular lakes, each with its ring of ejecta, a few with peaked central islands or a ring of islands parallel to their shores, and with dark quarter-moon circles formed by crater walls. They lay in the bright light from the moon and from the belt of equatorial orbiting cities, shining like silver. If he hadn't known what they were or how they got there, Jak might have found them breathtakingly beautiful; he glanced sideways at the Rubahy, whose expression never changed because they don't have expressions.

"My ancestors have much to answer for," the Rubahy said, as if reading Jak's thoughts, "and yet for all the suffering it involved, this part of your world has become very beautiful."

"I've never been here before," Jak said, "and it *is* singing-on beautiful."

After all, he reflected, the Rubahy homeworld was a sterile nightmare that they were still waiting to re-gaiatize, because of what Jak's species had done to it. Not for lack of trying, but the Rubahy had left humanity in considerably better shape than we had left the Rubahy. And besides, the night landscape of white and blue mirrors of the circular lakes and the deep blue-green of the forests, cut by big lighted roads and dotted with towns and buildings, *was* very beautiful, even if it was not the desert that had been here before.

The wing deployment began with a creak and a smash, but given how old the *Vespertilio Tartari* was, for all Jak knew that was normal. The wings gripped air for a moment, and Jak felt the craft bank, a sensation he'd read about and seen pictures of all his life, but had never actually felt before. He felt the strangeness of a full g pulling down and a half g pulling sideways as if the launch had tilted on its side, but the front window showed him the world at the wrong angle; it was disorienting and sickening, though he knew Earth people would think of this as ordinary, normal flying.

A shudder ran through the launch, amplifying in seconds to violent shaking and deafening thunder. From the screams of the passengers around him, Jak knew that this couldn't be a normal landing.

The noise stopped abruptly with a low boom, and the launch flipped over on its back, continuing into a roll that became a spiraling dive. The Rubahy looked up and said, "Hmm. This does look worse. We've lost a wing. Perhaps I shall have to comfort myself with your honorable company after all; I wonder if this craft is maneuverable at all with just one wing."

As if to answer his questions, there was a sharp bang and the cold jets came on, yanking the launch out of its spiral and turning it belly first into the line of its fall again. They were so low, now, probably not even twenty kilometers up, that Jak could still see a little horizon through the front window, a deep black streak, menacing and cold, below the safe, friendly stars. Earth reached up with her brutal gravity to pull them into a deadly hug; the cold jets pushed them forward, sputtering and whooshing out the last of the propellant.

"Well, the machinery seems to think we can softland," the Rubahy said. "It's trying to get a little extra lift."

The cold jets farted to a stop, leaving them with no sound but the praying of a passenger, in the front row, two seats ahead of Jak, who was running through the Short Litany of Terror, a traditional subset of the Principles of the Wager used when in fear of death.

"'144: Death happens, anyway,'" he chanted. "Therefore '062: Since it doesn't change anything, go ahead and fear death if it makes you feel better,' because '009: Fear is an excellent way to pass the time when there's nothing else you can do,' but remember that '171: Courage is fear without consequences.'" The man, whoever he was, drew a deep shaking breath and began again, "'144: Death happens, anyway,' therefore '062...'"

Other passengers took up the chant, following him in

it; Jak wanted to, but now, as he watched the dark horizon crawling up the sky, wiping the moon and the orbital
cities and the stars and every other familiar and comfortable thing from his view, he realized that he had never
really dakked the Wager at all. He looked around and the
only other person not chanting was the Rubahy. Their
eyes met.

"I guess there wasn't enough in the cold jet tanks to
back us all the way down," Jak said.

"More likely the robot is saving a little for last-second
maneuvers, to spin us around and try to brake down on
whatever is left of the hot jets," the Rubahy said. "It will
have to do that—if it can—just before we land. At least
if I were flying such a miserable old ship, so badly damaged, that's what I'd try. So the robot's behavior is consistent with rationality, which is quite comforting in the
circumstances."

The chanting grew louder and Jak saw that the black
horizon had now crawled up to halfway across the window.

"One thing does worry me a bit," the Rubahy went on.

To Jak's amusement, he found himself laughing.
"Well, I'm glad that you're able to be worried."

The Rubahy made that weird gargling sound, and Jak
realized that they were sharing a joke like two toves.
Being a few seconds from a wreck certainly did strange
things to your mind.

The whistling scream of air past the torn metal pro-
truding from the launch almost drowned out the loud
recitation of the Short Litany of Terror, so it was hard to
hear. The Rubahy leaned over and said, loudly, in Jak's
ear, "I don't know if the robot can actually do the job. It

has a very long reaction time—probably they stinted it on memory and it takes far too long to think of what to do next. So if we are lucky, and it's smart enough, it's calculating the singing-on moment to spin us and turn on the hot jets, to try for an on-the-tail landing. It may just not be smart enough or fast enough, and of course if we're out of fuel for the hot jets, we're on entropy's bad side."

"What do you think our chances are?" Jak shouted.

"If the robot can do it, and there's enough fuel in the tanks, fifty percent. Otherwise, one percent."

Jak was beginning to wish that he could bring himself to chant with the others, or at least to believe that if he did it would help, but that didn't seem to be part of his makeup, so he just watched the window as the dark Earth ate more and more of the night sky. They seemed to be leveling off, a little; perhaps they were moving fast enough so that the keel got more lift, or perhaps Jak's hopes were fooling him. At any rate, it now felt more like an uncomfortable full gravity and less like high acceleration, and that was a slight improvement.

The sky dwindled to a small upper part of the window. Now Jak could see individual hills and clumps of trees that dotted the grassland. They streaked over a herd of animals who were wandering across the plain, on their way to some purpose that made sense to them, and despite the feeling that he would be dead in a moment—or because of it—Jak was glad, just once, to have seen so many animals all out wandering free.

At just the point where Jak had decided that either the robot was too slow, or there was no fuel for the hot jets, or both, the cold jets spewed a stream of white vapor across the view, the launch whirled 180 degrees, and the hot jets cut in at full power. An instant later, the pile of corpses by the forward bulkhead flew back down the cabin, caroming over the seats to smash against the aft bulkhead. Jak had just time to bend forward and hug his knees when he saw a corporate type, coverall still impeccable and briefcase still clutched in his dead hand, but with his slightly dented head hanging at an unworkable angle, fly from the forward bulkhead. One dragging shoe ticked the seat in front of Jak and scraped his bent back, stinging.

Sounding exactly as bored, in exactly the same way as it had before, the robot pilot said, "You see what happens when you don't wear your seat belt?"

The hot jets roared against their direction of flight, pushing back against Mother Earth as she tried to crush them to her breast, and the thunder seemed to go on forever, though it could not have been as much as a minute. The Rubahy shouted to Jak, "This is all very well done by the robot! His designers should be proud! If it is possible for us to survive, the robot will see that we do! If not, thank you for the honor of your company!"

"And thank you for the honor of yours!" Jak shouted. In all the intrigue-and-adventure stories that he had been gobbling down ever since he could remember, they had always said that only when you faced death did you find out what sort of person you really were. *Apparently, what I really am is really* polite. *Even to a terrier. Though he* is *about the only person around here not behaving like a gweetz.*

The chanting continued, unable to match the full-on

blasting of the hot jets for volume, but making up for it with pure intense passion.

With a loud thump and one last hard shove at their backs, the hot jets cut out. Jak had just an instant to hear the wild unison shout of "—an excellent way to pass the time—" before the loud smash and grind of impact; acceleration must have been high enough for him to black out because he recalled nothing more of the crash after that.

Jak returned to consciousness as if he were swimming up from deep, cold water that became warmer as he rose; then as if imperceptibly the warm water became a fog through which he flew; then finally as if a veil fell away from the world. When his eyes opened, he saw a white-haired man who might be a hundred or so, and a plain-faced, muscular young woman, perhaps five years older than himself, bending over him. "He's back with us," the young woman said. "Probably just blacked out from the acceleration; from the way the cabin whipped around, I bet he took the worst of it."

"From the way my head feels, I bet you're right," Jak said. It felt as if he were talking over a long radio connection to someone a few seconds' lag away. He sat up very slowly and looked around.

About a half kilometer to his right, the launch lay burning, lighting up the trees near it with a wobbly orange glow whenever the inky smoke blew out of the way.

"As far as we can tell, we're the survivors," the older man explained. "All the people in the first three rows. We landed flying backward, and the crash rammed the

engines up into the passenger compartment, to just behind where you and the terrier were sitting; everyone sitting further back than you were was torn to pieces or
crushed."

Two more faces joined the circle; a much older, badly
overweight man, and the Rubahy. "I am glad that you are
alive," the Rubahy said. "I sat apart till you awoke because I did not want you to wake up and see me; I can
tell my appearance disturbs you."

"Thank you," Jak said, feeling absurd, but trying to go
along with the Rubahy's formal, courteous way of
speaking, "and the fault is entirely mine. No doubt I'll
become used to your appearance soon."

The woman said, "He carried you out here; me and the
preacher dragged this heet." She nodded at the older,
heavy man.

"And I appreciate it," the older man said. "So everyone who could be gotten at, and was in a seat, got out. I
take it we were all traveling alone and we don't need to
go back and search for any friends or loved ones?"

They all looked at each other.

The one that the woman had said was a preacher took
out his handkerchief and wiped his face. " 'Principle
112: It is human to love some neighbors more than others and few more than yourself.' Or in other, shorter
words, I don't think we need to."

There was a burst of light as one of the trees by the
burning launch went up. "I'm surprised there was no explosion," the old fat one said.

"Nothing to cause it," the Rubahy said. "Cold jet fuel
doesn't burn and all the hot jet fuel was used up trying

for a soft landing. Probably the only things burning there are some of the cabin furnishings and the luggage."

"Well, now we know," the older man said, and sighed. "The moon's mostly full and it's all the way down to the horizon, so dawn is coming soon, right?"

Everyone shrugged and looked at him. "I speck you're the only one here from a planetary surface," Jak said.

"Well, I'm sure I'm right. Sun should be up soon. And the moon is setting, so that means that the direction away from it is east, so I'm going to start walking in that direction."

"Why not just wait for the rescue copters? They should be here in an hour or two, I would think," the woman said, reasonably.

"Because we might have guests before they get here, or the rescue copters might not be rescue copters," the older man said, getting to his feet and dusting off his tunic. "My name is Alo Fairrara, and you probably have never heard of me unless you stay up with the financial news, but if you do, then I probably don't have to explain any more." He looked around expectantly. Apparently none of them read the financial news. "Okay, I'll stop being coy. I'm going to walk to somewhere so that I don't return home by a too-predictable route, and so that I can get my own security people to pick me up. If someone deliberately set off the sandgun, I think I'm very possibly what they were aiming for. There's a seven-hundred-gigautil deal that could happen if I wasn't there to block it—and I have a real good reason to block it—so I have a feeling somebody decided to simplify the investment environment."

"Fascinating," the Rubahy said. Jak was getting used

to the whistle in his voice. "My name is Shadow on the Frost—most humans seem to prefer to call me Shadow, which is fine with me—and I had been about to say that I am on the outs with my blade-sworn sister-cousin, and that this was just the sort of crude thing I would have expected of her oath-bound children, who might show up any minute, and since from such a quarrel I can retreat without loss of honor, and I do have an important message to deliver to our embassy in Fermi, I am honor-bound to try to live and therefore not to give them too easy an opportunity to kill me. I was about to say that I was going to walk, myself."

Jak laughed, and sketched out his own situation in a few sentences, giving the primary cover story immediately. "And I would suppose the Duke of Uranium would have more than enough resources to have me eliminated, and if I were dead, he'd get an extra couple of months at least before he had to talk to any envoy from Greenworld—and the main thing he needs is time. So it might be me that the attack was aimed at. I hadn't gotten as far as specking it all the way, but if it's possible that someone is trying to kill me—and I guess it is—then by the same logic, I should be trying to walk away from the wreck, too."

The woman smiled and said, "None of you watches women's slamball, do you?"

They all shook their heads, embarrassed.

"Well, I'm Vara Cathana, and I'm the goalie for the Borneo Molybdenum Tigers, which is expected to be first or second in the league next year, and the season bets—the ones where you bet on the team's total record—just went down; the window closed as of nine hours ago. So if someone had enough bets down on Pepsi-Lockheed or on Brazil National, and BMT were to be suddenly out of it . . . they could make a pile. There were four gambling-related player assassinations last year, so I'm not just being paranoid. So, skipping all the familiar steps in the logic, it sounds to me like we're starting a walking party."

They all turned to look at the thinner of the older men, expectantly; he shook his head and said, "I'll be very happy to walk with you all, for the company, and because as a spiritual leader it's my job to be there to comfort and assist you spiritually after this traumatic experience, and of course if any of you is targeted, as any of you might be, it would be good to have you properly prepared in case the, um, eventually unavoidable should happen. Just in case. But all I am is a teacher of the orthodox version of the Wager—that is, the version taught on the Hive, which is of course the center of the Wager—just down here on Earth to give a few lectures at several conferences while my wife sees the sights, you know—and I don't have an enemy on the planet. Or any other planet. Or anywhere else. But I shall be happy to walk with you."

"What's your name, preach?" Alo asked.

"Paj Priuleter. Actually I was born Rif Priuleter, but after ten years of preaching, as an honor for my record of perfect orthodoxy, I was given the name—"

"You can tell us while we walk," Vara suggested, and got up and headed east; everyone immediately fell in behind her, the preacher trailing along last.

After half an hour of walking, Jak began to question the wisdom of the djeste. He was getting to know what the surface of a planet was like, and the answer, for this particular part of *this* planet, was "rough." On the *Spirit of Singing Port,* he had diligently alternated days walking a simulated five miles and running a simulated two miles in full gravity, trying to ensure that he would be fully mobile on Earth. It had seemed like endless hours of work, but as preparations for this, it had been far too light. The treadmill surface had been just the right combination of smooth and sticky so that he neither bumped his feet against anything nor slid for a single instant. The motion of the treadmill had told him at what pace to keep walking. And though for the last twenty days or so he had always made his workouts continuous, he had always known that whenever he wanted, he was just seconds away from a hot bath, a cold drink, and the comfort of microgravity.

Here, he was stumbling along in the predawn cool, tripping and slipping continually, and his only choices were more of the same or to sit down in completely unknown country. He was wondering, too, about all the things that showed up in intrigue-and-adventure novels; in school they had said that the Sahara had restablized, postBombardment, as a mix of grassland, scrubland, and forest, and that all sorts of animals were moving into it, their populations exploding in all the open country, but he had no idea what animals . . . tigers? cobras? if he saw an elephant, would it be dangerous and what should he do about it if it was? He was beginning to realize that although there was probably some useful information somewhere or other in the intrigue-and-adventure stories that he loved, he had never paid any attention to it. In the stories, the hero just knew things; it was part of his job;

perhaps Jak should have paid more attention to whatever it was you were supposed to know.

Oh, well, it was as useless as wishing that he'd paid attention to Uncle Sib; really you just couldn't. If he had paid attention to the information in the stories, he'd have found the stories boring, and not read them.

Eventually, they settled into a pattern of Vara walking on point, Shadow and Jak walking side by side at the rear, with the two older men in the middle, with everyone two or three meters apart. At least the way they were proceeding, Jak thought, if Vara steps on a deadly stonefish and dies of poisoning before our eyes, like in *African Maelstrom,* it will be her and not me. Except that it probably wasn't going to be a stonefish or any kind of fish . . . those were aquatic . . . maybe some kind of snake?

The way his luck was going, they'd be set on by a pack of wildebeests and all eaten, anyway.

As the moon sank into the distant horizon, everyone found more interesting ways for rocks, clumps of grass, and bits of fallen tree to grab their feet, so that they all stumbled along as if they were drunk or exhausted. Every so often Paj Pruileter would helpfully remind them that Principle 155 said that "If you stumble often, watch your feet and look for patient friends," and that Principle 138 was "Mistakes in an unfamiliar environment are still mistakes and no discount is awarded." After he had been reminded of each principle three times, Jak said, very quietly, "I really liked it better when he was reciting the Short Litany of terror, and I'm starting to have an idea about how to get him to go back to it."

Even more expressionless than usual, in the dim light, the Rubahy beside him asked, "That's human humor, isn't it? You're expressing a purely ironic intention, not one you intend to carry out?"

"Yeah, Shadow, that's right."

"I thought so. Pity."

It was darker for the few minutes after the moon set, when the light mainly came from the dozen or so orbiting cities above the horizon, but Jak could still see. He had specked that the strange little knobs that popped up and whistled and went away into recesses again were little animals going in and out of holes; perhaps they were what was drawing the attention of the big winged creatures circling above the little party.

Jak kept thinking about a more immediate question; he hated to second-guess leadership. After all, Principle 88 was "Ostentatiously obey, and quietly disobey, anyone with power." Nonetheless, as they came to the top of a ridge, and he looked back to see that the wreck was still in sight and still burning, he specked that they could have covered no more than three kilometers so far, and they had been at this more than an hour.

"Was there a particular reason for picking east?" he finally asked, out loud.

"Well, I was figuring that Fermi is most of the way across Africa," Alo said, glancing back and stumbling. (Paj said "Principle 155" but didn't elaborate.) Alo seemed to badly need the rest, and sat down on a boulder, after first looking all around it—Jak specked that he was not the only person who had read far too much intrigue-and-adventure fiction.

After he caught his breath, Alo went on. "I was figuring that there's a few dozen big north-south roads and a lot of smaller ones all through here, with usually an aqueduct running under the roads and irrigated land around it, so once we found farmland, we'd find a road, and once we found a road, we'd just follow it till it joined a bigger one, and so forth until we found someplace with a town. I didn't want to use my purse to call anyone for obvious reasons."

"I could use *my* purse, though," Paj said. "And I wouldn't have to mention who was with me. Just a party of survivors. There hasn't been any activity back behind us, and nobody seems to be even coming out to investigate."

"You could at least check where we are," Vara said.

Paj talked to his left hand, then held it up. "If I understand correctly, we are in an 'anchored erg,' whatever that is, and if we walk due south for three days, we'll find farmland. That's the closest and easiest."

Vara made a face. "I begin to see a flaw in Alo's plan."

Alo sighed. "Me too. All right, we're not any of us exactly backwoods experts, are we?"

Shadow coughed politely and said, "Actually, I had quite a bit of training in it, part of the warrior schools, you know."

"Then why didn't you say something?"

"I thought you knew where you were going, you hadn't made any serious errors yet, and anyway, I can walk for a very long time without food or water, so it wasn't me that would be suffering."

Jak sat and admired the logic in that, in an abstract sort of way; somehow it didn't precess him at all. Maybe he was growing tolerant.

Everyone else, he realized, was sitting quietly trying to get up the courage to make a decision. "Well," Jak said, "the situation is this. Probably not more than one of us is a target. Paj Priuleter is *not* a target. Other than Shadow, none of us will live more than a couple of days out here without help, and in any case we're not going to manage to walk to human settlements anytime soon. So I'm willing to gamble the possibility that it's me that the malphs are after, and that calling for help might get me killed, against the certainty of dying out here if we don't. Anyone else willing to take the bet?"

Shadow on the Frost nodded emphatically. "I think it's a good bet, and well put."

Alo shrugged. "I think I'd be dead in less time than anyone else. Sure, let's gamble."

Vara sighed. "I wish we'd thought of this back at the wreck. Okay, Paj, call for help, and let's see what turns up."

Jak looked around. The circling birds seemed to be coming lower, but not as if they were going to land. As he watched, a vivid orange light spread along the horizon beyond the wreck, and then a smear of gold light poured out across the blue landscape, putting it into vivid color and relief almost at once. Two trees by the wreck, now tiny and far away, were still ablaze; other than that, the grassland around them was as still as if the world had just begun with that dawn.

Two hours later, all except Shadow were moderately uncomfortable (and no one had asked him; what he could endure and what he found pleasant were probably separate issues). Small biting insects infested places that otherwise looked inviting to sit. The temperature was rising rapidly with the rising sun, and they had no water; far off to the east they could see a little brown creek, but it seemed silly to try to walk to it when the copters were supposed to arrive soon, and anyway Jak and Alo both remembered from casual reading that often there would be some reason you couldn't just drink from open water, although both of them had to admit they couldn't remember just what.

Taking pity on them, or perhaps just tired of hearing two people who knew nothing discuss it at great length, Shadow summarized: "Several things can be wrong with that water or the area around it, and at least some of them will be present at almost any standing water in country like this. Disease, mineral toxins, various poisonous animals, muck deep and soft enough to drown in, and possibly large predators, especially around dawn. That would be a great deal of risk for a drink of water, and quite a long walk in order to take such a risk, when help is coming—how soon, Paj?"

The preacher looked at his purse again. "Supposedly thirty minutes."

"So if we'd kept walking," Vara said, "we could all be dead around the creek by now."

"More or less," Shadow said. "We might have been lucky enough to miss that part of the experience. But we wouldn't have been any better off." In the dawn light the Rubahy seemed to belong more; he was like some fantastic monster out of the dim memory of the species, perhaps a residual trace of the dinosaurs left in the squeaking rodent hindbrain of humanity, with his flat expressionless face, mighty jaws, and overall look of a feathered reptile. Jak thought to himself that anyone who had looked closely at them could not call them "terriers"—"raptors" perhaps, but there was nothing doglike in reality, whatever the pictures might suggest.

The helicopters came out of the southeast, very fast and not very loud, popping above the low hills on the horizon and racing in toward them quickly. They all stood up and waved, and the helicopters circled in to land on the flatter ground below them. As they descended the hill, Alo commented, "Well, so far, at least, they haven't opened fire on us . . ."

Vara grunted. "All that shows is that if anyone is after one of us, they're smart enough to make it look like an accident."

"If there *is* anyone after any of us," Shadow said quietly. "It occurs to me that those who travel into space are a relative financial and political elite, and murder is fairly common among the elite in both my society and yours. Four out of five of us had some reason to fear it, true? So very likely in the twenty or so dead passengers, there might have been fifteen who were possible targets. If there was a deliberate killer, perhaps the killer has lost interest because the victim is already dead."

" 'Principle 120: Never neglect the null hypothesis, however dull it may be,' " Paj Priuleter said. Jak thought that it would be just spiteful and petty to kick him, now.

"Precisely," Shadow on the Frost said, and Jak noted that although they don't have the muscles for facial expressions, the Rubahy have no problem with being quite clear in their vocal expression—the Sahara around them felt momentarily polar.

By the time the survivors got down the hill to the helicopter, the soldiers or pokheets or whatever they were had already set up a table with a terminal on it, and an officer sat at the terminal, apparently to process them in time-honored bureaucratic fashion. "From transponder signal, we think we have a correct roster of you survivors," he said, "and another crew will be going over to the crashed launch to confirm that you are not among the dead, so don't worry, we should have all records pertaining to you immediately available. Now, let me just run through our role—Paj Priuleter, is he here?"

He asked Paj a few questions, seemed satisfied with the answers, and motioned him into the largest of the three helicopters. Then he asked, "Alo Fairrara, is he here?" and did exactly the same process with exactly the same questions; then the same for Vara, and finally even for Shadow on the Frost, before reading off, "Jak Jinnaka. I presume you must be Jak Jinnaka?"

Some odd tension in the officer's voice, asking not quite the form of the question that Jak was expecting, with everyone too alert for any sign that he might be catching on, almost gave him enough warning to get away. He hesitated for just an instant, not because he was suspicious yet but just because something felt different, and that instant caused two of the soldiers to pull handcuffs out of hiding. Jak reacted before he even knew they were handcuffs; he kicked the table upward, hard, as the best diversion he could manage in the second he had to do it, and turned and ran.

He covered about thirty meters before he felt the closest one go for his legs; he jumped forward and pivoted to hit the man coming in, getting him with a right knee to the face, but the next instant he felt control gel sprayed on his face, and before he could even raise his hands it had hardened into an airtight opaque rubber mask that wrapped the whole front of his head. He tried to lash out based on sound and kinesthetic sense, but they had been waiting for that; his wrist was grasped, his arm bent, and he was driven to the ground, the mask protecting his face from the gravel, but still suffocating him.

Another one of them grabbed his other arm, and he was cuffed behind his back an instant later. The ankle cuffs were secured to his feet as he kicked and tried to breathe through the horrible smell of the mask, and just before he passed out, he felt them pulling his ankles and wrists together into a hogtie; the moment the lock snapped shut, they sprayed the mask off his face with something foul-smelling that dissolved it at once but left him choking and retching.

"This was really quite unnecessary," the officer said. "Not entirely your fault, of course. I didn't even want to handcuff you out here; we could have dropped off the others and then taken you along, and after all, your ticket was to Fermi itself, so there'd have been no problem. But I'm just an underling here, I do what I'm told, and you know how it is, the boss gets a bright idea—especially one that's highly dramatic—and there you are, stuck carrying it out. So I do apologize."

"Thank you, I think," Jak said. None of his bonds was the least bit loose, yet another difference from the stories he was so fond of.

"It would be nice if you could apologize to Jentepe, who you bashed in the face," the officer added. "I'm sure he'd feel better."

"Aw, hell, Skip, leave the kid alone, it was my fault, I

got careless trying to tackle him and he took his best shot. Taught me a lesson, you know? If he'd been armed, it would've really served me right."

Perhaps it was a lingering effect of too many hours spent with Paj Priuleter, but Jak recalled Principle 194: "Never hesitate to abase yourself when you are powerless, at worst it does not harm you and at best it may make the other side careless." He sighed and said, "Well, I'm sorry that your face hurts, and I'm sorry that I'm the one who caused it, and I appreciate your understanding that it was all just business."

"See?" Jentepe said. "The kid's all right, Skip. I'm glad we're just locking him up for a few months."

"Me too. Killings are depressing, especially younger people; I can't help feeling that way, even if it's part of the job. So, luckily, today we don't have to deal with anything like that."

Jak thought he might express his own approval but decided it was better to just remain silent; there are times when added attention is just not desirable.

The officer said, "Now, Jak Jinnaka, unfortunately you have revealed a proclivity for escape, so I truly am sorry about this, but we'll have to load you onto a dolly and take you back strapped down. Those are strict orders. But at least it's a short flight—you're not going all the way to Fermi—and you won't be too uncomfortable, and once you get there, it's rather like a very spartan hotel room without any doors. You'll see. Really, there's not much to get upset about."

Jak didn't agree, but saw no good reason to say so. He listened as the helicopter took everyone else away, and the officer gave a series of incomprehensible orders that seemed to involve nothing but strings of acronyms.

In a few minutes, the dolly came crawling over on its treads, and, not urgently, they tied him to the framework. It was all metal tubing without padding, so it hurt a little as the dolly crawled back to the copter, but it was only for a few minutes and it wasn't any worse than it had to be. As the tractor crawled into the passenger space, Jak saw that the inside of the copter bore several plaques with the insignia of the House of Cofinalez, as he had expected. He might be in gentle hands, for now, but they were the hands of the enemy.

CHAPTER 9

A Comfortable Place
With a Little Bit of Style

People moved to Tjadou for the climate, if they couldn't stand the cold or the damp, because it was only about ten degrees off the equator and because even with the drastic revision of the Earth's climate by the Bombardment, there was still sunshine there almost every day. So since people, mostly older people, moved there for the sun, the warmth, and the dry clean air, the buildings and streets were laid out to shelter them from sunlight and to provide cool spaces, and huge pipelines were run in from the catch basins at the feet of the glaciers that covered Italy, bringing in immense quantities of fresh water, so that people could plant gardens as big as they liked, filling the air with water and pollen that would eventually make it impossible for people like themselves to breathe, which was likely to be the only limit on the growth of the town.

Because this process was far from complete as yet, more people were still moving in all the time, and aside from its constant population of the elderly, the place was something of a boom town, as a bedroom community for the industrial areas of central Africa. Many of the officers of the Duchy of Uranium's local garrison chose to live here permanently, because it was a fine place to raise a family and the climate could hardly be equaled, and there were superb homes available at very reasonable prices. In fact, as a kind of hobby or sideline, many of the Uranium Army's officer corps had become so fond of the place, and so familiar with the good things that were available, that they had become real-estate brokers here in Tjadou.

This was particularly useful for political prisoners to know, because the Duchy of Uranium adhered to all international conventions regarding the comfort of prisoners, so that most of them were ultimately released on monitored house arrest within the city of Tjadou, where they might well find that they had to live and work for decades. It was, of course, regrettable that some perfectly fine people who no doubt were good citizens of the places they came from had so grossly inconvenienced the Duke that it was necessary for them to be taken out of circulation, but still there was a world of difference between being thrown into a dungeon or buried in an unmarked grave, as opposed to merely finding oneself in a fine, growing, modern community—one that in fact many free people were moving to voluntarily.

Jak learned all of this, but in much more detail, as the helicopter circled the city, waiting for clearance to take him to the maximum security prison. He was dreading it, although all the soldiers continued to assure him, in between discussing the merits of the various neighborhoods of the city, with special emphasis on rapidly appreciating real-estate values, that very few people remained in maximum security for long, and that there was a good chance that within a month or two he would be living in a small apartment "somewhere convenient where you can walk to the main prison campus for your required visits, with good access to shopping and banking. There are a lot of nice little places just inside the patrolled area, and we can fix you up in a comfortable place with a little bit of style."

Uncle Sibroillo had always told him that if nothing else, you could always be thinking, analyzing, getting a handle on your situation, and the major thought running through Jak's mind right now was that these people truly had an incentive to make sure he didn't escape, so this was all going to be much harder.

The copter finally set them down on the roof of the main prison facility, and they wheeled Jak out to an elevator and took him down to the main office to do the paperwork. "We're not exactly booking you," the officer explained, "because Uranium officially has no laws about political behavior, and after all it's not as if you were going to have a trial or talk to a lawyer or anything. But we do need to make sure that we know things like how to get in touch with relatives, any special allergies or phobias, hobbies and interests, that kind of thing, so that the prison administration can serve you better."

"That's sort of nice," Jak said.

"Well, we realize that most prisoners will at least think about escaping, because most of them have acted on some idea or other in their belief system—and we try to respect everyone's beliefs, we don't ever pressure anyone to change their feelings or commitments, because we respect that if they've taken action about it, it matters to them, and it's only the action, not the belief, that should be our concern. So we know that you haven't given up your ideals or whatever it is you have, and you'll still be trying to find a way to act on them, and that means you'll be trying to escape. We try to take the sporting attitude—we do what it takes to keep you here but we aren't mean about it. Anyway, since naturally, being a prisoner, you're already inclined to run away, and as a political prisoner you already have some reasons to dislike being here in particular, things are already biased in a bad direction. We don't want you to keep being reminded to think about running away, even more, because you hate the food or your laundry is itchy or your room is too warm at night. After all, we aren't in the business of punishing people here; all we do is keep them from leaving."

Jak sighed internally, but aloud he said, "Well, then, I guess we'd better get going on the paperwork." Apparently, wherever he went, life was going to resemble gen school, and the pokheets would find a way to take your feets away.

The AI that interviewed him was correctly polite about everything, and as he'd been told, it mostly was information about how to make him comfortable. He wasn't asked to confess to any crimes, real or invented, nor was he asked to discuss any co-conspirators or associates or whatever the other people involved would be, officially. He supposed that this was because if they just held him here in Tjadou long enough, either Sesh would be won over and marry Psim Cofinalez, or else she'd escape by some other means, and either way, he'd then be irrelevant. The thought was not especially comforting.

When they had absolutely finished noting down every possible way in which Jak might be made comfortable while being held prisoner, they neutered his purse, installing a new operating system loyal to them rather than to Jak. He wasn't sure how to tell them that he would never be able to tell if his purse was disloyal, given how little it liked him anyway. He pulled it back on his left hand, checked to make sure that his personal files were still in place, and accepted it all with a shrug.

His room featured a reasonably comfortable bed with the usual adjustments but no luxury features, a table, chair, and lamp where he could eat or read, and a large screen to plug into his purse. Calls to Uncle Sib were blocked, as were calls to anywhere on board the *Spirit of Singing Port,* so he didn't have much of anyone to talk to. The Cofinalez family was too affluent, and their jail management people too shrewd, to force any doubling up in rooms, so there was no roommate to get to know. It was as the pokheets had said; he had all the feets he might want in a trivial way, and none at all otherwise.

Jak dialed up the prison regulations to see what he had available and what he would be permitted to do, and discovered that he was confined to five different buildings surrounding a courtyard, that meals, laundry, bathing, and other necessities were free at common facilities but there were entrepreneurs who would be happy to sell you better versions of them, and that his time was more or less his own; the officer who had picked him up had been the deputy warden, who was also the sponsor of the prison's daily calendar and gazette via his advertising banner across the bottom of the screen, which promoted his real-estate agency with the catchy slogan, "Coming up for parole soon? Just released and nowhere to go? Being a hostage doesn't have to mean living in a hovel!"

At least it looked like Jak would be able to secure basic comforts; he'd spent much less than his allowance while on the *Spirit of Singing Port,* so he had more than enough for the foreseeable future. And most of the screens assured him that people rarely stayed in the main prison for more than a few weeks—it wasn't necessary for most people, because Tjadou itself, an isolated town in scrub-desert country, with rugged bare mountains and little potable water nearby, was a reasonably effective prison, especially when combined with constant monitoring. Jak glanced down at his purse, which now worked for the malphs and was charged with turning him in, and said, "Curiosity about this. I withdraw the question if it is sensitive. What do you do if I try to take you off? Sound an alarm, call for help?"

"Both of those," the purse said. "Also I've had my energy storage enhanced, so I can run for quite a long time—exact time classified—without body heat to recharge me."

"And how does it feel to be working for them instead of me?"

"I'm not really the same purse any more with the new operating system, so I don't experience the direct channel to my old memories in quite the same way, but as far as I can tell, on the level where all the old memories interact and form emotions and opinions . . . I'm really, really enjoying this. Please do try to escape soon. I can't wait to be there to see what happens to you."

Jak thought, sourly, that the machine had found a very novel way to follow the built-in requirement that it try to encourage safe behaviors in its user.

There was a knock at the door; Jak opened it. A broad-shouldered, handsome young man with a vampire-brunette complexion, thin dark mustache, and weight-lifter body was leaning against the wall in the corridor. "I heard we had a new one here," he said. "You can call me Black—first name, last name, it's what everyone uses."

"Jak Jinnaka," Jak said.

"I know, it's displayed over your door," Black said, pointing. "The guards don't usually bother showing anyone where the free services are because they all get a cut out of the profits from the pay services. And they don't provide any orientation because they speck that if you're uncomfortable, you'll be all the more eager to buy or rent a place outside of the prison. Would you like a quick tour of where everything free is, with a few notes about local customs? Showing new heets around is one of the few things that breaks up my days."

"Sure. Do I have to do anything to tell them where I've gone?"

"They'll know. Your purse informs on you constantly, remember?"

"He forgets to blow his nose if I don't tell him," the purse volunteered.

"Let me guess. Your purse is feeling its feets for the first time."

"Yeah."

"It happens a lot. So, you want to see the rest of the prison? We can include lunch in the tour, and it'll kill a good part of the afternoon."

"Toktru, I had no other plans," Jak said, and closed the door behind him.

Black was of the once-over school of tour-giving; in rapid succession, they passed the free laundry, the free baths, the dispensary, and the "necessities shop." "It's not a bad idea to spend a little cash instead of going here," Black added. "They have pretty well everything you really need—if you don't mind toilet paper that you can sand metal with, bars of soap that will take most of your skin off, toothpaste that tastes like it should have been the laundry detergent, and so on, then this is your place. Otherwise, well, the three little shops inside the prison grounds all have ridiculous prices, but they also have the usual brands of things."

"Thanks for the note," Jak said.

"It's really the least I can do," Black said. "I happen to be the only long-term prisoner here, so I'm the only person who's had a chance to learn the ropes. I assure you I'm not being held for any evil I've done—the Cofinalez courts are perfectly fine for ordinary crimes—but because I'm an inconvenience to the present Duke and his heir, who nonetheless are treating me with surprising decency. At least, knowing them as well as I do, *I'm* surprised. Really, it's just the boredom that gets to me. I have access to news channels and viv and all that sort of thing, but somehow just being here with nothing to do does grind me down after a while. I've thought of writing memoirs but I'm afraid they would consist of an account of being a spoiled upper-class brat until I was locked up, and then of being a spoiled upper-class brat in a prison afterward. When one day is a great deal like another, describing them all would be masochism for writer and reader alike, masen?"

"I see your point," Jak said.

"Well, let's go up the view tower here," Black said. "It's one of the nicer features we've got—a view of the surrounding countryside."

Jak had never been much of a fan of scenery, and he was already getting somewhat sleepy after everything that had happened, for he had been awake for about eighteen hours so far. But it was still his first day on a planet new to him—in fact his first day ever on a planet—and Black seemed nice, probably just very talkative because he'd been lonely for a long time, and desperate to enjoy Jak's company before Jak was moved to an apartment. And he had been very helpful in showing Jak the place. So though his legs rebelled at climbing stairs in the insanely high gravity, his eyelids seemed to want to close, and he couldn't imagine its being worth the effort, Jak followed Black on up the winding staircase to the open platform on top of the tower.

The moment he stood there, he was glad he had made the effort. It was a wonderfully clear day and the midmorning sun was at just about the forty-five-degree angle that is perfect for vision. Low blue mountains lay to the east, still partly shaded from the rising sun behind them; farther away, to the west, barren brown rock stood out in sharp relief. Below the mountains there was a broad, scrubby plain, desert but not the dryest of desert, with plenty of low trees and little tufts of grass, broken in four places by the low, crumbling rises of the crater walls, mute and ancient witnesses to the Bombardment. Jak could see into the nearest pock; it was half full of muddy green water, and not at all inviting, either the half that looked black and poisonous in deep shadow or the half that looked like thinnish pea soup in the bright sunlight. Jak judged it might be a couple of kilometers away.

The city itself extended almost halfway to the horizon, but in the hot morning, it was blurred by rising warm air, and less clear than the distant mountains. It formed a pattern like runny graph paper: deep green fuzzy lines that ran straight as lasers and formed the grid itself between lumpy gray-white areas. The straight deep green lines had to be irrigation canals, with trees beside them, and the gray-white squares they marked out must be filled with buildings, but Jak could see little detail through the wavery air, as heat was already rising from the paved, smooth, harsh white area, 150 meters wide, that surrounded the prison.

"Are they raising those trees commercially? What kind are they?"

"It's one of the best pieces of genie-work in the solar system," Black said. "Each tree puts out a dozen different fruits. Some of them are old standards like apples and pears. Others are special flavors like a pineapple-lemon hard-shelled fruit that looks sort of like a honeydew, and the main crop looks like a blue rubber coconut and is a nearly pure saturated solution of fructose inside, which they sell for industrial use, as a sweetener and as a feedstock for grain alcohol. The genies have set it up so that everything grows only on the side that overhangs the water, and the tree drops them when they're ripe, but only when it gets a particular ultrasound frequency through its roots.

"Robot boats sail up and down the canals, with an ultrasound generator on their undersides. They carry big catcher nets spread out between poles to form sort of a funnel down to the hold. Whenever the fruit is ripe, it drops into the nets of the next passing boat; when a boat has a hold-full, it turns off its noisemaker and heads back to the center to be unloaded.

"Along those canals, walkways and Pertrans routes connect all those whitewashed houses and shops that make up the town, so that you travel everywhere in the shade, and on a sunny day like this, the canal will be lying in deep shadow, dappled with sunlight, tilapia rising to the surface now and then, and lots of people out just walking and enjoying it; now and then a boat goes by, and you watch the fruit fall into it. If there's a nicer place to walk in the solar system, I'd be surprised."

Jak thought it would be ungracious to suggest how much it could all be improved by just taking the gravity down by about seventy percent. "It sounds very beautiful," he said. "And you sound very familiar with it."

"I grew up in Tjadou. Or as much as I ever actually grew up, I grew up in Tjadou. My family had a place here and it was where I preferred to be, and I was the sort of child who always got his way, eventually." Black grinned, and Jak couldn't help liking him very much just then—there was such pleasure in his self-deprecation. "Of course, toktru some people might say I still am the sort of child who always gets his way, eventually. But 'eventually' is coming rather slowly these days."

"Is there any chance that you'll ever get to live outside the prison, so you can at least live in a town you love?" Jak asked. He was bothered by the thought that Black was such a short distance from his beloved canals, trees, and town.

"Not if the ducal family knows what they're doing, and alas, I do not believe that there are many fools in that family; there are fools in every family, masen? But no great abundance of them in the Cofinalezes. I am afraid that I'm right where I should be, looking at it through the lenses of the people currently ruling Uranium."

"You're very forgiving."

"'Principle 118: Forgiveness costs nothing and saves energy.' But, to tell you the truth, I'd be doing exactly the same thing if our situations were reversed, and so it's hard to work up much rancor."

Jak watched the face of his new friend closely, and saw nothing but honesty; though some might have found the chalk-white skin framed by dark black hair and deep red lips to be eerie, Jak rather liked it, and it made the pale blue eyes all the more dramatic.

"Well, then," Black said, "I know you're tired and would like to rest, but let me at least suggest that we go get some lunch before you lie down; as busy and stressful as things have been for you—the guards were saying you survived that launch crash?"

"Yeah. It was pretty damned scary, actually."

"Well, so you've had an immense number of shocks and scares since you slept last. That drains blood sugar from the brain, or so they tell me, and if you want to wake up at all cheerful, and without a headache, you'll have to eat, so come on down and do it with me, and then after that I'll leave you alone, I promise, and you can get your nap."

"It's a deal," Jak said.

The public free cafeteria was all the way down the stairs and diagonally across from the view tower. It faced south into the courtyard, toward the building that held Jak's—room? cell?—neither seemed quite the singing-on word . . .

Shadows were long enough to put a few outdoor tables in shade, and they sat down there. "Let me use my purse, since yours is a bit hostile and still reveling in the chance to get back at you," Black suggested. "Sit anywhere." He talked to the fingerless glove on his left hand. "What's on the menu today?"

"Nominally split pea soup, peasant oat bread, and a cheese and fruit tray," the purse replied, "but actually a massive power failure." At once the lighted display of the food dispenser went blank and dead, and the background hum of the hundreds of unobtrusive machines, always present wherever there were people, ceased. In the abrupt silence, guards could be heard running and shouting to each other. Black stared at his purse. "The whole system has been virused. It's an attack."

The shouting and the thumping of boots could be heard for barely a few seconds; then there were a few more seconds when it competed with a growing low rumble, whose pitch seemed to climb from subsonic to bass to baritone in mere moments. The roar stabilized somewhere in the upper part of the baritone range, and Jak realized it was coming from above. The shadows around him disappeared.

He looked up to see a bright light, like looking at the sun, which grew rapidly. Jak looked down, blinking, try-ing to get the red afterimage out of his vision, and so he only saw the fins of the big rocket touch down in the

courtyard, and heard the *whakka-whakka-whak* as its automated guns cleared the guards from the walls.

He looked up, his vision clearing, to see a ramp drop
from the side, and two men ran out, one bounding down
the ramp and leaping over its side to position, the other
hurrying but apparently unused to the high gravity. They
carried beam pistols and immediately assumed firing position, as if expecting an attack from any door. A moment
later, a slender boy—no, it was a young woman, in a
fighting coverall—ran down the ramp, and shouted, "All
right, I'm going to check this building first, you toves
just—well, dip me in shit and paint me blue. He's standing right here."

She raised her visor. It was Myxenna Bonxiao,
Dujuv's demmy, whom he'd last seen back on the Hive.
"Come on, Jak, no time to waste, we're breaking you
out, tove. Don't bother to pack, run to me."

Jak ran forward, and he could feel Black at his heels.
As they came onto the ramp, Myx asked, "Who's this?"

"His name is Black. I think he's a friend. Anyway he's
some kind of enemy of the Cofinalezes."

"Not their enemy, but they don't much like me, and I
would like to escape if I could," he said. "And I can assure you that if I escape, they will look for me much
more eagerly than they will for Jak."

"Great, you're a diversion," Myx said. "Come on
aboard, both of you."

"Company, Myx," one of the combat-helmeted figures
shouted, and began blazing away at the doorways on his
side of the courtyard. Unarmed as they were, Jak and
Black scuttled into the door of the rocket, Myx right with

them, and a moment later they were squashing along on the padded flooring of the bottom cargo room.

Jak started to ask "How—" but at that moment the two men, combat-helmeted, spinning to fire last shots behind them, came backward through the door, and one of them hit the emergency door release, causing the metal door to slam closed with a great ringing boom. He shouted, "We're all in, Sis, jettison the ramp and get us out of here. Everybody lie down on your back *now!*"

Jak dropped backward, slapping to break his fall, and stretched flat on his back just an instant before the rocket roared to life, a sound like being inside a drum that someone is belt-sanding. They boosted at max. It was like being run over by a huge wheel, but not as comfortable, and like being kicked in the gut and face simultaneously, but not as much fun. It went on for the better part of two minutes, before a familiar voice, amplified to the point of distortion in order to be heard over the terrible howl of the engines, said, "Shutting down. We're going to coast over to a landing field in Australia. We'll have about half an hour of free fall."

The dreadful thunder shut off, and the weight vanished with it. At once Jak was in normal, healthy, ordinary free fall, floating off the padded deck easily and comfortably. It was hard to believe that he had only missed this for a day; his joints and muscles seemed to rejoice in one great symphony of creaks and pops.

Black grabbed Jak's left hand and, before Jak knew what he was doing, stripped off the purse. Then he pulled off his own, airswam to the emergency station, threw its cover open, and stuffed both purses into the biowaste disposal. After a few brief, piping screams, the two purses were autoclaved into black sash. "That will make us harder to trace," Black said. "Hope you didn't have any un-backed-up data that was essential."

"Naw, and anyway I never liked that purse's attitude." Jak looked around; Myx had pulled her helmet off and was breathing hard. The helmets came off the two men, and Jak saw why they had seemed familiar. It was Dujuv Gonzawara and Piaro Fears-the-Stars. He looked from one to the other, trying to speck what to say to his toves, and finally he said, "Let me guess. Phrysaba is flying the ship? And probably Pabrino is navigating?"

Piaro shook his head. "Phrysaba's handling both," he said. "Pabrino wanted to come along but his folks wouldn't let him. But he's helping us with logistics and strategy for the operation, and he's monitoring everything from the *Spirit*."

"Well, just so there's at least one reasonably responsible party involved," Jak said, grinning. "All right, how did you all meet up and happen to be here? And does this have something to do with why you never wrote, Duj?"

Dujuv shrugged. "Your Uncle Sibroillo really did not like the idea of you doing all this with no backup, to begin with, so he approached me about it, and I said sure, and Myxenna volunteered to come along."

"It's good for my résumé for the PSA," she pointed out. "Public service to a friendly nation, namely Greenworld. Plus I know Sesh a lot better than anyone else and that might come in handy."

Dujuv continued, "A Hive Spatial warship was headed out to make a port call here, and it was taking one of those superfast energy-wasting orbits that just drops down to gain orbital velocity and then pops back up to wherever it's going, so we left a month after you did and almost got here at the same time. We were supposed to watch you and see how it went, and we'd just gotten you located in time to see the launch crash," Dujuv explained. "By the way, that is one *great* way to worry your toves."

"Toktru," Piaro agreed. "Sis was just idly watching— or at least she wants me to think it was just idle—and she called me as soon as she saw what had happened. There's a Spaceborn Grief Center on Singing Port— that's where you go to have professional counselors break bad news to you, and it's also usually the fastest place to find out if your friends or relatives are still alive. And we ran into Myx and Duj there, found out you were alive from the fact that you were being checked into the Duke's prison, and after discussion with your uncle, we discovered a rocket of untraceable registry that was available for immediate rent, and it happened to contain a small arsenal in its hold. And so here we are, more or less at your service. Depending on whether you have any good ideas beyond this point."

"Well, getting me out of prison was the best idea I've heard in a long time," Jak said.

"And Myx—Myxenna, is it?—let me add, thank you for taking me along on the ride," Black said. "I think I can say that I'll make sure you don't regret it."

"You're welcome." From the way her eyes twinkled at the handsome, older heet, Jak judged that Myx already had no regrets, but he suspected Duj would have enough for both of them. It was really just like being home.

"Ending free fall in two minutes," Phrysaba's voice said, over the speakers. "We're landing gentler than we took off, but it's still going to be quite a ride. Get stretched out on the padding, and stay that way."

The cargo area swung rapidly around them, cold jet noise echoing through the little ship, and after a few sickening seconds, settled back into ordinary weightlessness. Jak made sure he was comfortable on the padding.

"Acceleration in five, four, three, two, one, now," Phrysaba said, and the engines thundered to life again. This time they ran at a fraction of full power, and the descent was mostly at around two gravities; if Jak had really needed to, he could have very carefully gotten up and moved around. As it was, he lay there, trying to feel positive about the fact that shortly the two gees would go back to a mere one.

The minutes crept by and then Phrysaba said, "All right. Touchdown in twenty seconds . . ." The engines became almost muffled in their thunder, and acceleration decreased to a mere one gravity; they must be almost hovering. "Descending . . . coming up on it . . ." There was the barest of bumps, and Piaro said, "Singing-on piloting, Sis," even before Phrysaba cut the engines and said, "Well, we're here. Everybody out—this rocket is not going to be a healthy neighborhood for long. Pabrino tells me that his data trace shows that the Duke's pokheets have a singing-on fix on us, they've got where we've landed pegged within three meters, and are getting it together right now."

CHAPTER 10

Extremely Rude
and Unprofessional

As they emerged from the rocket, Black said, "Well, this is where I disappear, and I'm going to take a suborbital to North America—that ought to get most of them chasing me, while you and your friends get on with your business, Jak."

"Thanks," Jak said.

"Not a problem. They would chase me anyway—you might as well get some benefit from it."

"Do you have credit?" Myxenna asked.

He favored her with a deep, winning smile. "The next time we have a chance to talk, we can *both* enjoy how funny that question was. But for the meantime, yes, everything is fine, now that I'm out of that pen. I won't forget this, my dear toves." He turned, darted down a passageway between two buildings, and was gone.

"Strange kind of a heet, but I'm getting to like him," Jak said.

"So what do we do?" Phrysaba said, practically, as she climbed down the ladder from the rocket. She was carrying a large, heavy bag. "We have all these weapons left to use, but we've kind of lost the element of surprise. And Pabrino tells me we have about fifteen minutes to get away from this spaceport before all kinds of trouble starts happening here. He suggests that we grab the first ship out and improvise from there."

There was a suborbital excursion hopper leaving in six minutes, so the five of them got onto that, and breathed a sigh of relief when it took off for Buenos Aires without incident.

Jak had hoped to get a nap in free fall, and he tried, but he was only able to doze in the constant noise. The robot tour guide nattered on about weather conditions over the Pacific Ocean, and as they reentered and made the close overflight of South America, it spent an unbelievable amount of time explaining how odd it was, on Earth, to see a plain with no pocks; because Alpha Draconis is far to the north, with a declination of just over 69° N, anywhere south of 21° S had been spared the Bombardment, so that the Argentine pampas had been untouched. You wouldn't have thought that there'd be much else to say about pocks that were not there, but the guide seemed to be determined. Aside from Jak and his toves, the only other occupants of the ship seemed to be a few teenage couples who took private rooms, probably for free-fall making out.

The suborbital touched down on the linducer track at Buenos Aires, selling off its momentum and gliding in to refuel. It announced that they now had one half hour to visit the observation tower above the refueling station, and that it would leave without them if they were not aboard. Jak stretched and yawned and said, "How's our credit supply?"

"Plenty," Dujuv said. "Are you specking what I'm specking? Good time to change vehicles?"

"Yeah. Isn't there one of those—what do they call'em, the thing that's like a big Pertrans that runs between fixed stations?"

"Trains. Yeah, there's one to Africa from here," Phrysaba said, checking her purse. "It even stops in Fermi. We can catch a taxi, whatever that is, to get there." She stood up. "All right, let's go."

After they left their compartment, Jak reached back inside and pushed the privacy button, locking the compartment closed; the little tourist craft probably wasn't very sophisticated, and there was a good chance that the compartment would register as still occupied, if anyone looked into it, which he thought likely.

Right next to the steps marked "TO OBSERVATION TOWER" there was a sign pointing down a stairway: "GROUND TRANSPORTATION AND TAXIS."

"I wonder if that means that taxis, whatever they are, fly, and you're supposed to land here, whether you're flying a transportation or a taxi?" Myx said.

"Or maybe this is the place where they put people into departing taxis and recycle the old ones through the grinder?" Phrysaba guessed.

They didn't see any "ground transportation," whatever it might be, but when they got down to the curb there was a row of brightly colored wheeled vehicles, each labeled "taxi," so that seemed simple enough. They were robots who would take you to any address for a single fee, regardless of how many riders got in; they piled into one and authorized a payment.

It was just dawn as they shot out of the tunnel from the little secondary spaceport, headed for the train station, and though this was objectively the slowest part of the trip, it felt like the fastest and it was certainly the most terrifying. The taxi apparently monitored a real-time information system for ground traffic (Piaro pointed out afterward that since they never saw any law enforcement, this probably included monitoring where the pokheets were), and rerouted constantly to reduce trip time.

The taxi shot down big empty roads, made abrupt turns down steep ramps and plunged through narrow alleyways, wove between crowds of pedestrians in marketplaces, veered madly around buildings and through narrow spaces, absolutely destroying any sense of direction Jak had; everything seemed to be a blur and a smear of color, accompanied by the shrieking wheels of the strange little vehicle. It was bizarre how being less than a meter off the ground, and moving through such crowded spaces, could make speeds that were a fraction of one percent of orbital seem like the fastest he'd ever gone. The taxi didn't even go as fast as a Pertrans car, but a Pertrans ran in a nice sensible tunnel with no obstacles around—not in an open space with hundreds of other vehicles and people drifting about as randomly as the molecules in a gas, to Jak's eyes, yet miraculously not colliding. "Wonder when these things were invented," Phrysaba said. "Surely not before there were robots; I speck no human being could do this."

When the taxi pulled up at the train station, the sun

had not yet cleared the horizon, and Jak realized that the whole ride couldn't have been more than ten minutes. He decided that ten minutes in a taxi in Buenos Aires was probably as much time as he'd ever need to spend in his life. Myx staggered a little getting out. Even Dujuv just got out, without any stunts or vaulting.

They studied the displays over the train station counter carefully for a while. "I think I dak the djeste," Piaro said finally. "If everyone is going to share a train, then everyone has to leave at the same time, like a ship. So that's what 'departure time' and 'arrival time' mean—everyone going to the same place gets on *the same* train and goes at the same time. Then there's a fee for a particular trip." He raised his left hand to his face. "Confirm?"

"You've got it right," his purse said.

"What are the classes?"

"Classes are names for qualities of accommodation. 'First class' for long distance means a private space where you can lie down and sleep if you wish; 'second class' means small enclosed areas, bench seating within them; 'third class' means row seating—"

"Thanks, that's all I needed," Piaro said. His purse clicked off.

"So in first class I could get a nap?" Jak asked. He was amazed at how tired he felt; he had been up a long time and had already been more than all the way around this unnecessarily big and heavy planet.

"The train that goes to Fermi leaves in about forty minutes," Phrysaba said. "And it looks like it takes about twenty-five hours to get there. And since none of us is in a hurry, and we can get a luxury suite that lets us all wash up, sleep, and eat for a while, I'm in favor of it."

Afterward, Jak thought of the train ride as one of the most interesting things on the trip. The train only moved at slightly over 600 kph, but it moved continuously, and very smoothly, and unlike flight in aircraft or spacecraft, you were right there, however briefly, with whatever you were looking at.

He slept for about ten hours, so that when he awoke it was utterly quiet and dark; they were in the Recife-Banjul tunnel, a few kilometers below the floor of the Atlantic Ocean, and he realized that about as soon as he realized that Phrysaba was snuggled into bed with him, naked.

He gently disentangled her arm and climbed out into the luxury compartment; he could see by the dim blue lights, when he turned those on, that there were three other beds in there but only two of them were occupied. He hoped that Piaro was by himself. Otherwise this was going to be a classic case of Myx-awkwardness, which, toktru, he really wasn't in the mood for, just at the moment.

When he checked, he found that he had been asleep for almost ten hours, and that they were most of the way to Africa, but still under the Atlantic. They had bought an anonymous exchange card in Buenos Aires, deliberately walking up the street to buy it where the ground shuttle for the spaceport left, and using one of the "super-clean" account numbers that Uncle Sib had given Jak for emergencies; with luck, the malphs looking for them would have gotten no further than realizing that they had to search through the memories of dozens or hundreds of taxis, and since taxis were arriving and departing constantly at the port where they'd come in, that could be a long and inconclusive process.

He could also hope that the malphs were all busy chasing Black, and that Jak and his friends were no longer being pursued at all, but hopes like that were probably not wise to harbor. Jak hoped that Black was all right, and something about the man inspired confidence, maybe more than the situation warranted.

Well, anyway, he had troubles enough of his own, and thinking about Black's wouldn't make his any better. He quietly dressed and called up a quick meal from the foodmaker; that helped a lot as well. He was beginning to feel ready to take on the world, which was good because that was just what he might be doing soon.

He went up to the observation bubble on top of the car, though there was nothing to see in the tunnel itself; he wanted to be sure he didn't miss their emergence, since he had guessed that it would be impressive.

He had more coffee and food up there, having staked out a good seat at the front end of the observation bubble, finished eating, and sat quietly, just waiting for the moment.

His guess proved to be singing-on.

There was just an instant's warning, as the top surfaces of the cars ahead of him flashed into bright light surrounded by a semicircular patch of blue sky; then almost as if it had been turned on with a switch, African morning leapt into being around him, the high bluffs sweeping back behind him, a herd of wild horses and some kind of horned animal racing momentarily beside the track. The train hurtled on, climbing up through the low, ancient mountains. An hour later, they descended into the soft grasslands that had been all erg and dust just a thousand years before; here, they were far enough north so that every twenty kilometers or so, they passed by a Bombardment pock, sometimes dry, sometimes a small circular lake, its walls still sharp as if it were on the moon or crumbled and eroded as if it were a million years old—it all depended on what sort of soil and rock the fist-sized ball of quartz had penetrated at light speed, and what sort of weather the area had had since. Jak wondered what it had looked like, right down here on the ground, as it had happened. In school they had said that if you had been there, you couldn't have seen the arrival of any of the rocks—just a sudden flash of bright light and a tower of dust many kilometers high, like a fusion bomb set off just below the surface.

He thought about seeing it the day before, with the Rubahy, and wondered what Shadow on the Frost might think, seeing his species's handiwork all over the Earth. He had said it was "much to answer for" and yet "beautiful." What did he, or any Rubahy, really feel about it? Did it make him proud—*we almost beat you bastards— serves you right for that trick you pulled with our sun?* Did it fill him with awe that his ancestors had been able to do that, whereas now a puny remnant of his species clung to a couple of frozen snowballs, far out in the dark, on sufferance of the people they had dreamed of conquering? Did it hurt him to see such wounds in a living world? Were the pocks "just there" to him, something that had happened once and had nothing to do with him? Surely not that. Surely the Rubahy had some feelings.

"The others are moving around and will be up soon," Dujuv said, sitting down beside him. "I just reinforced your order, so there's some more coffee and some rolls coming. And some eggs and meat and bread and cereal. And some other stuff."

"It's Uncle Sib's credit line," Jak said, "and the good old gwont is loaded, or at least he is until we get done spending it."

Dujuv vaulted the seatback and sat down next to Jak, comfortably spread-legged, and began unfolding the table. "How long till we get there?"

"A good part of the day, still. Late afternoon. And as close to the equator as Fermi is, it gets dark right around six. So what we want to do, I think, is talk a little bit about what we're going to do when we get there, and then get long naps and be really up and ready, so that the moment we arrive, we're in business. I don't think I want to be surprised again; 'Getting surprised is distinctly unpleasant, and it nearly always suggests something is wrong with you,' as Uncle Sib is so fond of saying."

Dujuv stretched and yawned, his panth muscles straining against his coverall. "Weehu, that night of sleep felt good."

"Tell me about it. High gravity agrees with you," Myx said, plopping down in the forward seating area, her hair a muzzy tangle, a kittenish smile playing across her face. "From the way you slept, I was thinking, toktru, that I had finally killed you."

Phrysaba slid in beside Jak and rested a hand on his arm; Duj gave him a slight twitch of the eyebrow, which was about as much as he would ever raise the Sesh question—he'd known Jak long enough. Myxenna would not even lift the eyebrow, ever; unlike her mekko, she not only didn't have a double standard, she had pretty well no standard at all.

Piaro joined the group a few moments later. He was "very clearly not a morning person—I've seen livelier corpses," Myxenna teased. While he was rubbing his face with his hand, as if either trying to get it on straight or to just wipe it off, Phrysaba added, "Well, he's never been exactly singing-on lucid in the morning, no, but he makes up for it by being completely incoherent later in the day."

"As soon as I have three brain cells on line, I'll have a riposte," Piaro said.

The food came out then, and for a while all anyone did was eat and watch the brown and green of the Sahara roll by. After a while, they passed through pastures, and then grain fields. "This was all desert, a thousand years ago?" Phrysaba said. "That's what the guidebook said."

"A lot of it still is, but not like it was," Myx said. "What they say in school, anyway, is that with more than thirty of the rocks landing in the sea every day for fifty years, so much water got pumped into the atmosphere that—"

"Do you want that roll?" Dujuv asked, through a face full of his.

When all of them had stuffed themselves, they ordered another round of coffee. "There's no one else in the observation bubble," Jak pointed out, "and it's no more likely that there'll be a hidden microphone here than that there would be back in the compartment. So it's about four hours till we get to Fermi. Anybody got any ideas about what we should do when we get there?"

Dujuv shrugged. "I noticed a long time ago that things go a lot better when you make the plans and I just supply the muscle and motivation, tove."

Piaro nodded. "Your mission—your call."

"Boys are so passive," Myx said.

Phrysaba giggled. "Let's give Jak a chance, though. Did you have anything in mind, or were you just asking because you were fresh out of ideas?"

"Almost both," Jak said. He really wished that he could explain the djeste, and lay out the plan that he still intended to carry out, but he had a feeling that what would happen was that they would veto it, since it involved his being taken prisoner and held for months, not to mention personally delivering a blackmail message to an extremely dangerous criminal. But he had to try it— as far as he could see, getting back on the original plan was still the best hope for getting Sesh released.

While he had been thinking, they had been looking at Jak, waiting for him to explain. They might begin to suspect that something was up, so he temporized. "I kind of have an idea but I don't seem to know whether it's a good one or not."

Myxenna chuckled. "Well, then, you've found the right friends. Don't worry, if it's not a good idea, toktru, we'll make sure that you know it's not."

Phrysaba leaned against him, resting her head on his shoulder. "It's not exactly like we're painfully shy or anything, masen?"

Jak nodded and said, "Well, all right, here's what I was thinking. My Uncle Sib always say, that when you don't know how to get into a place, you should at least speck knocking on the front door. Now, as I see it, we know nothing about Psim Cofinalez's palace, where Sesh is being held. None of us is really an experienced fighter, so chances are that we aren't a match for the guards, not even you, Dujuv."

"I'd like to find out, though."

"Well, let's just say that I don't want to be there while you're finding out, because you might not find out what you're expecting to find out, masen? Anyway, so I think that any attempt to penetrate that palace, either by sneaking in or by breaking in, is apt to be a disaster."

"And it wasn't a disaster that they tried to kill you by shooting down the launch?" Phrysaba asked.

"Or that they were going to hold you in prison forever?" Myxenna added.

"Well, first of all, we don't know that I was the target of the attack on the launch. There were some other pretty good targets, just among the survivors, and Nakasen knows how many others among the dead might have been the target. So let's set that aside for the moment, eh? Now, they could have just shot me out in the desert, after they took the others away, or they could have given me a good shaking and destroyed my message and then put me right on a launch back up to orbit. Or they could have even just flown me to Fermi and had me present the message. So it looks to me like, whatever's in the message I'm carrying, it's not as important as the fact that there is a message, or the fact that the message gets presented. I think those two facts are what actually change anything. Therefore, what I plan to do is just walk right up to the address I've been given, in view of as many petty officials as possible, and present the message.

"I think once the message is formally, publicly presented, they don't have very many options. Once they're forced to admit that they've received it, they pretty much have to start negotiating publicly with Greenworld, don't they?"

Myxenna nodded. "That sounds right. Why don't you give me some time to look that up? I might be able to find something about it in the rules of international diplomacy, or find some precedents in history, or something like that. But so far so good."

"Well, then, there's a heet I'm supposed to contact and talk to, and what I'd say is, as soon as we're in Fermi, we all go get a place in a hotel; then I go to someplace that isn't the room, because if anything goes wrong—no arguing, masen?—I want you all out of it. If everything goes right, I go see the heet and present the message, and then we see where it goes from there."

"Well, the djeste makes complete sense," Myxenna said, "assuming that having delivered the message will be enough to protect you, and that the message will get Sesh freed eventually. Which are two *huge* assumptions, but I don't know that I see any alternative to making them. So let's try it."

Phrysaba nodded. "I agree, and I'll run it by Pabrino."

Piaro sighed. "I probably consume too many intrigue-and-adventure stories, but somehow it doesn't seem toktru singing-on that this plan involves nothing but telling the truth and dealing directly."

Dujuv nodded. "It's probably a good idea but it yellow-lines my creepometer for just that reason."

Jak smiled. "Suppose I promise that as soon as there's the least reason to, I'll lie and cheat . . ."

"Might help quite a bit," Dujuv said, and Piaro nodded agreement.

An hour later, Pabrino had seen nothing wrong with the plan and absolutely no way that it might be made better, and Myx's research had turned up half a dozen rules and cases that seemed to indicate it might really be the best thing to do. With that settled, they all sat back in the comfortable chairs in the observation bubble, talking idly, sipping juice, enjoying the respite from danger and effort, while the central African landscape slid away behind them in the late afternoon sun, grassland alternating with scrub and brush, then yielding to farmland, and at last the farmland shading into tall, dark, cool forests.

It was sunset by the time they were crossing the causeway that ran across the gigantic Lake Ralph Smith; somewhere on its bottom lay the bed of the much smaller Lake Victoria, but in one of the freaks of the Bombardment, this area had been hit heavily and the crater rings had overlapped in such a way as to provide a gigantic dam, just before the worldwide rise in rainfall had hit; by the time the Bombardment had ended, the vast new lake had been well established, and was now thought of as one of the things not to be missed on a tour of Africa. Fermi sat on its eastern shore, a great glowing city, with the sun behind them and the city lights just beginning to shine in the deep twilight shadows.

"Bex Riveroma will see you now," the voice said, and Jak got up from the bench where he had been sitting by himself for over two hours, according to his new purse.

Jak was trying to be nicer to this one, and so far it was at least giving him information in a nonsarcastic way. A door appeared in the white wall in front of him, and he walked through it.

Bex Riveroma was an exceptionally tall man with very broad shoulders, and if there was any surplus fat on him, it must have been in his earlobes or the tips of his little fingers. He was completely hairless, lacking even eyebrows; his jaw was large and square, his eyes were a deep vivid green, and his full red lips stood out like a gash in his light tan skin.

"Now," he said, "to begin with, I hope you'll be willing to repeat what you said to me over the communications link; I have been in touch with Sibroillo Jinnaka, so I'm somewhat better equipped to receive the message."

"Sure," Jak said. "'I am carrying information from Sibroillo Jinnaka, and I am authorized to exchange it for a service from you. The information concerns the location of all the extant, court-admissible evidence regarding the Fat Man, the Dagger and Daisy, the business about the burning armchair, the disappearance of *Titan's Dancer,* and KX-126, including all such evidence regarding your involvement. The public key has already been sent to you. The private key, along with the way to retrieve the encoded information, has been coded onto an antigen group in my bloodstream. Here are the specifications for the isolation and decoding of the antigen group, and I will cooperate when you draw a blood sample.'" Jak pulled the envelope from his pocket; Riveroma tucked it into his own pocket, zipping it closed as Jak continued. "'We will proceed no further than that until you agree to—'"

Riveroma whipped a full-force kick at Jak's head. Jak blocked and ducked, but Riveroma's boot heel scraped across his forehead as he was thrown backward. An instant later Riveroma drew Jak's foot with a neat inside sweep, so that Jak hit the floor hard, and then Riveroma was around him, kicking him hard in the face and the belly, the toe of the black boot snapping into the bridge of Jak's nose, slamming his fist into Jak's belly, blows coming too fast for Jak even to know everywhere that he was hit.

He covered up and tried to roll out, but he wasn't thinking clearly in the blur of pain. Riveroma grabbed his collar, then his wrist, and in a moment had him trussed up completely. He turned Jak over, and before Jak could speak, Riveroma held a ball gag in front of his face and said, "Now, will you open up for this or—"

"What are you—?"

Riveroma's fist plunged deep into Jak's solar plexus, and Jak gasped in pain and shock; the ball gag went deep into his mouth, and Riveroma touched the ends together and set them to autotighten, so that they clamped the ball deeper and deeper into Jak's sore, swelling mouth. When it was thoroughly painful, and Jak was wondering whether he would be able to breathe in another instant, or whether the increasing force of the tightening gag might dislocate his jaw, Riveroma touched it again, leaving it agonizing but not damaging.

"You can tell Sibroillo from me," Riveroma said, very calmly and pleasantly, as if the two of them were just having a friendly discussion, "that although I may very well want to take whatever deal he is offering me, or I may be forced to bow to whatever threat he is making—

whichever it should turn out to be—that I do not accept orders from him and in particular I resent the tone of that nasty little note, and you may remind him that I have told him about this before. His whole way of communicating is extremely rude and unprofessional and he shows no respect for the moral equivalence that is key to everyone's getting along. Do you think you can repeat that to him?"

Jak nodded eagerly.

"Good. Let me add, young man, that whether by choice or accident, you are working for one of the rudest, most obnoxious, and most egotistical bastards in the business, known to one and all as an arrogant ninny, and you really must try not to pick up any of his bad habits, because not everyone would make the allowances I am making for your youth and inexperience, and of course for your bad training.

"As for your mission, an even slightly more experienced operative would have refused to deliver such a message, and rightly so. I hope you beat the hell out of Sibroillo for it when you get home—and you probably will be getting home, since at this point I see no reason to take more of it out on you than I already have. I'm assuming that you are a mere operative; if you meant anything to Sibroillo, if for example you were a blood relative, then I might be tempted to use you to send a further message."

He spread his arms wide and brought his hands in with a resounding, excruciating clap on Jak's cheeks. "That was mostly to show you how free I feel with you. I suggest you avoid Sibroillo's tone entirely. Now, I'm going to go away for a while, and then a nice person will come in to take some of your blood, and then after that is all interpreted and decoded, I'll be back for further discussion." He tore the envelope open and pulled out the paper inside; when he glanced at it, he roared with laughter. "Oh, my. So you no doubt are a blood relative. How very like Sibroillo to think that I would be afraid to touch you because of that . . . he always had *such* an exaggerated notion of his reputation! No doubt he sent you for that very reason! Well, it's possible that I won't have any strong reason to do anything too dreadful to you, and I am in fact quite a reasonable man once you get to know me, which you should nevertheless be hoping you will not do. So I don't think there's anything more to worry about than you already had.

"Anyway, the next person will come along to take your blood, and then I'll be back, and then depending on everything, perhaps I will take that gag off you and we'll have further conversation. Or perhaps not. Anyway, whether or not you ever talk to me—or talk—again, *I'll* be talking to *you* later."

Riveroma left, still chuckling merrily; just before the door closed, Jak heard him mutter "Sibroillo, Sibroillo, Sibroillo," like a teacher thinking about a memorably dreadful pupil.

Jak ran through everything he knew for such a situation; it wasn't much. There was no slack to work in his bonds—Riveroma was far too much of a pro for that. Unlike any villain in any intrigue novel, Riveroma had not left the keypad for the molecular lock attached to the bonds, so there was no hope of specking it, and anyway even if he had, the things had nine-digit combinations, so Jak would probably have had to work his way through some significant fraction of a billion possibilities before getting free. He'd be better off hoping to starve to the point where his wrists slipped free.

At least his jaw was going numb.

There was absolutely nothing in this slick-surfaced white room; after much squirming, he managed to spin all the way around in increments of ten degrees or so (at least he thought he had—he wasn't sure that he hadn't lost count of the number of corners he had passed) and thus confirm that he couldn't even perceive where the doors were. He thought he remembered, but if he thought about that too much, the memory would disappear in a fog of doubt.

He could speck nothing else. When he was unsure or afraid, as long as he could remember, he'd always been able to rely upon a thing or two that Uncle Sib always said, but just now he really didn't want to remember anything about Uncle Sib.

It had never occurred to Jak that his uncle might be anything other than the way he presented himself. The shock of discovering that the malphs thought of Sib with contempt, and that it was quite possible that Sib was not exactly the master of intrigue and adventure that he had presented himself to be, was in many ways far more severe than the shock of taking a bad wanging from a professional. Jak went from despair to disbelief to rage at Sib to rage at Riveroma over and over and over, stopping now and then along the way to berate himself, but it neither loosened his bonds nor helped him to accept it, so after a while he began working the mental review part of the Disciplines, seeing whether he might get relaxed enough to gain some slack.

He had gained none by the time that a tall, older woman walked in, yanked his trousers down, and took a very unnecessarily large sample of blood from one of his buttocks; while doing this, several times she addressed him as "cutie" and accused him of getting excited. Jak knew that old tactic, at least—Uncle Sib had not given him a wholly erroneous impression of the world—and simply breathed deeper, concentrating more on relaxing. By the time the woman departed, with a final "Now be a good little bitch and maybe I'll take more blood later, the way you like it," he was merely mentally recording her voice, for later identification, if necessary.

He lay there and kept concentrating. There was no real slack in his bonds, but at least he was beginning to sweat more; he concentrated on making his hands and wrists feel warm, and finally he had budged things about a millimeter—but was no closer to getting free—when Riveroma returned and sat down beside him.

The huge man's voice was oddly gentle. "Well. Your uncle is offering a truly wonderful, once-in-a-lifetime deal, and I dearly wish I could take it, Jak, because it would make my life so much better in so many ways. But as I was forced to explain to him, at the very moment that I removed several of those dangling swords from above my head, I would be—to mix a metaphor savagely—putting two hounds at my heels, to wit all of Uranium and all of Triangle One. This is because anything I do to help your Princess Shyf escape, or to let her go, is going to be absolutely transparent to everyone, for a variety of reasons. It therefore follows that I simply can't take the offer, Jak, much as I would like to—and you have the word of one you can't trust at all that I am telling the absolute truth in that regard.

"Now there is no good reason for me to murder you, or indeed to harm you any further, except that it's possible that some earlier part of our conversations might have been heard and might have put some suspicion in my direction, because sad though it is to say, in this very distrustful world, both Triangle One and the Duchy of Uranium tend to watch me the way a rabbit watches a snake in its cage. Personally I don't know why anyone pays good money for someone they're afraid of, but there you have it.

"So I took the liberty of pumping a few good hard electromagnetic pulses through this room, and following up with a little hard gamma—oh, don't worry, you won't even lose any hair, they'll barely be able to detect it in your blood chemistry in a few weeks—and setting up a watch-and-scramble that I'm wearing at the moment, and for just now we can talk freely, you see? Or rather I can. You're still gagged.

"Anyway, a couple of quite technically proficient fellows are now going to take you over to a guardhouse for a quite mild beating, which I hope you will understand is in the nature of a cover and not intended at all to cause you much distress—it won't be nearly as bad as what I already did to you. I've already given the orders, and I— oh, here they are."

Riveroma stood, and Jak could see his shiny black boots on one side of his peripheral vision, and the boots of the guards on the other. "I was expecting Rab Beversen," he said. "That's the one I use for things like this. This can't be done by unskilled hands—there's a real precise level I want you to hit. Along with some real precise parts of young Jak Jinnaka here."

"Beversen got called over to Station Four," one guard said. "Just a second before we came over. We could take the prisoner over there."

"I'd appreciate that, if it's not too much trouble," Riveroma said. "And make sure Beversen has this"—he handed them a sheet of paper—"I already sent it, but everything is being screwed up today, you know, so let's just see if maybe we can get this right. Make sure that Beversen knows that under no circumstances is he to administer anything more than the level I tell him to."

"I believe he already got the order, sir," the guard said, "but I'll make sure he gets this copy, and I'll have him call you if he has any questions, before he starts."

"Good," Riveroma said. "Adieu, dear Jak, and I surely hope not to see you again—you must be feeling much the same about me, masen?" He left through a door that appeared suddenly in the wall; another door appeared, and the guards dragged him through it. Toktru, Jak wished he could faint.

CHAPTER 11

The Duke of Uranium

They threw Jak into a ground car, not gently but with no more roughness than was incidental to the process, and took off at great speed; probably the Duke's guards didn't have to worry about whatever traffic regulations there were in Fermi, if any. "Station Four," the guard said. "Can you believe he still makes us say 'Station Four'?"

"Shut up. There's a hostile present."

"Right, and six of the biggest media outlets, and a dozen viv programs, all have run and rerun that big story by Mreek Sinda, the one called 'Secrets of Station Four.' And there's a chain of flashclubs in ten cities at least—including this one!—called 'Station Four, Fit for a Princess!' So nobody knows that Station Four is really—"

"You heard me. Shut up. I'm not getting punished for you being a blabbermouth. Not for the third time this year, not ever again, nunh-unh. So shut up."

Jak had specked it already, of course; well, he was getting closer to Sesh, probably into the outer guard areas of Psim's palace. He saw no way that this could be helpful, but it was something to know about. He pushed himself into deeper concentration, hoping to be mostly self-hypnotized by the time his beating began.

They used a power dolly to move him inside the big building at the other end of the trip; Jak couldn't look around, so he had no way of confirming that he was in the palace, just yet, but he tried to make sure he stayed fully as alert as if he were.

"Rab, we brought your guy here. Riveroma's orders. Here's a copy in case you tossed the ones you already got."

"Thanks—I had. Weehu, what a day. One contradictory order after another. I don't know how they do it, I really don't. All right . . . hey, how long has he been bound?"

"I don't know. Riveroma didn't say—"

Jak felt rather than saw Rab Beversen bending over him and probing—"Weehu, and weehu again. Lots of areas on his skin that are cold as a lizard. I can't work on that. The pain monitors will read all wrong and there's a risk of doing way too much tissue damage, bruising him way more than the orders—and these orders are the strictest I've ever seen. We'll have to untie him and let him recover for at least an hour, so he can get his circulation back and his joints can get back to normal. If it isn't one thing, it's another!"

Jak felt absurdly grateful—it's absurd to be so happy at being untied entirely for the purpose of being beaten, and yet to be released from those bonds was still, somehow, the best feeling in the world. He lay on his side, gasping, working his jaw, stretching his legs and arms, trying to control the unbearable tingling on the side of him pressed against the floor. The sensations rushing through his body were overwhelming, and for a long time he concentrated entirely on those, trying to get his motor control and sensation back at least a little before they would realize he had it.

Gradually the sensations of being rubbed with sandpaper, pricked with a thousand cold needles, and dropped into a saltwater bath with a live electrode all diminished to the level of mere discomfort; he could have moved, but he was careful not to, waiting to see what chance he might be able to find in the next few seconds.

The places where Riveroma had kicked and hit him hurt terribly, but none of them was vital, and toktru it was no worse than losing a dozen rough rounds of catch-as-can. He might very well have taken a worse thumping than this at gen school championships a couple of years ago. Though he was having all sorts of doubts about his other training, he was grateful to Uncle Sib for having made sure he trained enough to really dak pain; that was critical right now, the knowledge that things hurt badly, but that *he* wasn't hurt badly.

As he was able to return his focus to the room around him, he realized that there were only two people left in it; Rab had switched into his dress uniform "because her princessy-ness is always coming up with more annoying things for us to do, I think she just wants to make sure she doesn't make any friends here!" Apparently if you were really a specialist at beating people up, there was a special beating-people-up uniform you had to wear to do it just exactly singing-on right, and Rab had already taken his beating-people-up uniform off, so while Jak was recovering, a surly private, who was quite sure it was not part of his job description, had to be bullied into going to Beversen's quarters, getting that specialty uniform, running it through a quick fresh-up, and bringing it back here. "And hurry—I don't have much time but I have to do this one absolutely singing-on right!"

"I'll be back in four minutes, Sarge, you can place a bet on it that I will. And with it all cleaned and freshened. Really!"

"All right. You're on. Beer tonight on me if you get it here in four minutes. Ready, go—"

The door closed. Rab Beversen paced around impatiently; after a moment, he grabbed a chair and took off his coat, hanging it neatly over the back. He draped his belt and sidearm across the coat. Then he removed his tunic, which he laid across the seat and smoothed flat. His boots came off next, and he placed them carefully under the chair, presumably so that no one would trip and scuff them.

His trousers were just at his calves when Jak shot from the bed in one smooth motion, driving a shoulder into the sergeant's buttocks, smashing headfirst into the wall before he could reach forward to catch himself. It didn't make much of a sound; the wall seemed to be solid stone. Jak slipped the butterfly strangle on him, squeezing the man's carotid fiercely, and in a moment felt the body go limp. He grasped Rab's jaw, turning the unconscious body to face him, and slammed the man's head against the wall as hard as he could, hoping to give him a concussion or perhaps a fractured skull. "After all," Jak muttered, tugging the pants off the unconscious body, "you'd have done the same for me." He specked he had no more than two minutes left before the other guard returned—after all, beer was riding on this. Jak had no idea how to lock the doors in this place, so he just finished dressing in Rab's uniform, noting with mild distress that the sleeves and legs were about a centimeter long, enough for a smart person to notice.

He thought for an instant about picking up the sidearm but then remembered that it was sure to be keyed to Beversen's thumb and index finger prints, and that if Jak tried to take it, it would sound an alarm and turn on a transponder. Hating having to go unarmed, he hurried through the other door.

He emerged into a courtyard, and at the other side of it he saw what was clearly an internal checkpoint. Chances were that each internal checkpoint would mark one step closer to Sesh. Therefore, crazy as it all was, he'd have to head straight into this one.

Ninety seconds to come up with something beyond what he had already improvised. He had no idea, so he walked straight and tall, headed directly through the checkpoint, and saluted the guard standing there.

The guard looked at him coldly; seeing only corporal's stripes on his arm, Jak said, "Well, aren't you going to ask me the password?"

The guard pulled his stun baton. "I don't expect an escaped prisoner to know it," he said, closing in.

Jak struck with the best disarm of his life, and followed up with an elbow to the head. The man went down and Jak went through; about ten seconds of freedom left, now, and still no plan.

The gate had turned out to open into a courtyard, and in the center of the courtyard there was a high-walled building; far above, Jak could see branches of trees from what had to be a rooftop garden on the building. That *had* to be where Sesh was being held, he realized. He looked wildly around; there were more than enough handholds on that wall, because it was all in faux-medieval broken stonework, but he'd be at least an hour getting up its twenty meters. He picked a direction at random and dashed left, trying to suppress the image of being found running aimlessly around the building.

On the back side, there was a small platform elevator, hanging from cables, just two meters off the ground, and two masons were slowly, contentedly tuck-pointing the wall.

Jak sprang onto the platform, toppling the bucket of mortar and knocking one mason to the ground. The other, clutching the cable to stay on the elevator, hastily saluted, and Jak, remembering that he was still in a sergeant's dress uniform, returned the salute, sketchily and badly. "Emergency!" he shouted. "The princess is in danger! I am commandeering this elevator as an emergency transport for the Duchy of Uranium. Take it to the top, now! Full speed—uh, up!"

The mason saluted again and yanked at the controls; the open platform shot upward, Jak clinging to the cable to stay on. He made the mistake of looking down just once, and realized that twenty meters was several times the fall needed to catch a bad case of dead. After that he kept his eye on the wall and the approaching top parapet.

With a thump, the elevator stopped. The top edge was still two meters above their heads. "This is all the further it goes, sir," the mason said.

"I knew that," Jak said. He firmly told himself not to look down; the gap between the platform and the wall was only about a fifth of a meter or so, at closest approach, as the platform swayed gently. He reached out, got a grip with one hand, got a grip with the other, and jammed a boot into a crevice in the stonework.

At his first step upward, the boot came off his foot, and he was glad he hadn't worn socks, because he had a better grip with his toes anyway. He kicked the other boot off and concentrated on going up carefully; he'd done many rock-climbing vivs and at least this tower didn't feature ledges with snakes or eagles who swooped in to peck out your eyes. Also, it was really only about two and a half meters that he had to cover, even if the two and a half meters had a very unpleasant long drop under them.

Grip, reach, grip, reach . . . he wondered why this tower wasn't smooth. Probably one of those decorator touches—the hereditary nobility liked to pretend that their titles went all the way back to the European, African, and Asian feudal periods, so they were forever building fake ruins . . . grip, next grip, check that, foot, other foot, stay in close . . . grip—that was the top of the parapet, he realized, and a couple more moves got both his arms over it, and then his hands were over onto the other side of the wall. Groaning at doing it in the full gravity, he flipped over and dropped neatly into a fishpond, water flying everywhere.

He stood, shaking the water from his eyes, and found himself looking into the surprised eyes of Sesh, who was just clutching her torn, and now soggy, tunic over her breasts. A small, unpleasant, and strangely familiar man was gasping for air, having caught most of the pond with his face. Surmising the basic situation, and very uninterested in any mitigating details, Jak snapped the ball of his foot into the little man's face, knocking him backward over a bench, and said, "I don't speck any hope of getting you out—"

"Nonsense," Sesh said. "All the guards just ran down the stairs or piled into the elevators." She ran; he followed. Within seconds she'd yanked the EMERGENCY DELIVER CAR TO GROUND FLOOR/LOCKDOWN button for both elevators. "It's boring up here," she said, "apart from the occasional visit from His Rudeness, and I had a lot of time to study everything just in case. Now there's just the few guards on the spiral stairs—they'll be turning around any second."

She turned and dashed again, losing her tunic as she went and not bothering to retrieve it. Jak, awkward in his too-long soggy pants and bare feet, was a few steps behind as she reached the door. "How many?" he gasped, staring at the narrow staircase. He could already hear cries and pounding feet far below.

"I don't know, twenty, maybe," she said.

"Don't know how I can fight them all if they have weapons but if they come at me one at a time—"

"Oh, weehu, don't be stupid, old tove," she said, slamming the door shut and dropping a large bar across its hasps. "They never specked that they might need to be able to get in; they thought they might have to secure the stairs against a rescue attempt. That door may look like something out of old oak from a dramatization about the Middle Ages, but it could probably smother a small atom bomb. Now all we have to do is call in the rest of the rescue team—surely you had aircraft standing by . . . tell me you had aircraft—"

Jak's heart sank. "I came here to bargain to get you back," he said. "Till about fifteen minutes ago, there was no rescue plan."

Her face fell. "There's no one you can call?" she asked.

Jak looked down at his purse. As far as he knew, all of his friends on the planet were sitting in a coffee shop waiting for him to call in with a progress report. He could call them, but he didn't speck them turning up with a helicopter in the next two minutes, given no warning. Even the most loyal and competent friends have their limitations.

Jak stood there, dripping, barefoot, bruised, and exhausted, facing Sesh, naked to the waist in her long skirt and heeled shoes, in the middle of this absurd garden in the sky, and very seriously thought about just sitting down and giving up. He'd done pretty well for a heet who was making it up the whole way. Now he was utterly out of ideas, and even if he had had an idea, he didn't see how the best idea in the world could help now.

With a loud thud, the door to the stairs behind them went over, and Bex Riveroma strode across it. Behind him there were a dozen guards.

Sesh turned and ran; Jak thought about standing and fighting for perhaps a millisecond before his common sense took over and he ran after her. They fled down a broad aisle between pleasant fruit trees, with Riveroma and the guards rapidly closing in on them. The nasty little man who had been assaulting Sesh when Jak showed up rushed from between the trees, trying to tackle her, but she had momentum on her side; she threw an arm out and knocked him flat. Jak jumped over him and kept going. The little man got the attention of most of the guards, but Riveroma and a few more stayed right on the track, losing only a step to go around.

The top of the tower was only about 150 meters square, and in just seconds, the parapet was ahead of them. Sesh veered left and Jak followed, hurdling a hedge after her as she tossed aside the hampering skirt. Now they were only three paces at best ahead of Riveroma, and from the shouting all around, Jak knew other guards must be closing in and heading them off. The parapet was getting nearer, just a second or two away, and neither he nor Sesh could possibly climb down fast enough, nor was there anywhere to jump.

Something thundered up above the parapet in front of them.

At first it was just a strange bluish blur, then metal— and to Jak's astonishment, a helicopter drifted in toward them, just off the ground. He thought at first it was the last reinforcement for the pursuit, but then it pinged and rang as the guards fired on it with their small tranquilizer pellet pistols, the only weapons they had.

Sesh darted for the helicopter door, ducking low, no doubt betting that if the guards didn't like it, it was friendly to her, and Jak followed. The door opened and Jak's friend Black, from the prison, pulled Sesh inside, and beckoned Jak on. Jak was just reaching for Black's hand, himself, when his legs went out from under him— Riveroma had tackled him. He tried to turn and fight, but the big man was strong enough to drag him away from the copter. The other guards closed in around him.

With a screeching whistle, rather like a gut-shot teakettle rising into audio feedback, something hit one of the guards in the back, knocking him down, then leapt over Jak's supine body and laid into Riveroma, who shouted in terror.

Jak rolled over and sat up, seeing Riveroma, blood running down his face and an expression of pure horror, before Jak realized that he was also seeing the back of a Rubahy, the rage-spines standing straight out. The other guards were fleeing as fast as they could. Riveroma fell backward, hands over his face.

"Into the copter!" Shadow barked at Jak. Jak jumped to his feet and dove through the open door of the slowly drifting helicopter. Shadow followed, jumping over him to claim a seat. Before Jak had the door all the way closed, Black whipped the copter around and put it into a shallow climb. They streaked away to the north.

Clinging to a seatback, Jak carefully closed the door and looked around. Black was flying the helicopter with a big, happy grin. "Now this is the way things should get done," the man said, his eyes twinkling.

A series of "bloop-bloop-bloops" came from Shadow on the Frost, as his rage-spines retracted into his back. "A splendid day with plenty of honor," he agreed.

Sesh was sitting on the seat, not quite aware yet that she was wearing only briefs and one high heel; no doubt she'd realize in a moment.

Meanwhile, Jak said, "I would really like an explanation for all this."

Below them, the great city of Fermi swept by; there was plenty of air traffic, as always, but it seemed to be being routed around them, leaving them with an open bubble in the sky.

"And there will be one," Black said, "but just now we

have to go meet your friends at the spaceport. They had to get the last part of this mission accomplished, or we're going to have even bigger problems than we've had so far. Shadow, would you mind—?"

"Of course." The Rubahy lifted his left hand and pointed it toward his face; "Get me the blue team," he said to his purse.

"Full secure?"

"Yes." There was a long pause while the purse established a multiple-indirect-route encrypted connection.

"Here they are. Go ahead," the purse said.

Jak was startled to hear Piaro's voice. "Everything's fine. No casualties on either side. The package is in hand and will stay in hand for a little while longer. But we are surrounded by B&Es and they seem to be trying to speck how to get the package back without damaging it."

"Tell him we'll be there in two minutes," Black said, "and to just keep stalling and avoid any shooting. We don't want anyone hurt."

Shadow repeated the orders. As they neared Fermi's spaceport, the tall buildings of the city gave way to pleasant suburbs, and then to the sort of suburbs that are only occupied by people who can't afford better, and are punished for that by being subjected to constant rocket takeoffs and landings. They flew across the green safety belt, toward the military part of the spaceport where the warcraft sat parked on their landing gear or reared back and ready to roar up the catapults. The spaceport drew nearer, and Black angled toward a complex of buildings where people were running around like a kicked anthill.

Black got on the air and talked to a couple of people,

apparently worried about possible violence, and not getting any of the reassurance that he really wanted.

"How did you meet my friends?" Jak whispered to Shadow.

"I had followed you to the prison—I was planning to break you out, but your friends got there first," the Rubahy said. "I knew your friends would be bringing you to Fermi sooner or later because that was where your mission was, so I accomplished my own errand at the Rubahy embassy here in Fermi, and then thought that before starting my next assignment, I'd look in to see if I could help you, and thus I found your other friends, who all behave as if they owe you an even greater debt of honor than I do. You must be an extraordinary person among humans, Jak Jinnaka, to have so many and such fine friends, and I am honored to have taken an honor-oath with you back on the launch."

Jak realized that there was probably something the Rubahy was misinterpreting, but this would not be the time to try to straighten him out.

"So," Shadow went on, "this fellow here"—he gestured at Black—"was kind enough to engage my services as warrior, and also very interested in these other friends, and not long after you went to negotiate, he looked them up at the cafe where they were waiting. He hired them, also, to be the blue team for this operation. We would have swooped in to rescue you sooner, but as it happened, the blue team was delayed with getting their package—"

"The blue team is Piaro, Phrysaba, Myxenna, and Dujuv?"

"That is correct."

"And the 'package'—"

"Oh, of course, you weren't there for the planning," the Rubahy said. "It must seem very confusing to you. I apologize for that. By 'getting the package,' of course, I mean 'hijacking a warshuttle.'"

As they approached the spaceport, Black took the helicopter lower and lower, until finally it seemed to Jak that they were just skimming the roofs of the warehouses. Black was now talking constantly into his microphone, sometimes to Piaro, mostly to what seemed to be military officers, and it sounded to Jak more or less as if he were working out some kind of a complex auction arrangement, though Jak could understand neither what was being bought or sold, nor the medium of exchange.

They came up on the edge of the field, where the warshuttles were parked, and it was immediately obvious which one had been seized; it was the one surrounded by B&Es, who crouched behind barrels and trucks, or around the corners of the warehouses, their weapons aimed at one craft. The warshuttle's ground protection guns wavered ominously as they automatically sighted in on anything that moved; if anyone inside gave the command, the warshuttle would at least go out shooting.

About thirty more beanies lay prone on a rooftop as the helicopter zoomed over them, their weapons also pointed toward the warshuttle, and crouched behind a chimney there was a man with a large radio booster plugged into his purse. Black waved at the man with the radio booster, who waved back and shouted to the men on the rooftop.

A few of the beanies on the roof turned and started to sight in on the helicopter, but for some reason or other, their comrades immediately wrestled them to the ground, ripping their weapons from their hands. Jak was puzzled, but he was getting used to not understanding things.

The copter slowly descended between the ship and the B&Es, in a wide bare area, and as soon as he'd stopped the rotor, Black hopped out and walked out onto the heat-scarred tarmac. He looked toward the ship and beckoned; looked toward the B&Es and beckoned; and in a moment, the captain of the warshuttle, in his full-dress uniform, emerged and walked toward Black. A few seconds later, a B&E, this one in combat gear, emerged from one of the barricades and walked over to join them.

The captain arrived first, snapping a brisk salute and then kneeling. The B&E seemed taken aback, but kept walking; then he obviously recognized Black, and did the same salute-and-kneel. Black gestured for them to rise, and after a few brief words, the B&E officer and the warshuttle captain went back to their posts, talking vociferously into their purses. In a moment, the B&Es were standing up and stowing arms; the ground protection guns of the warshuttle were pointed harmlessly at the sky; and it was abundantly clear that whatever the crisis had been, it was now over.

Black turned back toward the helicopter, made a "come-on" gesture to Jak, Sesh, and Shadow, and turned to walk toward the warshuttle's ramp. Jak and Shadow followed at once—something about Black didn't let you think of disobeying. Sesh kicked off her remaining shoe. "Eeep," she commented as she ran across the hot tarmac in her bare feet, trying to keep her breasts covered with her hands. "Eep."

All over the spaceport, sirens were sounding and people were running and shouting, but there were no bangs from projectile weapons and no hisses of beam weapons. It didn't sound so much like an impending attack or an accident, as like mass confusion. They ran up the ramp into the warshuttle. The ramp lifted behind them, and a bell rang. "This is the captain. Everyone grab an emergency security surface and stay on it. We're taking off."

Because warshuttles so often accelerate suddenly, there are almost always several acceleration couches within few meters of you; Jak, Shadow, and Sesh pulled three down from the wall and lay on them. "Wonder where we're going?" Jak said.

"Low Earth orbit, or else somewhere else on Earth. Those are actually the only available choices," Shadow on the Frost said.

"Earth or somewhere close," Sesh said. "That helps a lot."

Shadow made that bubbles-in-a-bucket sound. "Your demmy has a sense of humor as fine as your own, Jak Jinnaka."

There was a tremendous roar and they boosted at what had to be at least four g, mashing them down hard into the acceleration couches. After a few minutes, the acceleration cut out, and the captain said, "We're in orbit; move around if you need or want to."

Jak unbuckled, floated free, and looked out the viewport; sure enough, they were perhaps five hundred km above the planet, now.

A door opened, and Dujuv, Myxenna, Phrysaba, and

Piaro swam in. "You have splendid friends," Shadow on the Frost said. "It speaks well of one who has chosen to share honor with me."

Myx and Duj immediately scrambled to hug Sesh and make sure she was all right. Sesh was suddenly acutely aware that she was all but naked; Dujuv pulled off his tunic and gave it to her, where it fit like a bedsheet over an end table, but at least provided some modesty.

Jak noted that Phrysaba had taken a firm grip on his arm, and she breathed in his ear, "Well, at least this way everyone got to find out what you see in her."

Trying to disentangle himself gently, he said, "I arrived right when Psim Cofinalez was trying to rape her—"

"He did *what?*" Dujuv said, turning and staring.

"Not me," said Black, coming in through the same door. "I didn't have the luxury of giving Jak quite the elaborate explanation I gave you. That unpleasant little turd of a person who was up in the garden with you, Princess Shyf, was Pukh Cofinalez, the heir to the throne of Uranium, a creepy little man, and incidentally already married. Or not so incidentally. He needed to get you into a line marriage with him, which would have broken his old marriage, not to mention capturing Greenworld for us and thereby getting him in good with Pop. But since Greenworld would hardly have allowed the courtship, and would have fought a war to keep you out of that situation with a married fellow, he needed to be an unmarried one—so he just borrowed my identity. Since my picture doesn't get around much, for security reasons, nor does his, for esthetic reasons, and he had noticed I was building a very pleasant palace where I intended to live myself, but which could be perfectly adapted as a cage for kidnapped princesses, he just grabbed me while I was sleeping one night and sent me off to Tjadou, where the family stores all the inconvenient prisoners. Pop doesn't get out much anymore and isn't all that sharp when he does, so he didn't ask any awkward questions, and Pukh had things pretty much his way unless and until I could escape and rally family forces loyal to me. Jak's escape gave me a way to escape, and the rest will probably be history once it's all declassified."

Sesh looked bewildered. "But to marry him with full consent, as a marriage-of-lines requires, I'd have had to find out that he was Pukh, not Psim—"

"You'd also have had to fall really, sincerely in love, contrary to both your political and personal interests, with a man who had you kidnapped and held for months or years against your will. Pukh is not what you'd call the brains of the family. Or the looks. Or indeed much else, in the family, at all, now, (I am de*lighted* to say!) because I've already sent over the details of the sorry djeste to Pop, and though he's not as sharp as he once was, perhaps, he's more than sharp enough to recognize inept treachery, which is the one kind he can't tolerate. Pukh is out, I'm in, and I'll be Ducent for Pop and then Duke thereafter. And though it's not in the nature of the positions of our houses and holdings to be friends or even allies, Princess, I hope we can avoid being enemies."

"You're doing very well so far."

"Well, good then. Within an orbit or two, the captain should notify me that our forces are holding everything important in Fermi, and then we'll be able to ground and sort things out. It will take some time, first with getting confirmed as Ducent and then with all the things I have to do as Ducent, but we should have everything straightened out in a few days, if everyone will bear with me."

Fermi was a charming, beautiful city (at least when one was not being chased through it) but it did have an African climate and full gravity. While they waited to hear what arrangements the new Ducent had made, they all elected to move up to one of the hotels owned by the Cofinalez family, as part of their personal property, on Singing Port. If things seemed a little—well, extremely—tense between Phrysaba and Sesh, that was something that Jak could deal with by simply spending time sparring with Dujuv and Piaro, and playing Maniples with Shadow on the Frost, who had such a different approach to things that Jak felt he was making extraordinary progress with his game. Twice, in the period of a few days, they all came together to experience, by live viv, Pabrino playing some planet-class opponent; the sporting-and-games news media were already calling him the "spaceborn phenom."

When Ducent Psim Cofinalez was finally able to get time to meet with all of them, it was not for the small dinner or party he had hoped for. It was really just a short, friendly meeting in a conference room before the new Ducent attended four more meetings in the hotel and then flew back to Fermi the next day. "Well," Psim said, "I would really rather do this more gradually, but I didn't want to keep you all in suspense any longer, and I know the importance of gratitude to friends, so let me tell you what I'm planning to do. Remember Principle 159: 'Money changes everything.' "

He turned to Phrysaba and Piaro, and said, "One way that money can change everything is that what's a disaster for some of my friends is no more than writing a couple of checks for me. I'm going to buy the cargo of the *Spirit of Singing Port,* at a price which will get you part of the way out of debt with enough credit to get the ship fully repaired and up to spec, and then have you take it to Mercury for me, which should make enough profit to pay off the rest and keep you flying as free merchants." Piaro's and Phrysaba's jaws dropped, and then they bounced up as to embrace him, but he waved them off, clearly embarrassed. "Oh, now, now, let's not exaggerate the importance of this. I know your sunclipper is your world, but for the House of Cofinalez, it's about forty-four minutes of profit. Not to mention that we aren't always eager to have everyone know just what cargo is going where, and friends among the spaceborn are always good to have."

"You know you have them on the *Spirit of Singing Port,*" Piaro said.

"Well, then, your next destination after Mercury is the Aerie, where you will be dropping Princess Shyf off, and I'll pay for a premium passage for her."

Piaro smiled in a way that Jak wasn't sure he liked. "Well, that will be great."

Phrysaba and Sesh were not-looking at each other as hard as they could.

The Ducent went on. "Shadow on the Frost will be joining my little cadre of Rubahy mercenaries for a while, which is a much better job than he was headed for."

Shadow nodded graciously.

"How is it better, Shadow?" Jak asked.

"Though my oath-bound cousins-club has granted me honors, the fraternity of my voluntary parents found that those honors were an affront to their sense of grandiose prolixity, and the fact that my honors were not unbalanced has somewhat shamed my uncle-group, which was already displeased with me and therefore was going to assign my next mission as something very high risk, to see if I survived, and thereby re-won them the honor I had cost them," the Rubahy said, calmly. "Er, that's a tough translation but I didn't want to include too much about the secondary connections. Anyway, luckily, this offer will pay well enough so that I can buy myself out of the displeasure of every group to which I belong and into whose bad graces I've fallen. We have a saying rather like one of your Principles of the Wager: 'Honor is without price but can often be cheaply bought.'"

The Ducent nodded. "Principle 159 remains my favorite. Jak and Dujuv, are you aware of the PSA's foreign trainee program?"

They glanced at each other and shrugged. "Not at all," Jak said.

"Well, your administrative types, among the wasps, are among the cleverest administrators that the solar system has ever known, and so one thing they do regularly is offer slots at the PSA for aspiring bureaucrats from all the thousands of other nations in the solar system, to come and learn the wasp way of doing things. It is always presented, of course, as a very altruistic way of assisting the functioning of the whole human race, which I suppose it might be if you really think the human race would function better if only it were run from the Hive. And pretty well no other nation, especially not one of any power or size, ever takes advantage of the offer, because we all understand perfectly well that what this will do is eventually fill our civil service with wasp agents, many of whom won't even know that they're wasp agents, because they think that the way in which they have learned to make everywhere as much like the Hive as possible is merely 'good administration' or 'modern management.'

"Well, along the way of things, my intelligence service, which does quite a good job of supplying background information, discovered two very deserving young citizens of the Hive who didn't get into the PSA, and what I propose is this: I'll declare you both to be subjects of the Duchy of Uranium, and send you to the PSA as foreign exchange students. In exchange for that, I ask only that you promptly defect to the Hive when you're all done with school, and that above all else you don't come back here and introduce all that public service nonsense into my administration! I have nice trustworthy officials who take bribes on everything that doesn't matter, so that business gets done, and are terrified of my secret police about everything that does matter—I don't believe I have a single bureaucrat who cares about fairness, procedure, or principles, which is why Uranium is such a pleasant place to live, with plenty of slack always and no worries about some idiot in the Underbureau of Classification making a mess, or committing treason by deciding to do something for the greater good. So . . . if I do send you both to the PSA, I assume I have no worries about your coming back here and trying to reform and improve anything?"

"None at all, Your Excellency," Dujuv said.

"You should know us better than that, sir," Jak added.

The new Ducent laughed and clapped them both on the shoulders. "Well, then, the ship is saved from bondage, everyone is going to where they belong, and we have all the elements of a happy ending in place."

"Uh, was there anything you were going to do for Myxenna?" Jak asked, not wanting a tove left out of the bounty.

She turned on a radiant smile, the kind that she normally got while watching the buttocks of an attractive young man, or when suggesting that she knew a good private place to talk; Jak had seen that smile focused on himself a few times and privately—that is, never in any way the panth might be aware of—regarded the times when he'd received that smile as high points of his life. "Well," she said, "we haven't exactly specked what would be appropriate"—Jak had never before realized how perfect the word "appropriate" is for purring—"but Psim and I are having dinner tonight to talk about that very question."

Jak glanced away, not wanting to see Dujuv's reaction. Phrysaba and Sesh were looking at each other as if each were contemplating how pleasant it would be to wear the other's entrails as a feather boa. A moment or two later, after the Duke had left, Jak grabbed Shadow, Piaro, and Duj and suggested that they all go someplace for a large meal to celebrate, "just us heets."

Halfway through a third plate of glutles, the panth looked up and said, "She called him by his first name."

"Well, I guess that's what he has a first name for, so people can call him by it." Piaro dove back into his plate of Tranquility Scallops, clearly hoping he'd closed off the conversation.

"He's a duke. Or a ducent, anyway."

"Way above her, so he won't be interested," Jak said, firmly.

Shadow nodded. "In your social order, he is going to be the top, she is going to be underneath him, eh? And I am sure that they are not unhappy with that. She is a loyal person of respect and she will very much enjoy being under him."

Dujuv, appearing to have been poisoned, got up and went into the rest room. After he had gone, Shadow on the Frost began to shake, and to emit the familiar burble of bubbles in a metal bucket. "You evil bastard," Piaro said, "you speak Standard better than that!"

"Absolutely cruel and evil," Jak said.

"Horrible thing to do," Piaro agreed.

The metal bucket burble got stronger and louder, and Shadow on the Frost was now shaking like a spastic monkey, his feathers fluffed up in pure glee.

"Funny, though," Piaro said, giving way and laughing, and Jak joined them a moment later, admitting to himself that for an evil feathered lizard, Shadow wasn't a bad heet to hang around with.

CHAPTER 12

The Two of You Could Have Shaken Hands . . .

Gweshira had arranged to spend a while talking with Jak, and since she was practically family—toktru, he liked her a lot better than the only family he had, just now—he had to admit, at least to himself, that he was hoping she could patch things up. When she joined him at the little cafe, there was no one else there; it was in the back parts of Entrepot, notorious as places where people went for a romantic rendezvous, and Jak was mildly amused at the thought that he might be mistaken for a gigolo, before sternly reminding himself that if Gweshira had wanted one, she could have afforded something far better than Jak.

When she arrived and they had ordered the Seven Tisanes tray, she looked at him and said, "Now, look, the very first thing you have to remember is that Sib and Bex go back a very long way. In fact I met Sib before I met either of my husbands, may their atoms drift in peace, and by that time he and Bex Riveroma already had a long, deep history of hatred. They were two of the favorite students of one of the greatest Disciplinarians, *and* two of the favorite students of one of the great social engineering practitioners, and in short they were rivals for everything, all the time. So of course they bad-mouth each other. Of course they say dreadful things about each other. That doesn't make what either one says about the other true. Sibroillo is sentimental and good-hearted, but he's not incompetent; Riveroma will do anything at all to advance his interests or the interests of the mission, but he's not without honor and there's no one better at what he does."

"It's not that," Jak said. "I mean, I realized he was just trying to send some insults to Sib and maybe sow some dissension in the family. I knew that Sib hadn't taught me *that* badly, and I knew that even really good plans can go wrong and that people can misjudge a situation for reasons that have nothing to do with ego or foolishness. I know all that. I'm just mad at him for . . ." He stopped and poured himself a calming tisane, sipped it. "Well, it's not easy to say it because it really sounds childish."

"That's strange, Jak. Usually Sibroillo doesn't misjudge you that much. And I can tell that he thinks you are angry at him because of the beatings you got and the way things happened so differently from the script he gave you, and it's killing him to feel that way—he feels like he failed you, and at the same time, as a pro, he knows that nothing ever follows the script and improvisation is the heart of the djeste, so he can't see any way in which he could have done anything other than fail you."

"It's not that," Jak said, again. "It is toktru not that.

The big problem is just that I speck I'm being toktru childish. That kind of keeps me from talking about it."

She shrugged. "All right, but I can't be much help until you do."

He sighed, poured more tisane, stared out at the mostly unoccupied corridor beyond the big window, and said, "Well, all right, here goes. Try not to make fun of me, and I'm warning you right now, you'll be tempted to.

"What I couldn't stand was finding out that the whole time I was fleeing from him, Bex Riveroma was setting it up and manipulating it. He even *told* me that he couldn't appear to be helping Sesh, and that if he did look like he was helping her it would kill his job and just possibly get him killed. And I still didn't realize!

"Then Riveroma set up a completely bizarre situation—which I now know Uncle Sib *scripted, collaborating* with Riveroma, because Uncle Sib knows what kind of entertainment I like—I mean, really, a guard left alone with me taking off his clothes and turning his back to me while I wasn't tied up! That's exactly the kind of thing I've been gobbling up for years in those intrigue-and-adventures stories I like.

"Doors kept opening in just the singing-on moments and places, things kept being right singing-on where I needed them, every little coincidence was singing-on. Nobody ever had a lethal weapon if they crossed my path—and the whole time, even though I was scared out of my mind and not really appreciating it, I was also proceeding just as if all the cheap intrigue-and-adventure stuff was the way the world was! It was like I was tricked into playing a role in a viv. And to add to the overall foolishness, this reporter, Mreek Sinda—she's written and produced the whole story just as if the djeste of it were real-life intrigue-and-adventure!"

"Well," Gweshira said, mildly, "rights to it will at least ensure that you're affluent for a long time, and if it should be a hit, you'll be wealthy."

"But I feel like a gweetz! All I was doing was following someone else's plan; the whole time I thought I was boldly improvising and winging it as best I could, and it turns out that Sib and this heet Riveroma were pulling the strings the whole way; everyone was right on top of me. It was like I was just playing a game and I thought it was real. And that makes me feel, toktru, like a complete, total, utter gweetz. So having a viv out there that makes a hero of me just seems like more mockery. And I feel like hiding under a rock for a thousand years, and the last heet in the universe that I want to see is Uncle Sib."

"Hmmph," Gweshira said. "And exactly what parts of life do you expect will not involve playing a game, as if it were real?"

"But this whole thing was like a viv script!"

"And what happens in viv if you just sit back and do nothing? Or if you freeze and cower in a corner—some people do, you know, when a viv gets too real, the rescue squads are out every day retrieving people from those vividly imaged hells. Or if you're a lousy shot, or you make bad decisions when time gets short, or any of the thousands of other things that can go wrong in both viv and real? The only difference between viv and real, as far as nerve and skill and being good in a bad spot are concerned—and what else matters, really?—is that in viv there's a do-over, and in real life there's not.

"If you'd moved too slowly, or fallen from that tower, or slipped and fallen when you needed to be up and running, or let Riveroma get his boot on your head—well, things would be very different, and there would be no do-over. It was your nerve and your skills that got you through, even if the situation wasn't exactly a hundred percent pure improvised reality. I don't see why it makes such a big difference to you, and I don't see why you hold it against your Uncle Sib that he set that situation up, any more than you hold it against him that he sent you on the mission in the first place. You were the one who had to do everything; he was helping, but you really did do an excellent job. If I thought you had the slightest interest in what's going on in the world, I'd be predicting that someday you'd be a fine agent."

Jak watched a very nice-looking young woman walk by; she didn't have the hard lean body of Phrysaba or the sheer grace and beauty of Sesh, but it was occurring to him that she'd do in a pinch . . . or perhaps in a stroke of maybe an outright grope. With Sesh in the Aerie and Phrysaba back on the *Spirit,* a heet might need to do some shopping.

"Er, before you began optically molesting that young lady," Gweshira said, after a while, "I was telling you that you might someday make a fine agent. Obviously I'm hoping you would like to be one for Circle Four. Are you interested?"

He sighed. "Well, I like the kind of athletic side of things, the running and chasing and shooting and all, and the travel is interesting, but the rest of it's way too much like school."

Gweshira nodded. "Then let me tell you the other reason why I wanted to meet with you today. It seems your Rubahy friend did you a very strange kind of favor—a good one that may turn bad at any time. You may remember that buried deep in your body there's a sliver that contains a list of the physical locations of all the evidence needed to get Bex Riveroma executed a few dozen times over, in so many jurisdictions that an accurate count would be hard to come up with . . . ?"

Jak thought for one instant and his eyes widened. The whole room seemed threatening and he glanced around, looking for anyone tall who might be Riveroma in disguise. "You're right. And he knows I have it because he got as far as decoding the antigen group and reading the codes. He knows what's in it and he knows it's in me—he'll be coming after me!" And yet another thought struck Jak. "And now he doesn't have any reason to keep me alive anymore, either. He can just have me grabbed and they can cut it out of me—with or without killing me first. I could get shot and dragged off any minute."

"So could anyone; it's a dangerous world, it's just that most of the people who live here don't know that. But in the first place, he won't do that because he has to worry about reprisals. And he does worry about them, despite what he tried to convince you of. And also, it seems that Psim Cofinalez is indeed rather different from his brother and father, which at least means the Duchy of Uranium will be a different kind of entity from now on, which I would say is a good thing. One of the first things Ducent Psim did was to discharge Bex Riveroma, with a generous settlement package and a nice ticket out to Triton, where his talents are apt to be appreciated and it will be a long time before he comes back to Earth. It should be a year or two before we hear from him, since he won't bother to communicate until he can do it from someplace secure and where there's some ability to take action.

"When he does get back in touch, and he will, we'll see what can be worked out, and it's possible of course that the information in the sliver will be partly, or even wholly, out of date by that time.

"At any rate, that was where Shadow on the Frost did you either a big favor or no favor at all. Riveroma was about to capture you; that would have been when he could have extracted the sliver, and released you, and the two of you could have shaken hands in a nice professional manner, and that would be the end of it. Now Shadow didn't know that, and he saw that his honor-bound friend was in danger of capture—"

"What exactly does 'honor-bound' mean, anyway? To a Rubahy, I mean?"

"Didn't they cover that in school? I know that they have classes in dealing with the Rubahy."

"Toktru, Gweshira, when did I ever pay attention to anything in class? Especially when the subject was how to get along with feathered lizards, masen?"

She groaned and said, "Well, honor-binding places you both in a state of deep obligation to each other; you have to look out for each other in all sorts of situations, and come to each other's aid, and if either of you fails in the obligation for any voluntary reason, you instantly become mortal enemies. So I suggest you look up honor-binding in any good encyclopedia and make sure you know the rules, because if you ever fail in them, Shadow on the Frost won't stop trying to kill you till he's dead himself, and even then it's possible his cousins would be obligated to keep trying. On the other hand, as you may have noticed in the process of getting rescued, there are certain advantages to having a Rubahy honor-bound to you, and it would probably be a good thing to maintain that situation."

"How did I become honor-bound to a Rubahy in the first place?"

"Well, that's why you should have paid attention in class. When a Rubahy says that you honor him by being there to die with him, and thanks you for it, that's just politeness to a comrade, but if you then return the compliment and say the same thing, you're honor-bound. It looks casual to us because our culture is so steeped in reciprocity, but the Rubahy are not a very reciprocal society, as you're no doubt finding out, and extending reciprocity in any form is always a deep, heartfelt courtesy. That's why you hear people say 'never say "and you too" to a terrier,' because no matter what they said, you just made the situation extreme.

"Now, before you insult or hurt your friend—and thereby make an extraordinarily deadly enemy of him— I suggest that you spend some time studying up on Rubahy customs."

With as much contrition as he could manage—which was always very little—Jak nodded his head and said, "All right. I'll look it up, and"—the same young woman went by in the other direction, looking vaguely puzzled; Jak wondered whether she might be lost, or stood up by someone, or wearing anything under that thin shift, and need his help—"well, anyway, I'll do that."

"Of course you will," Gweshira said, in a tone that indicated that she didn't believe it but felt no need to press the point.

"Uh, I had one other question," Jak said, "and I was just wondering, since you got to read all the sealed files and so on about the case, whether it's a question that there's even an answer to."

"If I don't know the answer, I'll say I don't know. If I'm not allowed to say, I'll say I don't know. I won't give you any hints about which 'I don't know' that is. Otherwise, I'll answer."

"Fair enough," Jak said. "And it may just not be possible to know. Why did Riveroma have that launch I was on shot down? It must have cost a fortune in money, time, and effort to hack into the old sandgun system and do that, and he couldn't have been certain I'd be killed, and since he didn't know what I was coming to communicate about, anyway, why would he shoot me down before he heard the offer? The whole thing made no sense at all."

Gweshira laughed, long and hard, and said, "Jak, that was something we looked into right away. Riveroma had nothing to do with it. Remember Paj Priuleter, the preacher among the survivors? His wife was trying to kill him for the life insurance, and she wanted the kind of freak accident that gets double indemnity."

Jak laughed too. "Nothing ever goes exactly as planned, does it?"

"Nothing. Which is why I really want you to forgive Sib, look up honor-binding, and get on with things, because, toktru, old pizo, whether we try to lead a quiet life or go looking for trouble, none of us ever knows what's coming next." She stood up, so he did; they shook hands. "Well, I hope you have some fun in these few days before you start at the Academy."

"It just figures that for the first time in all those years of schooling, probably no one will ask me to write any essays about what I did on my vacation. Yeah, Duj and I have fun stuff planned; I'm supposed to meet him up at the pole in half an hour or so—Myx is coming in, finally, on that very conveniently scheduled warship from Uranium that just happened to have an extra berth. I speck Myx and Duj just want me to be the ref."

Gweshira smiled. "Whatever you do, don't stand between them. See you later."

She turned and walked away. Jak had a few minutes to kill before he'd need to call Rover and have it take him to the station, and since he knew Duj was always a few minutes late anyway, there wasn't much pressure of any kind. He decided to walk for a bit.

He heard a loud woman's voice; she sounded young. "What's the name of that club, again? I thought I knew it. I thought it was something about a flower—can you remind me?" Her voice was coming from around the nearest corner.

"I'm not equipped for that," the Pertrans reminded her in its flat mechanical tone.

When he came around one corner, Jak saw the beautiful young woman he'd noticed while talking to Gweshira. She was standing by a Pertrans at that stop. "Crane O'Hanna," she said, suddenly, "that's the club. But hold a minute."

Crane O'Hanna was the very lightest of the light dance clubs—expensive, but interesting.

"Hey," she said, "aren't you on viv? Jak somebody?"

"Yeah," he said.

"I've been through that viv a hundred times," she said, and sighed. She turned and got into the Pertrans car. "Crane O'Hanna," she said, again, very loudly.

The Pertrans car pulled away.

She had certainly had a nice body, and dressed to make sure everyone knew it. And she'd gone out of her way to make sure that Jak in particular knew where she was going.

He thought for less than half a second before he summoned Rover and headed for the same club, not knowing what he had in mind, but figuring it could develop. No doubt Myx and Duj would manage to have a perfectly fine fight without him. As Gweshira said, nothing, absolutely nothing, ever went according to plan.

ACKNOWLEDGMENTS

George Orwell said that writing a novel is like contracting a lingering illness; the metaphorical illness would have been much more severe and lingered much longer this time without gracious and judiciously timed pressure by Betsy Mitchell, my editor; efficient and prompt support on business matters by Ashley Grayson, Carolyn Grayson, and Dan Hooker, of the Ashley Grayson Literary Agency; and quick, voluminous, precise research by Jes Tate, my research assistant. Thanks to them, I kept more hair, gained less weight, and delivered almost on time.

ABOUT THE AUTHOR

JOHN BARNES lives in downtown Denver and writes full time. At various times he has worked full time as a gardener, systems analyst, statistician, theatrical lighting designer, and college professor. More than fifty entries by John Barnes appear in the 4th edition of the Oxford Encyclopedia of Theatre and Performance. His most recent books include *The Sky So Big And Black*, *The Merchants Of Souls*, *The Return* (wth Buzz Aldrin), and *Candle*.

WE PROUDLY PRESENT THE WINNER
OF THE WARNER ASPECT
FIRST NOVEL CONTEST . . .

WARCHILD
by
KARIN LOWACHEE

THE MERCHANT SHIP MUKUDORI ENCOMPASSES THE
WHOLE OF EIGHT-YEAR-OLD JOS'S WORLD, UNTIL A
NOTORIOUS PIRATE DESTROYS THE SHIP, SLAUGHTERS
THE ADULTS, AND ENSLAVES THE CHILDREN. THUS BE-
GINS A DESPERATE ODYSSEY OF TERROR AND ESCAPE
THAT TAKES JOS BEYOND KNOWN SPACE TO THE
HOMEWORLD OF THE STRITS, EARTH'S ALIEN ENEMIES.
TO SURVIVE, THE BOY MUST BECOME A LIVING
WEAPON AND A MASTER SPY. BUT NO TRAINING WILL
PROTECT JOS IN A WAR WHERE EVERY HOPE MIGHT BE
A DEADLY LIE, AND EVERY FRIENDSHIP MIGHT HIDE A
LETHAL BETRAYAL. AND ALL THE WHILE HE WILL FACE
THE MOST GRUELING TRIAL OF HIS LIFE . . . BECOM-
ING HIS OWN MAN.

ASPECT®

AVAILABLE WHEREVER BOOKS ARE SOLD

VISIT WARNER ASPECT ONLINE!

THE WARNER ASPECT HOMEPAGE
You'll find us at: www.twbookmark.com then by clicking on Science Fiction and Fantasy.

NEW AND UPCOMING TITLES
Each month we feature our new titles and reader favorites.

AUTHOR INFO
Author bios, bibliographies and links to personal websites.

CONTESTS AND OTHER FUN STUFF
Advance galley giveaways, autographed copies, and more.

THE ASPECT BUZZ
What's new, hot and upcoming from Warner Aspect: awards news, bestsellers, movie tie-in information . . .